"What I did," Thad said sharply, *"was my job.*

"I was a federal agent long before I ever met you. You knew that from the moment you got involved with me."

Lindsey stared at him.

"It's ironic, you know," he went on. "I wasn't the one who committed the crime, but I was the one you made pay for it." He shrugged. "So much for love."

With that, he turned and walked out, leaving Lindsey sitting there, eyes squeezed shut. She heard the click of the door closing behind him, and a moment later she heard the purr of an engine as he drove away.

So much for love. He'd sounded skeptical, as if he'd given up believing in love—at least in *her* love. But she *had* loved him, so much so that she still ached with it. *He* was the one who had ended it, who had destroyed what was between them—wasn't he?

Dear Reader,

Once again, Silhouette Intimate Moments is breaking new ground. In our constant search to bring you the best romance fiction in the world, we have found a book that's very different from the usual, and yet it's so appealing and romantic that we just had to publish it. I'm talking about *Angel on my Shoulder,* by Ann Williams. Ann isn't a new author, of course, but the heroine of this book definitely *is* something new. In fact, she's an absolute angel—and I mean that literally! Her name is Cassandra, and she comes to Earth on a mission. Her assignment is to save the soul of one very special man, but she gets a lot more than she bargained for when she takes on an earthly shape—and starts to experience earthly emotions. I don't want to tell you any more for fear of spoiling the magic, so I hope you'll start reading right away and discover for yourself the special nature of this book.

Another book is special to me this month, too, though for a more personal reason. In *The Man Next Door,* author Alexandra Sellers not only creates some very appealing human characters, she introduces some precocious felines, as well. And if you think Lorna Doone and Beetle are too good to be true, I feel honor bound to tell you that they're actually very real. In fact, they're both living in my house, where they're more than willing to cause all sorts of trouble. But now, through the vividness of Alexandra's writing, you can get to know them, too. I hope you like them—as well as *The Man Next Door.*

Marilyn Pappano and Lucy Hamilton, two more of your favorite authors, finish off the month in fine style. And in coming months, look for Kathleen Eagle (back after a long absence), Emilie Richards, Heather Graham Pozzessere, Kathleen Korbel, Jennifer Greene and more of the top-notch writers who have made Silhouette Intimate Moments such a reader favorite.

Enjoy!

Leslie Wainger
Senior Editor and Editorial Coordinator

MARILYN PAPPANO

Probable Cause

SILHOUETTE·INTIMATE·MOMENTS®

Published by Silhouette Books New York

America's Publisher of Contemporary Romance

SILHOUETTE BOOKS
300 East 42nd St., New York, N.Y. 10017

PROBABLE CAUSE

ISBN: 0-373-07405-0

First Silhouette Books printing November 1991

Printed in the U.S.A.

Books by Marilyn Pappano

Silhouette Intimate Moments

Within Reach #182
The Lights of Home #214
Guilt by Association #233
Cody Daniels' Return #258
Room at the Inn #268
Something of Heaven #294
Somebody's Baby #310
Not Without Honor #338
Safe Haven #363
A Dangerous Man #381
Probable Cause #405

Silhouette Books

Silhouette Christmas Stories 1989
"The Greatest Gift"
Silhouette Summer Sizzlers 1991
"Loving Abby"

MARILYN PAPPANO

has been writing as long as she can remember, just for the fun of it, but a few years ago, she decided to take her lifelong hobby seriously. She was encouraging a friend to write a romance novel and ended up writing one herself. It was accepted, and she plans to continue as an author for a long time. When she's not involved in writing, she enjoys camping, quilting, sewing and, most of all, reading. Not surprisingly, her favorite books are romance novels.

Her husband is in the Navy, and in the course of her marriage, she has lived all over the U.S. Currently, she lives in Georgia with her husband and son.

Chapter 1

Thad McNally maneuvered the car into a parking space in the second row, then shut off the engine and rested his hands on the steering wheel. The shopping center around him was similar to dozens of others in Atlanta. There were a grocery store, hair salons, specialty shops and a drive-through bank. And right in the middle, sandwiched between a record store and a dance school, was a card and gift shop, its broad plate-glass windows painted in graceful script with its name: Lindsey's Gifts.

Realizing that his fingers were wrapped tautly around the steering wheel, Thad deliberately turned his attention away from the small shop to its surroundings. The shopping center was less than two years old and was pleasantly designed with wooden benches and shade trees and dozens of planters overflowing with thousands of flowers. The sidewalks and about half of the storefronts were constructed with old brick faded to a soft dusty red, and the rest of the shops were built of wood, worn and weathered. Wood and brick pillars supported rough-hewn beams above the walkways, and a profusion of vines—he recognized wisteria and honeysuckle among them—were woven over and around them to provide a leafy shade below. Overall, he found it visually appealing, and apparently others agreed. The parking lot was nearly full on this Monday afternoon.

A familiar car parking in the row in front of him caught his attention, and he reluctantly forced his fingers free, automatically flexing them to ease tight muscles. He reached for the jacket on the seat beside him, then got out and shrugged into it. It snagged on his holster, and impatiently he reached back to pull it free, smoothing the rich fabric over the bulge.

Clint Roberts met him halfway between their cars. "Do you want to talk to her or should I?" he asked as he adjusted his own suit coat.

Thad removed his glasses, fogged by the sudden change in temperature from the air-conditioned car to the hot, humid air outside, and absently wiped them with a handkerchief from his pocket. He shouldn't even be here. This case wasn't his, but Roberts had invited him to tag along anyway because he'd known of Thad's connection to the earlier case, the one they had thought was closed. The one that, just last week, had been reopened. "You handle it," he said finally. Lindsey wouldn't listen to anything *he* had to say—at least, she hadn't the last three times he'd tried to talk to her.

They crossed the parking lot and walked along the sidewalk to Lindsey's Gifts. His hands were clammy, Thad noticed as they got closer, and he had to resist the urge to wipe them on his trousers. He'd taken an active part in literally hundreds of interviews in his career, but he couldn't remember a single one that had made him feel so nervous, so sick. Not even the one on the bridge with Donny Phillips.

He would handle this like the professional he was. He would forget that he had once been in love with this woman. He would forget that, if circumstances had been different, they would have been married by now. He would forget that she held him responsible for her brother's death. And he would forget, for the next few minutes, that in some way he *had* been responsible for Donny's death.

Roberts entered the shop first, setting the chimes above the door ringing. Thad had driven by here a dozen times or more, but he'd never been inside, not even when the only person present had been the teenage girl, Cassandra, who helped out after school and on weekends. He'd been afraid of running into Lindsey, afraid of seeing hatred or, worse, emptiness in her lovely brown eyes.

The first thing he noticed upon entering was the fragrance carried throughout the shop on the cool air. It was the fragrance, heavy on the vanilla and light on other unidentifiable spices, that always filled Lindsey's house and even her car. In the nearly eighteen months since he'd last seen her, he had never been able to smell any kind of spices without remembering, without hurting.

The shop was charming. The giftware—ceramics and crystal, porcelain and pottery—was displayed on shelves and low tables, the way they might be grouped in a home rather than in a store, and the comfortable chairs scattered around the room added to that impression. Stuffed animals filled a child-size sofa and were squeezed together on a low parson's bench, while handmade dolls all sat together in an old-fashioned tin washtub. The rest of the merchandise—cards and candles, wrapping paper and stationery—was displayed in equally unique and appealing ways.

The only thing that seemed out of place in the shop was the large card rack only a dozen feet from the door. It stood empty except for a pale yellow envelope and a sign across the top proclaiming Mother's Day in soft, romantic pastels. Since the holiday had been yesterday, Thad assumed Lindsey had packed away the unsold cards and would soon fill the empty shelves with graduation or Father's Day cards.

He had just picked up a small glass unicorn when a woman's voice called through the open door at the back of the room, "I'll be with you in a moment."

Roberts replied, "Take your time."

Thad grew still, even his breathing suspended for one long uncomfortable moment. Then he expelled the air in his lungs and unfolded his fingers from the unicorn he had clutched. When he realized the glass figure rocked un-

evenly in the palm of his trembling hand, he returned it to
its place on the mahogany table, careful not to disturb any
of the other fragile creatures that surrounded it.

Coming here with Roberts was a mistake. His head had
known better, had known not to get involved in the reopen-
ing of a case that had once cost him so dearly, but his heart
had overruled him. It had been so long since he'd seen
Lindsey, even longer since he'd spoken to her or held her or
loved her. How could he possibly pass up the opportunity
to be in the same room with her, to listen to her, to see if she
still hated him, to see if maybe she could forgive him?

But if she had forgiven him, she would have told him so.
Lindsey had no problems communicating. She was one of
the most open and forthright people he'd ever known. Her
silence these past eighteen months meant nothing had
changed. She still blamed him. She still hated him. So if he
had any brains at all, he would walk out the door right now,
before he saw her, before it was too late.

But even as he turned toward the door, he knew it was already too late. The clicking of her steps on the tile floor was
crossing the back room, pausing only briefly in the open
doorway before continuing down the center aisle toward
Roberts.

She had assumed Roberts was alone, Thad realized with
a sense of relief. Not expecting anyone else, she hadn't
glanced around the room but had instead focused her attention and her welcoming smile on the other man.

He took advantage of the brief reprieve to study her. A
friend had once commented disinterestedly that she was kind
of pretty, but Thad had always thought she was one of the
most beautiful women he'd ever seen. Her hair was dark
brown, nothing spectacular, and her features—brown eyes,
straight nose, full lips, sweet smile—were average rather
than stunning. And yet, there was something—the gentle-
ness in her eyes, maybe, or the vulnerability in her smile—
that made her achingly beautiful in his eyes.

Her hair was swept up in a chignon that should have
looked severe but instead was soft and touchable. She was
dressed as elegantly as always in a royal blue outfit that

closely followed the lines of her body and ended in a slim-fitting skirt an inch or two above her knees. Although tall at five foot seven, she wore narrow, three-inch heels in the same ivory shade as the belt around her waist.

"Can I help you?" she asked, her tone polite, her voice still the same throaty, Southern-accented drawl Thad heard in his dreams.

Roberts pulled his credentials from his coat pocket and offered them for her inspection. "Ms. Phillips, I'm Special Agent Clint Roberts with the FBI. There are a few questions I'd like to ask you."

From his vantage point alongside a rack of greeting cards, Thad could see the color drain from her face and her smile fade away. Now that her afternoon had been unpleasantly interrupted, it was as good a time as any to make his presence known.

His first movement, although quiet, caught her attention, and she turned in his direction. And he had thought she'd been pale just a moment ago, he thought grimly. Now she looked as if she might faint or be ill or both. What a wonderful response to stir in the woman he'd once wanted to marry.

As Thad joined Roberts, she took a step backward, then a few more, as if that small distance between them might offer her safety. In those few seconds, she masked her shock and dismay, then directed a cool response to Roberts as if *he* weren't even there. "What would you like to know, Mr. Roberts?"

"Have you seen or heard from your brother lately?"

The bluntness of the question chased away her mask. This time the shock was too much. She swayed unsteadily on her heels, recovering only when Thad instinctively reached out to brace her. Before his hand touched her, she drew away, turning instead to the support of the nearest chair.

"Is this some kind of joke?" she demanded when she was seated. "My brother died eighteen months ago. Didn't you know? Or are you people responsible for so many deaths that he was just forgotten in the crowd?"

Roberts drew a matching rocker over and sat down facing her. "Donny's body was never found," he needlessly reminded her.

She stared at him. "That bridge is ninety-eight feet above the water. The river is less than fifteen feet deep at that point, and it's filled with submerged rocks. The water temperature that day was in the low forties, and the air temperature was in the low thirties. You people told me that in your 'expert opinion'—" she mocked the words "—he didn't survive, that he *couldn't* have survived. And now you're here asking me if I've *seen* him lately?"

Thad winced at the strained disbelief in her voice. He'd been a fool to come here and a bigger fool to think he could stand back and let Roberts question her in his coldly efficient way without intervening. He couldn't.

"Lindsey, you know Donny was the only suspect in the Heinreid kidnapping," he began in an unnaturally quiet voice. "And you know he confessed to it before—before..." He needed a deep breath and more courage than he'd believed he had to finish the statement. "Before he fell from the bridge."

Fell. The word was a lie meant to protect her. Donny Phillips hadn't *fallen.* Facing arrest and a certain prison sentence—maybe twenty-five years, maybe life—Donny had chosen death instead. He had *jumped* off that bridge, and he had damn near taken Thad with him. But Lindsey didn't know that. All she knew was that she'd asked Thad to help her troubled brother, and instead he had somehow helped cause his death.

Her gaze was centered somewhere around his feet as he spoke. He was surprised she could bear to look at even that much of him.

"There was no evidence that Donny had a partner," he continued. "No reason to believe that anyone else was involved. We assumed that he'd hidden the ransom someplace safe, someplace only he knew about, and that it was probably lost for good. But some of the money has begun turning up locally, and Donny's fingerprints are on it."

There was a long silence. Thad watched her, but all he could see was the top of her bowed head. When she finally spoke, it was in a hoarse whisper. "Is he alive?"

"It's possible that he had a partner who sat on the money all this time," Thad said. "Or maybe someone found the cash wherever he hid it and has started spending it."

It was then that Lindsey looked up, and her eyes glistened with unshed tears as she looked directly into Thad's eyes. "Or maybe Donny's alive."

With a sigh, he yielded to her defiant challenge and told her what she wanted to hear. "Or maybe he's alive."

Lindsey sat in the rocker long after they'd left, grateful for once that business was slow, grateful to sit undisturbed and rock and think.

The Heinreid kidnapping. Although she hadn't thought about it in months—hadn't *let* herself think about it—she hadn't forgotten a single detail. How a man had forced his way into the Heinreid home and taken the old lady at gunpoint. How the kidnapper had demanded a ransom of two hundred and fifty thousand dollars. How, in spite of his threats, the family had called in the FBI and the case had been assigned to a team of agents that included Thad. How, finally, against the Bureau's recommendation, the family had paid the ransom and the elderly woman had been released, dazed and frightened but unharmed.

How, only a few weeks later, her brother had become the Bureau's prime suspect. How, shortly after that, he had died.

Or had he?

Maybe Donny's alive.

After Thad had admitted that, he'd let the other man take over again. Clint Roberts had asked her numerous questions—about Donny and her relationship with him, about his friends and the woman he'd been seeing before his death. He had even asked a few questions about her. Where had she gotten the money to buy the shop? How was business? And, most insultingly, if her brother was alive and she knew it, would she tell them?

Smiling bitterly, she tilted her head back. *She* was the one who'd turned them on to Donny in the first place. If she hadn't been so worried about him, if she hadn't asked Thad to help him...

Thad. She'd been stunned to see him. For months she'd made a conscious effort not to think of him, but there were still times when he slipped unguarded into her mind. When Cassie accused her of being a neatness freak, she remembered Thad's gentle teasing on the same subject, as well as his respect of her need to have everything just so. When she rolled over in bed and saw the wisteria blooms hanging heavy from the live oaks outside, she remembered countless mornings of awakening to the same sight with Thad's arms around her. When she was tempted to skip her daily run on weekends, she remembered his coaxing and bribing her to get out of bed and onto the street. Oh, how she remembered his bribes!

He'd had no right to come here, not after the pain and sorrow he'd caused her. Did he regret what he'd done, what they'd lost? she wondered. Did he feel the slightest guilt over Donny? She wanted to believe that he did, that the man she'd fallen in love with couldn't go through that experience and be untouched by it.

But she wasn't sure. There had certainly been no sign of regret or guilt in his eyes or his voice. He had been the consummate FBI agent today: professional, detached, unemotional. He hadn't let a little thing like the fact that they had once been lovers interfere with his ability to conduct a thorough interview. He hadn't let anything as unimportant as love, betrayal or heartache cloud his mind.

Donny had never quite understood how she'd fallen in love with Thad. He fit perfectly the stereotypical image of an FBI agent, Donny had insisted: he was straitlaced, uptight, rigid, inflexible and completely lacking in a sense of humor. Almost as bad to her twenty-three-going-on-sixteen-year-old brother was Thad's taste. How could she possibly love a man who listened to classical music, preferred public television over sitcoms and thought "casual dress" meant loosening his tie?

Of course Donny had exaggerated. Thad hadn't been as bad as he'd made him sound . . . although he *had* fit the FBI agent stereotype, she admitted. There had been only two times when impeccably dressed, impeccably groomed and suitably solemn had given way to tousled and sweaty: after his five-mile-a-day run and after their always passionate lovemaking.

Before the longing she'd kept buried deep for eighteen months could work its way free, she turned her thoughts to the purpose behind their visit. Maybe, as Thad had pointed out, Donny *had* had a partner. Maybe someone *had* found the ransom money.

Or maybe Donny was alive.

The possibility made her tremble, made her eyes fill once more with tears. She had cried hysterically when she'd seen her brother fall from the bridge into the icy, rushing river below, and she had cried every night for months afterward—for Donny, for Thad, for herself. In one terrifying moment she had lost the two most important people in her life: Donny through death, and Thad through betrayal. She had lost everything.

But maybe she hadn't lost Donny after all.

If he had survived, where had he been the past year and a half? Why had he let her believe he was dead? Where was he now? Did he blame her for his arrest, for the fall, for the terrible injuries he must have suffered? Did he hate her?

She had no answers and didn't know where to find them. She had known so few of Donny's friends besides his roommate, Shawn Howard, and Donny's girlfriend. She had remained close to Shawn and knew that he would have told her if he had any reason to believe that Donny wasn't dead. As for the girlfriend, she had married some sailor out at the naval station and moved away more than a year ago. After disappearing for a year and a half, Donny would have even less idea of how to contact her than Lindsey had.

Wearily she forced herself out of the chair and went to work again in the back. The Mother's Day cards were finally put away, she thought with grim relief. It was unquestionably one of her most profitable holidays, but she found it depressing. Her own mother had been dead for more than twenty years, and she had never developed a mother-daughter relationship with the aunt who'd taken over raising her. To make it worse, Donny, only four at the time of their parents' deaths, had never been close to Aunt Louise, either, so he had chosen, instead, to give Lindsey the hand-made Mother's Day cards that had been grade school art projects. In a drawer at home, she had cards from him for every Mother's Day from the time he was six until his death—or disappearance—at twenty-three.

With a sigh, she taped the last box and moved it into the storeroom in back, then turned her attention to the cartons that covered her desk and worktable, opening each one and sifting through the contents. There were graduation cards for everyone from preschool to graduate school, high school to medical school. Funny ones, serious ones, religious ones. Other boxes held a wide variety of Father's Day cards: for natural fathers, adoptive fathers, stepfathers, grandfathers and single mothers who had to fill a father's role.

She found the banners she needed—graduation in bright primary colors and Father's Day in subdued greens and blues—and replaced the Mother's Day sign on the empty rack. Next, she began the task of unpacking the cards and sorting them into similar categories. She had to stop periodically to wait on customers, but she was finished with the graduation cards by the time Cassie arrived.

Her only help in the shop, Cassie Newton was a high school junior, lively and energetic and young. Lindsey couldn't remember ever being that young herself. But Cassie was also reliable and unfailingly responsible. Although her father had abandoned her mother with three younger children, Cassie intended to go to college after graduation next year, and virtually every penny Lindsey paid her went into the bank toward that goal. And every spare minute went into studying in order to earn scholarships to help, as well.

"I met the mailman outside, and he gave me your mail. Do you want to look at it now or later?"

"Later. Just put it on my desk, would you?" Lindsey stepped back to study her work, bent to straighten a stack of red envelopes, then smiled. Every card and every envelope was neatly lined up. There were no bent corners, no sun-faded edges, no cards out of place and no blue envelopes stuck in with green. For probably the only time in their brief season on this rack, the cards were displayed to perfection.

"Whoops, you must have missed this. That card is at least half a millimeter higher than the others." Cassie pretended to straighten the bottom stack of cards, then grinned at her boss. "You're so *precise* about everything. I bet when you cook and the recipe calls for half a teaspoon of salt, you use exactly half a teaspoon and not one grain more, don't you?"

"Don't be silly," Lindsey said, turning away to hide her guilty flush. Although she wouldn't admit it to Cassie for the world, her habits—fussiness, her aunt had called them; obsessiveness, others less kind had said—did follow her into the kitchen. She was one of the few cooks she knew—all right, the *only* cook she knew—who followed recipes precisely. She never tried to guess at a dash of this or a pinch of that. Just as she would never mix different colors or sizes of envelopes here in the shop, she wouldn't sprinkle an unknown amount of seasoning into a dish whose recipe called for exactly one half teaspoon.

It was all because of her parents' unexpected death—at least, that had been Thad's theory. Her life had suddenly been ripped apart: she had lost her parents, had been taken from the only home she'd ever known and had faced losing Donny, too, until their aunt had agreed to take them both in. In the strangeness of a new home with a new family, she had needed to control every aspect of her life that a ten-year-old could manage. She had needed to establish familiar routines, familiar habits, familiar places for the things important to her—every photograph, every precious gift from her parents, every single item that was *hers* and not her aunt's and not a hand-me-down from her cousins, had to be carefully accounted for.

"Want me to get started on the Father's Day cards?" Cassie offered. "You can come along behind and tidy up after me."

Lindsey gave her a fond smile. "Sure, go ahead. I'm going to put some of these empty boxes away." She gathered as many of the cartons as she could carry and stacked them on the shelves in the storeroom, then sat down for a moment at her desk. It was neat, as usual. Like Thad, Cassie had learned to respect her quirks. She had laid the mail carefully next to the phone, and her schoolbooks and purse were at the smaller desk in the corner where she studied when the store wasn't busy.

She didn't pick up the stack of letters and sort through them yet. The only mail that came here was business related—suppliers, distributors, utilities, insurance. Come to think of it, that was the only mail she got at home, too. Bills. The only family she kept in touch with and the few friends she had lived right here in Atlanta. She couldn't remember the last time she'd gotten something personal in the mail.

Then her forehead wrinkled in a frown. Yes, she could. It had been only a few weeks ago, but because something about it had disturbed her, she had tried, successfully it seemed, to put it out of her mind. It had come only a week after the write-up in the monthly magazine, *Atlanta Business,* about her shop and the line of greeting cards she had recently launched. She remembered looking at the pink envelope with its sloppily typed address and thinking that it was the same quality paper and one of the same delicate hues that she herself used with her own line of cards, Lindsey's Blooms. Count on a friend, she had thought fondly, to buy one of her own cards for her.

The card inside *had* been one of hers, with a blooming azalea on front and a congratulatory message inside. There had been no note, no signature. Just the blank card, the typed address and an Atlanta postmark. She'd tried to tell herself that it had been a perfectly harmless gesture—perhaps from an admirer too shy to sign his name—but it had still made her oddly uncomfortable. She had put the card in the bottom drawer of the rolltop desk in her living room and willed herself to forget it. Until now.

Could it have come from Donny? If he had survived the fall, if he was in the Atlanta area, he could have somehow come across the magazine article and wanted to congratulate her without giving himself away.

Then she gave a shake of her head. Donny reading *Atlanta Business?* When his reading material had rarely extended beyond the backs of cereal boxes and *Playboy?*

Maybe she was clutching at straws, taking too much hope from Thad's grudging concession. Maybe she wanted more than she'd realized for her brother to be alive and well. Maybe she desperately needed one part of her life to be right again.

A headache was forming behind her eyes, and she rubbed her temples to ease it. She could thank Thad for this. Both his sudden reappearance in her life and his news had been more than she could handle in one afternoon. Seeing him had made her remember once again all the hurt, all the sorrow. It had made her feel so sharply, once again, the emptiness he'd created within her.

And it had brought her hope. Hope that her brother was still alive. Hope that he would contact her, that someday he would forgive her for her part in his arrest. Hope that, if unfounded, could destroy her.

It was nearly six-thirty when she got home that evening. The shop stayed open until seven, but Cassie was more than capable of handling things. Lindsey collected the mail from the box, then let herself into the foyer. She put her purse on a shelf in the coat closet, dropped her keys into a porcelain dish on the hall table, checked herself in the adjacent mirror and laid the mail on her desk before turning the air conditioner on and heading upstairs to change.

She had fallen in love with the house—a neat, two-story Victorian in an older Atlanta neighborhood—the first time she'd seen it six years ago. Even though it had needed a great deal of work, even though its three bedrooms were more than she could use, even though the monthly payment had, until recently, been a strain on her budget, she had scraped together the money to buy it. She had moved in immediately, fixing it up one room at a time, living for months surrounded by the chaos of remodeling and never regretting one minute of it. For the first time since she was ten years old, she'd had a real home, a place that was all hers, a place where no one could tell her what to do or how to do it.

She smiled faintly as she entered the master bedroom. As much as she loved the house, she didn't know if she would make the same decision today. Six years ago she had been younger, more naive, more optimistic. Six years ago she had believed that she was working for her future, that one day she would share this place with that "special man," that they would fill the house with love and the extra bedrooms with children.

Now she knew better. The future she saw didn't include a special man or children or love. Her future appeared no different than her recent past: just Lindsey. Alone.

She traded her blue silk dress for nylon running shorts and a T-shirt, her three-inch heels for a pair of thickly padded and very expensive running shoes. The chignon came down, and a ponytail took its place, and a few moments at the sink removed the light layer of makeup she'd worn to work. She added a headband in peach—the same color as her shorts and socks—and thought ruefully as she faced the mirror that she was as fussy about her appearance as Donny had accused Thad of being. Instead of looking like a serious runner, she looked like one of those women whose primary concern in working out is how pretty they look while they do it. But she *was* serious. Five miles a day every evening in warm weather and every morning in cooler weather had given her the muscles to prove it.

She was on her way to the door when she remembered the mail sitting on her desk. Detouring that way, she swept up the stack of envelopes and thumbed through them. Junk, a bank statement, an insurance bill, a credit card bill—the usual stuff. Then she came to the last envelope.

Her address had been typed on the soft lavender paper with a faded ribbon, and one letter—the *l*s in her last name and the city—was barely distinguishable, as if the character hadn't struck the ribbon with enough force. A mistake on the street name had been corrected not by erasing but simply by typing over it—a quirk that she remembered from the last card she'd gotten.

Hands trembling, she sat down in the padded leather-and-wood chair, not hearing its protesting squeak, and carefully slit the envelope with a silver letter opener. She knew that when she pulled the card out, it would be one of Lindsey's Blooms. Would it have a note this time? Would it be signed?

When she saw the card, the pain was like a blow. It *was* one of hers—a heavy cluster of wisteria hanging from the Spanish moss-draped branch of a live oak—and embossed in silver script across the bottom was the message. Happy Mother's Day.

It *had* to be from Donny. He was the only person in the world who'd ever sent her a Mother's Day card, and he would know that the spring-blooming wisteria was her all-time favorite flower. Six years ago he had helped plant the vines that surrounded her own live oaks outside.

Breathing deeply, she forced herself to open the card. She ignored the verse she'd written months ago and went straight to the bottom. As before, there was no signature, but this time there *was* a note, neatly printed.

Lin, I left a gift for you at the bank. I love you.

For a long time she simply stared at the card, until tears blurred her vision. Then she laid it on the desk, bowed her head and cried. Donny was alive. Eighteen months of mourning, eighteen months of sorrow and regret and despair, were over. He was alive, he was in Atlanta, and if he'd hated her, he had forgiven her.

And he was also wanted by the FBI.

If your brother were alive and you knew, would you tell us, Ms. Phillips? Remembering Clint Roberts's question made her shudder uncontrollably. Only a few hours ago she had been offended, even insulted, by it. Of course she would, she had haughtily informed him. As much as she loved Donny, she didn't condone what he had done. She knew that if he had survived, if he had come back, he would have to pay for his crime.

But that had been easier to say four hours ago, when his survival had only been a remote possibility, when she'd been too numbed by the news to really understand what it meant. And what it meant was that she might have gotten her brother back only to lose him to a lifetime in prison. What it meant was that she would have to betray him again, the way she had betrayed him eighteen months ago.

Could she hide the card, keep it a secret, protect Donny and tell no one? Could she live with herself if she did?

Could she live with herself if she didn't?

Anchoring one foot on the floor, she pivoted the old oak chair from side to side and leaned her head back, studying the ornate molding where the wall met the ceiling. She had been raised first by her parents, then by her aunt and uncle, to respect the law and authority, to recognize right and wrong, to do the right thing. But she had also been taught to take care of her younger brother. What no one had ever told her was what to do when one conflicted with the other. Sentencing Donny to spend the rest of his life in prison certainly wasn't taking care of him, no more than protecting an admitted kidnapper was doing the right thing.

Opening the card with the tip of one finger, she read the note again. *Lin, I left a gift for you at the bank.* The bank? Remembering the unopened envelope from her bank, she frowned. She had automatically assumed it was a statement, but she'd gotten her checking and savings statements less than two weeks ago. They were filed in the bottom left drawer of this desk.

A gift at the bank. Suddenly a sick feeling took hold in the pit of her stomach. Dear God, not money, she prayed as she reached for the bank envelope. Not *ransom* money.

When she slit open the envelope and reached inside, she found a single slip of paper that showed a deposit made to her checking account over the weekend. A deposit of two thousand dollars.

Swallowing hard, she let go of the deposit slip and watched it flutter down to rest on top of the card. Her questions were answered, her doubts resolved. Reaching for the telephone, she dialed a number that, after all these months, she'd never forgotten. When she got an answering machine with its straight-to-the point message, she took a deep breath to control her trembling and said, "This is Lindsey. I—I have some news about Donny. If someone could call me... I'm at home now. The number's the same."

If he'd gone for his daily run alone, the way he used to, he would probably keep running after five miles, Thad thought as they rounded the corner onto the block where his apartment, part of an old two-story house, was located. He certainly had the energy to go on—nervous energy, he knew, from seeing Lindsey—but his running partner was already grumbling about the five miles Thad had insisted on. Deke Ramsey didn't take pleasure from the exercise itself as Thad did, but rather jogged from necessity. Being a deputy U.S. marshall required that he stay in good shape. And being the father, at the age of forty-five, of a lively almost-one-year-old son required that he get in even better shape.

They slowed their pace along the sidewalk until they were walking; then Thad led the way onto the porch and to his door. "How's the family?" he asked as he opened it.

Deke waited until they were inside to answer. "Tess is pregnant."

Thad had gone directly into the kitchen to get a couple of bottles of juice from the cabinet. Now he turned and studied his friend across the breakfast bar. "Is that good or bad?" he asked quietly. He knew Tess had had some problems conceiving the first time, and the pregnancy had been one crisis after another, resulting in the five-weeks-premature birth of their first—and, he had assumed, only—child.

Deke shrugged unhappily. "She's thirty-eight years old, and she spends twenty-four hours a day taking care of a miniature tornado. I know she wants more kids, but I'd rather try to adopt than see her go through another pregnancy like Andrew's."

"What does the doctor say?"

"That we'll see how it goes." Deke didn't sound reassured by that.

Remembering the juice bottles he held, Thad offered one to Deke, then uncapped his own, drinking deeply. He understood his friend's concern. Deke had been through two bad relationships and a lot of years alone before he'd met Tess Marlowe. The difference she'd made in his life had been amazing. For a time Thad had thought he and Lindsey had shared that kind of special love, but he'd been wrong. What they'd had hadn't been strong enough to withstand outside pressures and strain.

"What does Tess say?"

Slowly, unwillingly, Deke smiled. "That everything's going to be fine. Our mothers are taking turns helping her with Drew during the day, and she insists that she feels great and is stronger and healthier than anyone gives her credit for."

"People tend to underestimate her because she's so small," Thad pointed out. "She's also one of the most determined and obstinate people I've ever met. That's got to count for something." He pulled his glasses off and laid them on the bar, then noticed the blinking light signaling a message on the answering machine. He punched the button as he drained the last of the juice and was bending toward the wastebasket beneath the sink when the recording started to play.

"This is Lindsey. I—I have some news about Donny. If someone could call me... I'm at home now. The number's the same." There was a moment's silence, then a mechanical voice gave the time of the call.

He had missed her by less than ten minutes. He didn't know whether he was disappointed or relieved. After her reaction to his presence at her store this afternoon, he suspected the rush of emotion he felt was relief. All he had to do now was pass her message on to Clint Roberts. He didn't have to see her again, didn't have to expose himself to another icy, bitter reception, didn't have to subject himself to more pain.

"Lindsey?" Deke echoed. "As in Phillips?"

Thad tossed the bottle into the wastebasket and slowly straightened. "Yeah. We've reopened the Heinreid case. The ransom has started to show up in local banks with Donny Phillips's fingerprints all over it."

"You're not working this, are you?"

His disbelief made Thad smile faintly. Deke knew, better than most federal agents, the dangers of combining official investigations with personal relationships. So did Thad. His involvement in the kidnapping investigation a year and a half ago had ended his relationship with Lindsey. He would never make that same mistake again.

"No, I'm not assigned to it. But I did go with Roberts to interview Lindsey today. I—I just wanted to see her."

"Has anything changed?"

"No. She still blames me for Donny's death. She still thinks we handled it badly." He wiped the sweat from his face with a dish towel, then put his glasses on again. "The hell of it is maybe she's right. Maybe we—maybe I made a mistake."

"You told her up front that if her brother was involved in something illegal, you would have to turn him in."

"Turn him in," Thad agreed bleakly. "Not get him killed."

Deke made an annoyed gesture. "You didn't get him killed. He *jumped* off that bridge."

"But Lindsey doesn't know that. She saw us struggling, then she saw him fall."

"Why didn't you tell her the truth?"

"After he died, she never wanted to hear anything from me—especially that the brother she loved more than anything in the world took her along to that meeting *knowing* that she would be there to watch him die. He confessed to the kidnapping because he wanted a clear conscience before he died. Donny never intended to leave that bridge alive."

"So you sacrificed whatever chance you might have had with her to protect the memory of her dead brother?"

Thad avoided answering the question, focusing instead on the last words. "Maybe he's not so dead, after all. The

banks where the ransom has turned up are all in the area
where Donny lived and worked, and those *are* his fingerprints on the bills.''

''Fingerprints can be lifted from an item years later.''

''True. And the chances of him surviving that fall are in-
calculable. But if he did, that would explain where he's been
the last year and a half. He would have been badly hurt. He
would have needed time to heal, to recuperate.''

Deke shook his head, still skeptical. ''If he survived, it
would be a miracle, and I don't believe in miracles.''

''Don't you? You have Tess and Andrew and the baby.
Those are miracles.''

Deke's expression softened. ''Yeah,'' he agreed. ''They
are. And I'd better get home to them.'' He walked to the
door, then gestured to the answering machine. ''Are you
going to turn this over to the case agent ... or call her yourself?''

Thad found the right answer easily enough. ''It's Roberts's case, not mine.'' He said goodbye to his friend,
watched him run down the steps, then closed the door and
leaned against it. He would call Roberts and tell him to get
in touch with Lindsey. He wouldn't think about calling her
himself. He wouldn't even consider going over to her lovely
old house himself.

But when he moved away from the door, it wasn't to the
phone but rather, to the bathroom. He *would* call Roberts,
he promised himself, after he got out of his sweat-stained
running clothes and into a cool shower.

But fifteen minutes later, showered and dried, he didn't
reach for the phone but did reach for clothes. He *would* call
Roberts, he promised again, but it wouldn't hurt for him to
tag along again. After all, this had been *his* case originally;
he knew all the details, knew all the people involved. Roberts hadn't even been assigned to the Atlanta field office
until months after it had ended.

Finally he placed the phone call and arranged to meet the
other agent at Lindsey's house. Only then was he honest
with himself: it wasn't his interest in the case, professional
because he'd worked it originally and personal because of

his ties to Donny, that was drawing him out tonight. He wanted to see Lindsey again, plain and simple. In spite of this afternoon's unfortunate meeting, in spite of the pain at being reminded of how drastically things had changed between them, he wanted to see her, to talk to her, to be with her. She wouldn't agree to that woman-to-man right now, but she couldn't turn him down subject-to-FBI agent.

It wasn't much, but he would take whatever he could get.

Chapter 2

In a neighborhood of traditional, single-parent and blended families, Lindsey stood out as the only resident with no husband, no children and no roommates. Her house stood out, too—the neatest, prettiest, best maintained house on the block. Victorian in style, it was lavishly decorated with lacy scrolls, intricately turned spindles and detailed woodwork. Painted a soft blue and trimmed with bright white, it sat in the center of its lot, surrounded by lush grass, long beds of brilliantly colored flowers and a neat white picket fence. There were azaleas, now a mass of pink and white blooms, planted inside the fence, and three small crepe myrtles, their blossoms also pink and white, filled one corner of the yard.

How did she find the time, Thad wondered as he parked across the street, to keep the house looking as good as it had when it was built eighty years ago, the lawn in pristine condition and all those flower beds weeded, and still run her business? Maybe she had a yard service—but he doubted it. Letting someone else take care of her lawn and flowers would mean giving up some measure of control, and if he knew Lindsey, after Donny's disappearance she would have needed even more control over the areas of her life that allowed it.

Maybe this was her way of coping—keeping so busy that she rarely had time to consider what she'd lost. It had been that way for him, too, the first few months after their breakup. He had been driven, working late every night, making work on the few occasions when there was none to be done. He had increased his daily run from five to ten miles, had doubled his time at the gym, had spent more evenings with friends than ever before.

At last he'd realized that none of it was helping at the time when he'd needed help the most: late at night, alone in his bed. Those had been the worst times, when he remembered making love with Lindsey, holding her close while they slept or simply waking in the morning beside her. Gradually he had given up the long hours and resumed his normal schedule, in better physical condition than ever, but with his mental condition only slightly improved.

He crossed the street, then followed the sidewalk to the porch where an American flag hung limply in the still air. After ringing the doorbell, he glanced around at the wooden swing and the pots of bright red geraniums grouped around the furniture. The love seat and chairs were wicker, painted white—a weekend task Lindsey had recruited both him and Donny for—and cushioned in a soft floral patterned canvas. To thank them for their help, she'd taken them both out to dinner that Saturday evening; then Donny had left, and he and Lindsey had made love for the first—

His thoughts were interrupted by the opening door. Lindsey looked apprehensive—because she didn't want to see him again, didn't want him in her house again? he wondered—and she didn't say a word but merely gestured for him to enter. Sliding his hands into his pockets, he accepted her silent invitation, but stopped only a few feet inside the foyer. He didn't want to look around, didn't want to stir up the memories that were still so vivid—of times they had argued here, times they had made love, times they had simply held each other. He didn't want to breathe in the delicate scent of vanilla-flavored potpourri that he'd smelled earlier in her shop. He didn't want to see how little things had changed in her house and be reminded of how greatly things had changed in their lives.

Lindsey closed the door, automatically twisting the lock, then turned toward Thad. She wished she hadn't called him, but at the time, it had seemed like the right thing—the *only* thing—to do. Afterward, when she wasn't quite so shaken, she had looked in the phone book and had found the after-hours number for the FBI office. She could have called that number and spoken to some anonymous stranger, could have asked him to get in touch with the man who had come to her shop this afternoon, could have left Thad out of it entirely.

It was just like old times, she thought bitterly. Whenever she'd had a problem, she had always turned to him, too often without thinking it over first, and he had solved it for her. She had depended on him in ways she had never counted on anyone else, and he had never let her down...not until the most important problem of all. Not until Donny.

She stood there awkwardly, knowing what she needed to say but not finding the courage to do it. Finally Thad broke the silence.

"I called Clint Roberts. He's going to meet us here."

She nodded once, then glanced toward the living room. "Would you like to sit down?"

After a moment's hesitation, he went into the living room and sat in one of the two armchairs. She followed, moving an armful of embroidered pillows to wedge herself into one corner of the couch. They had spent so many hours in this room that it seemed natural to see him here, she thought, even though there was nothing natural about this meeting. They were awkward together in a way they had never been—not even as strangers meeting for the first time before the start of Atlanta's annual Peachtree Run. Of course, as strangers, they'd had nothing between them but the future. Now they had the past.

"So you still run."

Though his observation needed no answer—she hadn't taken the time to change from her gym shorts and T-shirt—

she offered one anyway, simply to break the silence. "Usually. I didn't make it this evening."

"That's where I was when you called—with Deke."

The mention of his friend filled her with the warmth, long forgotten, of deep affection. She had attended Deke and Tess Ramsey's wedding with Thad nearly two and a half years ago and, in the year that followed, had come to consider Tess one of her closest friends. But after the horrible scene involving Donny, she had cut not only Thad out of her life, but everything that had connected her to him. That had included his best friend's wife.

Tess had been a good friend. She had gotten Lindsey through those first few weeks when grief left her incapable of functioning, and had helped her plan the memorial service her cousins had wanted for Donny in place of a funeral. But Tess had been too close to Thad, and when she'd dared one day to gently suggest that Lindsey wasn't being fair to him, Lindsey had ended *their* relationship, too.

That had been a mistake, she could admit that now. After losing both her brother and her lover, the last thing she'd needed was to alienate her closest friend. At a time when she'd needed support badly, she had turned away from the only one left who could give it.

"How are Tess and Deke?" she asked softly.

"Fine. They have a son who will be one next month."

Lindsey smiled for the first time all evening. "That's wonderful. Tess had told me that she'd wanted a baby for so long. I didn't know she'd finally gotten her wish."

"How could you? You dumped them along with me."

She was caught off guard by the bitterness in his voice, and it chased away her smile. How could he make it sound as if *she* had been the one at fault, as if *she* had been responsible for the end of their relationship? Had he really expected her to overlook his role in Donny's death or disappearance or whatever the hell it was? To accept his sweet little apology and go on loving him? To forget that he'd destroyed what was left of her family, forget that he'd betrayed her love and her trust? "After what you did—"

The doorbell interrupted her, and she clamped her lips together in a thin line as she went to answer the door. Clint Roberts waited there, still in his suit and tie, as if his workday hadn't yet ended, which, she supposed, it hadn't, since this was definitely a business call.

"Ms. Phillips," he greeted her politely. "Is Special Agent McNally here?"

"Yes, he is. Come on in." She led him into the living room, but instead of sitting down again, she went to her desk. "I—I got this card in the mail today. I think it's from Donny." She didn't pick up the card or the envelope, but just waved her hand limply in their direction. She didn't know much about law enforcement, but she assumed they would want as few extra fingerprints on it as possible.

Both men approached the desk. Thad was closest to her, and she edged around until she was standing at the opposite end with Clint Roberts between them—subtly so, she thought, until she looked up and met Thad's knowing, judging gaze. Blushing, she dropped her own gaze to the card.

Roberts picked up a ballpoint pen and used its tip to open the card. He read the handwritten note out loud, then let it close again and picked up the deposit slip. "The gift?"

"I guess. *I* didn't make that deposit."

"Why would your brother send you a Mother's Day card?" Roberts asked curiously.

Lindsey folded her arms across her chest and leaned back against the wall. "Donny was four years old when our parents died. We were sent to live with an aunt and uncle who had four kids of their own and didn't want any more. They took us in out of duty, not desire." She broke off for a moment. This would be easier if Thad weren't here. It was ironic. Once he'd known everything about her, every intimate secret and every painful memory, including this one. But confiding in a man she was going to spend the night with—a man she was hoping to spend the rest of her life with—was a different matter altogether from confiding in a man who was conducting an official federal investigation.

Sighing softly, she continued, still directing her conversation toward Roberts. "Remember when you were in grade school and you made drawings and cards for all the holidays, including Mother's Day?" She paused only briefly before going on. "Well, Donny never felt close to our aunt, and he didn't have a mother, so he gave his stuff to me. It became a tradition."

"Who knew that?"

She gave it a moment's thought. "I suppose our aunt must have known when we still lived with her, and maybe our cousins. I don't think Donny would have told any of his friends. It was sentimental, and sentimentality embarrassed him."

"*I* knew," Thad said quietly.

All her secrets, Lindsey thought, feeling a twinge of pain centered deep in her chest. He had known everything—how much she'd loved him, how much she had loved Donny—and yet it hadn't affected his decisions in any way. His job had come first.

Ignoring him, she pulled the desk chair to one side and sat down, protectively folding her arms again. "I got one other card. It came a couple of weeks ago. There was no note, no signature, but the address was probably done on the same typewriter, and whoever typed it made the same mistake."

"Why didn't you tell us about it this afternoon?" Roberts asked.

"Because I had no reason to believe it was from Donny," she snapped, then made an effort to control the emotion in her voice. "It was a congratulatory card. The last issue of *Atlanta Business* did a feature on my store and my line of cards, and this card came a couple of days after the magazine came out. I thought—I thought it was from a friend or an acquaintance. I didn't know... I didn't suspect..."

"Do you still have it?"

She nodded.

Roberts glanced at Thad. "I'll get the evidence kit out of the car. We can run them for fingerprints and check with the manufacturer to see how many markets in the Atlanta area sell these particular cards. It's a long shot, but maybe we can find out where he bought them."

"There are forty-seven outlets," Lindsey said numbly. "Forty-two of them are in this area."

Both men looked at her curiously.

"This is *my* card," she explained. When that didn't seem to enlighten them, she leaned forward and pulled a birthday card from the bottom desk drawer, tossing it facedown on the desk. Centered on the back was a drawing of a single delicate rose, and forming a graceful arch above and below it was the name of the line, Lindsey's Blooms.

Thad picked up the card and turned it over. The paper was a good quality stock, heavy and textured and pure white, and the artwork—magnolia blossoms floating in a woodland pool—consisted of simple, clean lines that gave a sense of serenity to the scene. The verse inside, printed in flowing black script, was unabashedly sentimental—but then, Lindsey had never been embarrassed by sentimentality. That was part of the reason she'd spent so many hours fixing up this old house, part of the reason she'd gone into the gift-shop business to begin with.

It was also part of the reason she hated him.

He turned the card over again and studied the logo while Roberts asked if she had a list of her buyers. Of course she did, Thad thought, and then heard her say that it was filed away at the shop. If Roberts would stop by the next morning—she made it clear that the invitation didn't extend to Thad—she would give it to him.

Roberts left to get the evidence kit, and Thad finally looked up. "I've seen these in the store." Seen them? Hell, he'd *bought* them—for Andrew's birth, his mother's birthday, his parents' anniversary, for the only woman he'd seen with any regularity after Lindsey. He'd noticed the name on the back and had thought it only a painful coincidence. He had never imagined that the Lindsey of Lindsey's Blooms was *this* Lindsey. *His* Lindsey. "They're nice. I didn't know..."

She didn't say anything. She just sat there, jaw set stubbornly, staring at nothing, as if he hadn't spoken, as if he weren't even there.

It made him suddenly angry—this silence, this bitterness between them. They had once been too important to each other to wind up this way. He wanted to grab her, to shake that haunted look right out of her eyes, to make her understand that he'd had no choice in the things he'd done. He wanted to make her see that he had paid for them every bit as dearly as she had. He wanted...God, he wanted to touch her, just for a moment, to hold her the way he'd held her countless times in the past, to know that, just for that moment, she could stop hating him and could remember loving him.

But he didn't take a step toward her, didn't reach for her. She would never forgive him and would never stop hating him. That hatred had given her the strength to deal with Donny's disappearance. It would get her through these next few weeks or months until Donny was found. She relied on it, trusted in it, far more than she'd ever trusted in *him*.

Roberts returned, letting himself into the house. Using tonglike forceps, he placed the card and the envelope into separate plastic bags, labeled and sealed them. He repeated the process with the second card, carefully fishing it from the back of the bottom drawer.

Once it was sealed, too, Thad compared the addresses on both envelopes. Lindsey had been right. They appeared to have been typed on the same typewriter and probably by the same person. It was a manual typewriter, he suspected, one with a defective key and a well-worn ribbon. The lab could tell them more once they'd had a chance to study the envelopes.

"We'll need your fingerprints, Ms. Phillips," Roberts said, "to compare against whatever we find on these cards. Can you come by our office tomorrow?"

She nodded. "It'll have to be early. And I might as well bring the list of buyers with me then."

After collecting his equipment and the three evidence bags, Roberts glanced from her to Thad. "I'll see you tomorrow," he said to neither one in particular before he left.

Thad knew he should leave with him, but there was something he wanted to say, and this might be his last chance. He shifted uncomfortably, then slid his hands into the hip pockets of his trousers. "What I did," he said sharply, referring back to her accusation that Roberts's arrival had interrupted, "was my job. I was a federal agent long before I ever met you. You knew that from the moment you got involved with me. You knew that when you told me you were worried about Donny. You *knew* that if he'd done something illegal, I would have had no choice but to arrest him."

She stared at him, her brown eyes cold. "Arresting him and killing him are hardly the same thing."

"It doesn't look like he's dead, does it?" he reminded her sarcastically. Then his anger faded, and the bitterness returned. "It's ironic, you know. You claimed to love both of us, yet you can forgive Donny for kidnapping a terrified old lady and holding her prisoner for five days for no reason other than money. Greed. But you can't forgive me for doing nothing more than my job, for being the cop who arrested him. Donny was the one who committed the crime, but I was the one you made pay for it." He shrugged. "So much for love."

With that, he turned and walked out, leaving Lindsey sitting there, eyes squeezed shut. She heard the click of the door closing behind him and a moment later heard the purr of an engine as he drove away.

So much for love. He'd sounded skeptical, as if he'd given up believing in love—at least, in *her* love. But she *had* loved him, dear God, so much so that she still ached with it. *He* was the one who had ended it, who had destroyed what was between them . . . wasn't he?

You're not being fair to Thad, Tess Ramsey had told her so long ago. Lindsey had known his obligations, had understood the demands his job placed on him. She had known he couldn't turn his back on a crime simply because

it was her brother who had committed it—and not just because he was an FBI agent, but because that was the kind of
man he was—honest, principled, upright.

But that didn't change the fact that because of him, her
brother had nearly died. If Thad had handled things differently, if he had come to her and told her what Donny had
done, she could have helped him. She could have convinced her brother to turn himself in. She could have prevented that terrifying scene on the bridge.

And none of *that,* she admitted miserably, changed the
fact that she missed Thad. That losing him had, in its way,
hurt more than losing Donny. That while she had accepted
Donny's loss months ago, she still mourned Thad's.

The sound of the doorbell pulled her from her thoughts.
Had Thad or Clint Roberts forgotten something? she wondered, taking a quick look around as she rolled the chair
back into place at the desk.

It wasn't either of them at the door, but Shawn Howard
instead. He was twenty-five, blond, good-looking and always a pleasure to have around. He had been Donny's
roommate for two years, his friend for years longer. He was,
besides her shop, the only bright spot in her life. When she
was depressed or sad, Shawn could cheer her up. He could
always make her laugh. He could always make her feel that
life was worth living after all.

He hugged her when he came inside. "I came by earlier
and saw that you had company. Are you free now?"

She nodded.

"Then change your clothes and come to the club with me
tonight. I'm trying out a new routine, and I could use the
support."

The club was the Comedy Spot, an Atlanta nightclub that
featured up-and-coming comedians. Shawn appeared there
several times a week, fine-tuning his act, polishing his style,
hoping for the break that would lead to bigger and better
things. He had already established a solid reputation as one
of Atlanta's premiere comics, and he had his sights set on
upgrading that to one of the nation's best.

Normally Lindsey was more than happy to go with him. She enjoyed all the acts and offered Shawn a different perspective on his routine. But this time she smiled a little sadly and shook her head. "I can't go tonight, Shawn," she said apologetically. "But could I have a few minutes of your time? I need to tell you something."

He immediately agreed and followed her into the living room. He always gave her whatever she asked for, she reflected. In eighteen months he'd never turned her down, whether she'd needed a sympathetic ear or a shoulder to cry on, he had always been there for her. That made it easier for her to break the news to him.

"Two FBI agents came to the shop today. They think that Donny—" Tears welled in her eyes, and she had to swallow hard and start again. "They think Donny might be alive. They think he's back in Atlanta."

Shawn stared at her, his blue eyes wide with shock. "My God, Lindsey... Where is he? Is he all right? Has anyone seen him? Has he tried to get in touch with you?"

"Some of the ransom has turned up in local banks with his fingerprints on it. And I've gotten a couple of cards that I think are from him. They're not signed, but I'm sure he sent them."

He stared at her a moment longer, then his mouth curved into a big smile. "God, Lindsey, he's *alive*. But where has he been? And why hasn't he come to see you?"

"Maybe he blames me for what happened." Although the thought had occurred to her this afternoon, it hurt to put it into words now.

Shawn gave her a quick hug. "Of course he doesn't blame you. You're his *sister*. You practically raised him." Then, more thoughtfully, he added, "But maybe he's concerned about what would happen if he contacted you. Maybe he doesn't know that you aren't seeing McNally anymore."

He must have seen something in her eyes, Lindsey guessed, because suddenly his own grew dark and cold. "Was he one of the agents who came to see you?"

She nodded.

"That bastard. Doesn't he have any consideration for your feelings?"

She rested her head on his shoulder. "It's his job," she said numbly. "His job always comes first."

They sat in silence for a moment, then Shawn tilted her chin up so he could see her face. "How did it feel seeing him again?"

"It hurt."

"Do you still love him?"

She shook her head slowly. "How could I after what he did? He never gave Donny a chance—never gave *us* a chance. He treated Donny like any other suspect in any other crime. He *knew* him, *knew* what kind of person he was, but he didn't let that make any difference in the way he handled the case."

Shawn didn't say anything, and Lindsey was grateful for that. Grateful that he didn't remind her that Donny had committed a serious crime. Grateful that he didn't agree that yes, Thad had known what kind of person Donny was—immature, irresponsible, immoral and greedy. Grateful that he didn't ask her if she could have loved a man, a government agent, who let his personal feelings influence how he did his job.

"I sound foolish," she admitted sheepishly. "My head knows it's wrong to put all the blame on Thad...but my heart can't help it. I still feel so betrayed."

"Because he put his job first?"

After a moment's thought, she nodded. After her parents had died, she had never been really important to anyone. Aunt Louise had raised them because she felt she had to, and she had always met the needs—emotional, physical, financial—of her own kids first. Donny and Lindsey had only gotten leftovers, hand-me-downs. But she understood that. They weren't Louise's. She hadn't loved them the way she'd loved her own kids. But Thad...

He'd said he loved her more than anything. He had even, a few times, talked about marrying her, about having a family with her, about spending the rest of his life with her. But when he'd been forced to choose between loyalty to her and loyalty to his job, he'd chosen his job. And he had done his job coldly and efficiently, destroying her family, her dreams, her future and her love.

The clock on the mantel chimed softly, and she withdrew from Shawn's embrace and stood up. "You'd better get going or you'll be late," she said with a sniff.

"I can cancel tonight and take you to dinner instead," he offered.

"Thank you, but I wouldn't be good company. I—I think I need to be alone."

"You're alone too much, Lindsey. It's not healthy for a woman as young and pretty as you." But accepting that she wouldn't change her mind, he bent to kiss her forehead. "I'll be at the club until midnight if you need to talk or anything, okay?"

She nodded, then went outside and watched him leave. When his car was out of sight, she slowly went back into the house. Alone too much. There was no question of that. She hadn't had a date since the last time she and Thad had gone to dinner two nights before Donny's arrest. Thad had known then what was going on, had known that he was going to arrest her brother, but he'd pretended that nothing was wrong. He had acted—

She drew up short and slowly sank down to the nearest seat, the bottom step of the stairs. That wasn't true. He had been quiet, preoccupied, the entire evening. He had been more serious than usual, and she hadn't been able to coax more than one or two faint smiles from him. She hadn't been able to coax him into spending the night with her, either, as he usually did. Instead, he had kissed her good-night on the porch and for a long time had held her in a silent but fierce embrace.

Because he'd known what was going to happen? Because he'd felt badly about not being able to confide in her? Because he'd suspected that after Donny's arrest she might not give him another opportunity to hold her?

Determinedly she got to her feet and checked the laces on her shoes. It was after eight o'clock and nearly dark, but she was going to run a mile or two around the neighborhood anyway. It would give her a break from thinking. From remembering. From feeling.

It would give her a break from hurting.

Early Tuesday morning she went by the shop and picked up the file containing her distributor lists for the cards, then drove to the federal building downtown. She had been there a few times in the past with Thad, so she was vaguely familiar with the offices.

If Thad was around, she saw no sign of him as Clint Roberts led her back to the area where he would take her fingerprints. Of course, Thad had other cases to work on, and there was no reason to think he might be hanging around here just because he'd known she was coming by this morning. Besides, it wasn't as if she *wanted* to see him.

So why did she feel something disturbingly close to disappointment at his absence?

"Have you ever been fingerprinted before?" Roberts asked as he rolled a thin layer of ink across a sheet of glass.

"No."

"Don't turn your fingers. Let me do it for you."

He started with her right hand, rolling her thumb across the ink, then repeating the action in the appropriate square on the fingerprint card. Lindsey concentrated her attention on a mark on the wall. It wasn't easy making her fingers limp, letting someone else control their movements. She had to fight the urge, when he reached for her other hand, to tell him that she could do it without his help this time.

Was it natural to feel so uneasy about being fingerprinted, even when she knew she hadn't done anything wrong? she wondered. She decided it must be. After all, how many average, law-abiding citizens had their fingerprints on file with the FBI? She could be identified now by anything she touched for the rest of her life. It gave her a strange feeling.

When the agent was finished, he gave her a moment to wash the ink from her hands, then escorted her out of the office and back to the elevator. "Thanks for coming by, Ms. Phillips. If anything comes up, we'll be in touch."

She knew he didn't mean they would keep her informed. Thad certainly hadn't done that. She'd had no idea Donny had done anything serious until that day on the bridge when the two men had begun to struggle. She hadn't found out what crime he *had* committed until hours after he'd fallen, when the search for his body had been called off for the night, when the news was already in the papers and on television, and even then it had been Deke Ramsey who'd told her, not Thad.

Of course, she shamefully reminded herself, just a few hours before that she had accused Thad of murdering her brother and had hysterically slapped his hands away when he had tried to hold her, to comfort her. She had screamed at him through her tears, had said horrible, hurtful things before two of the other agents present had taken her to their car and driven her home. One of them, at Thad's request, had called Deke, who had picked up Tess and met them at her house.

She had seen Thad only three times after that. Late that evening he had come to her house, asking to see her, to talk to her, but she'd told Tess to send him away. A week later he had tried again. There had been no one with her that time, so she'd been forced to answer the door herself, to confront him herself. That was the first time she had truly hated him. By then she'd had seven days without her brother, seven days to experience the emptiness his death had left in her life, seven days of relentless grief, and she had hated Thad for every miserable minute.

The last time she had seen him after that night was at Donny's memorial service. A month had passed, bleak and lonely, and she had survived the cheerless holiday season, Christmas coming and going without her noticing. Although Donny's body had never been found, the FBI had been convinced that he'd died in the fall, and the case had been closed. Pressured by her cousins and Aunt Louise to arrange some sort of service, Lindsey had given in and done it with Tess's help, and Thad, no doubt informed by Deke, had been there.

She remembered thinking that she should make him leave, that he'd had no right coming to pay his respects when it was his fault that Donny had died. But she'd been too drained, too empty, to create a scene, so she had shut him out of her mind, the same way she had shut him out of her heart. She had ignored the haunted look in his eyes, the lines that sorrow had etched into his face and the rough edge grief had given his voice. She had ignored his words of apology, of sadness, of guilt and of love. She had let him speak, then had walked away without a word.

Was that when he'd given up? When he had realized that there was nothing left between them to save? When he had accepted that Donny wasn't the only casualty that day on the bridge? It must have been, because he had never called her again, had never tried to see her again. He had gone on with his life, and she had done the best she could with hers. Gradually her grief had faded, and she had filled all the empty spaces in her life with work—first as executive assistant to her last boss, then for herself. She had accepted and dealt with Donny's death, and she had told herself that she'd accepted losing Thad, too.

Even though it wasn't true.

"Ma'am? Are you going down?"

The voice intruding into her thoughts made her start. She blinked, then focused her gaze on the elevator car in front of her, doors open, and a half-dozen passengers waiting impatiently. She remembered Clint Roberts pressing the button before he'd walked away, but then she had gotten lost in her memories. She hadn't heard the bell ding when the car had arrived, hadn't seen the doors open. The past could do that to her.

Giving a shake of her head, she entered the elevator with a murmured apology. Lost in her memories, she said silently as the doors slid shut. She'd spent most of the last eighteen hours there, lost in the unhappiest time of her life. If she had to relive the past, why couldn't it be better times? Why couldn't she remember joy instead of sorrow, hope instead of despair? Why couldn't she remember the twenty-three years she'd had with Donny instead of the eighteen months without him? And why couldn't she remember loving Thad instead of hurting him, hating him, losing him?

Chapter 3

Friday afternoon found Thad sitting at his desk, his fingertips pressed together to form a steeple, which he studied intently while listening to Clint Roberts talk.

"Trying to find the store where Phillips bought the cards is like looking for a needle in a haystack," Clint said flatly. "We've only crossed three off our list so far. We have forty-four to go. We've also been interviewing some of his friends, his cousins and his aunt and uncle. No one admits to knowing anything. I checked with the sister's bank, and two thousand dollars of ransom money did turn up there over the weekend. One of the tellers remembers the deposit because it was mailed in and she thought that was odd, sending two thousand dollars' cash through the mail."

"What other choice did he have?" Thad asked, finally relaxing his hands and leaning back to rock in his chair. "All transactions in the lobby and at the night deposit are videotaped. We would have gotten the tapes and identified him."

"Or someone else," Roberts added.

"You think someone's trying to make it look as if Donny's alive?"

"We can't rule it out, not yet."

"What about the fingerprints on the cards?"

"The only ones we can match are Lindsey's. There are dozens of others—probably belonging to store clerks, customers and postal workers—but none of them are Donny's."

But all that meant, Thad speculated, was that maybe Donny had gotten smart, had learned from his earlier experiences. Instead of leaving fingerprints all over everything as he'd done before—the victim's house, the two ransom demands, the cabin where he'd held the elderly woman and the van he'd transported her in—maybe this time he was using gloves. As far as the prints on the money, as Deke had pointed out earlier this week, they could be old, left there from eighteen months ago when Donny was too dumb to know better.

"The envelopes were definitely done on the same typewriter," Roberts continued. "The lab is comparing the handwriting on the Mother's Day card to the ransom notes. It looks the same to me, but we'll know for sure Monday." He fell silent for a moment as if going over a mental checklist. Satisfied that he'd covered everything, he said, "You were the only one here who knew Phillips, right?"

Thad nodded.

"Does this seem like something he would do? Hiding away for eighteen months, letting his sister believe he was dead, then suddenly sending her money and cards?" He paused. "It seems kind of cruel—as if he's playing with her."

Thad removed his glasses and rubbed the bridge of his nose, then looked across the desk. Roberts was fuzzy, an indistinct form that melted into other forms. Everything was soft, hazy, with no sharp lines or hard edges. It wasn't a bad way to look at things sometimes.

Then he put the glasses on again, and everything returned to clear, harsh focus. "I don't know," he said finally, in response to Roberts's question. "Donny may have been twenty-three, but he was still a kid. He was spoiled. Lindsey spent most of her life not being just a sister, but mother and father to him, as well. She accepted responsibility for him when she was ten years old, and she's never given it up. I know she meant well, but as a result Donny never grew up. He never had to.''

"So he was spoiled, irresponsible and selfish. He depended on his big sister to take care of things for him. So why hasn't he let her handle the mess he's in now? Because he thinks it's her fault in the first place?''

Thad shrugged. "If he blames anyone, it's probably me. He thought I was a bad influence on Lindsey.''

"You didn't get along with him?''

"If Lindsey's relationship with him was motherly, I guess mine was almost fatherly. We got along, and we fought. There were a lot of things we agreed on, and a lot we didn't. I thought he was immature and that he took advantage of Lindsey. He thought I was too strict and that she could find someone better. He didn't take anything seriously. He never held a job for more than a few months at a time because something more important always came up—going to the beach in Charleston or playing basketball in the afternoons or hanging out with his friends. Life was a game to him. I think the kidnapping was a game, a challenge. He planned it, he carried it out and he almost got away with it.''

"And would have if not for you.''

Thad nodded. It was all in the case file. How Lindsey had come to him with her concerns about Donny. How he had seen the same changes in Donny that had alarmed her. How he had begun checking into the younger man's activities and had uncovered his sudden spending spree. How he had come across the information that the last company Donny had worked for, a large carpet dealer, had installed new carpet in the Heinreid house only two weeks before Mrs. Heinreid was kidnapped. How he had realized that the elderly lady's description of her kidnapper perfectly matched Donny Phillips, from his physical appearance right down to his personality.

The rest was in there, too. Thad didn't know how Donny had found out that he was being investigated—maybe one of his friends or former co-workers who'd been interviewed had passed the information along—but he *had* found out. Totally serious for probably the first time in his life, he had called Thad and requested a meeting. He had set the time—two o'clock on a cold December afternoon—and the place—a lonely road outside Atlanta where a bridge crossed high over the rushing river below.

Backed up by seven other agents who had remained out of sight, Thad had waited on the bridge, worrying a little about Donny and more about Lindsey. How would she react when he revealed that her precious brother was a criminal, a kidnapper who had terrorized a defenseless old lady? How would she deal with his arrest and the upcoming trial? How would she accept the fact that Donny would probably spend the rest of his life in prison?

But he hadn't had to tell her anything. Donny had brought her to the meeting, and from the safety of her car, she'd seen it all.

Sometimes he wondered how different things would have been if Donny hadn't chosen to jump from that bridge. If the arrest had gone as planned, if Donny were in prison right now, would Lindsey still hate *him*? Would she see that he hadn't been responsible for Donny's choices or for the consequences of those choices? Or would she still blame Thad? Would she still damn him for doing the job he'd sworn to do?

When the phone on the corner of his desk rang, he welcomed its distraction. He'd spent more than enough hours this week thinking of Lindsey and Donny. It was time now to put them out of his mind and regain control of his life.

But that wasn't to be. The voice on the line was soft and Southern and unbearably familiar. "Hello, Lindsey," he said in a carefully guarded voice.

There was a brief silence; then she spoke. "Someone's been in my house, and some of Donny's things that were stored upstairs are gone. Could you come—" She broke off, cleared her throat and tried again. "Could you ask someone to come over?"

"There's no evidence of a forced entry, Ms. Phillips," Clint Roberts said as he faced Lindsey in the broad hallway of her house. "And there doesn't seem to be anything out of place. What makes you so sure someone's been here?"

"I told you. The stereo was on when I came home, and it's tuned to a country station. *I* don't listen to country music. Donny does. The spread on his bed is wrinkled, as if someone sat down on it. Some of his stuff is missing. Some things in the living room have been moved—that silver picture frame, that angel figurine, that flower vase." Lindsey turned to gesture toward the items, knowing that her movements were jerky, but she couldn't help it. Ever since she'd walked into the house an hour ago, she'd been fighting for self-control. It was only when Thad, Clint Roberts and the other agents arrived that her trembling had stopped, that she'd begun to feel in control again.

Roberts dismissed the change in settings on her stereo as inconsequential, she saw, and he wasn't impressed by the rest of her claim, either. He didn't *know,* as surely as she knew her own name, that the picture frame had been turned in the opposite direction when she'd left the house this morning, that the angel had been exactly centered on the small shelf where it sat, that the vase had been a few inches to the left. He didn't know, either, that the frame held the last photo ever taken of Lindsey and Donny together, that the angel had been his last birthday present to her, and that the lopsided vase, its glaze now cracked and peeling, had been Donny's one and only attempt at pottery-making the summer he was fifteen. It had also been a gift.

"How long has it been since your brother lived in this house?"

She sighed. "Three and a half years."

"How long since you've been in his room?"

Again she sighed. This time her impatience showed. "Not since January of last year."

"So how can you be sure that the bedspread in there hasn't been wrinkled all that time? And how can you be sure that you didn't simply misplace these things you say are missing? Maybe you gave them away. Maybe they're packed up someplace else."

Lindsey opened her mouth for a scathing retort, then closed it again and took a deep breath. Before she was calm enough to reply, Thad answered for her.

"Lindsey doesn't misplace things," he said quietly. "She doesn't forget where she puts them. Look around, Clint. Everything is exactly where it belongs. It's one of her quirks."

The other agent did look around, and so did Lindsey, wondering what he saw with that detached, professional gaze. *She* saw neatly organized rooms, the living room behind her and the sitting room in front, with everything tucked into its own little niche—homey but not cluttered. She saw her home, her own private place, that had been invaded by somebody this afternoon, that was being invaded now by the agents who were dusting for fingerprints.

"Did Donny have a key to the house?" Roberts asked.

She nodded.

"What happened to it when he disappeared?"

"I guess he had it with him." Her voice was husky, and she cleared her throat before going on. "I packed all of his things from his apartment myself, and the only keys I found were an extra set for his car."

"And you stored everything upstairs?"

She nodded again.

"Did you get rid of anything—sell, give away, throw away?"

"Only his car." She felt Thad's gaze on her, and it made her uncomfortable. "I—I never got around to sorting through the rest of his stuff—the clothes, the books, the keepsakes." In the beginning, it would have been too painful, would have added a finality to Donny's death that she hadn't been ready to accept. Then, as the sorrow had lessened, she had put the items out of her mind. As long as she didn't need that bedroom at the end of the hall, she didn't have to think about the boxes it held.

"Will you show us his room?" Roberts asked.

Holding in a sigh of relief, Lindsey led the way up the stairs and to the last bedroom. She pushed open the door, then stepped back to allow them to enter. She stayed there in the doorway, not venturing into the room.

The wide closet doors stood open, and Thad walked over, looking without touching. The bar that stretched from end to end was filled with hanging clothes—one suit, two jackets, jeans and T-shirts, sweatpants and sweatshirts—and one empty hanger. Stacked on the floor were boxes, all of them neatly taped but one. It held a trophy for track, the only sport Donny had participated in in high school, a half-dozen cassette tapes, a couple of books, a small jewelry case—open and empty—and a blank picture frame.

"What's missing?" Roberts asked as he joined Thad at the closet.

"A brown leather jacket," Lindsey replied. "Also, a ring that belonged to our mother, and a photograph. It was a smaller copy of the one in the silver frame downstairs."

Thad turned from the closet and approached Lindsey. He had remained silent, more or less, since they'd arrived because this wasn't his case. He could tag along out of professional courtesy, but he couldn't get involved in this investigation. He wouldn't let himself. Still, he quietly asked her to recount everything that she'd found when she'd gotten home from work.

She took a deep breath, then began. "I left work early because I had a headache. As soon as I opened the door, I knew someone had been here. The stereo was playing—I don't even listen to it in the morning—and it was on a country station. I *never* listen to country music. I came in—"

"Why didn't you go to a neighbor's house and call us then?" Thad interrupted heatedly. "How did you know the intruder wasn't still inside?"

She met his gaze. Hers was level and calm, his sharp and angry that she'd been so foolish, so careless. After a long moment, she gave him a cool and distant reply. "My brother would never hurt me."

"Your brother isn't the only man in the city of Atlanta who listens to country music." Then, his mouth clamped shut in a thin line, he gestured for her to go on.

"As soon as I saw the things that had been disturbed, I knew it was Donny. I called his name and looked for him downstairs. When I didn't find him, I came up here. The bedspread was rumpled, the closet doors were open, that hanger was empty and the ring and the photograph were gone." She fell silent for a moment, then looked at Thad again. "*Then* I called you."

Roberts excused himself, passing between them, leaving them alone while he went downstairs to talk to his men. Thad rubbed the back of his neck, then dropped his hand to his side and said, "I'm sorry. But if your burglar had still been here and it wasn't Donny, you could have been hurt—or killed."

"But he wasn't still here, and it was Donny."

"Maybe."

The look she gave him was defiant. "It *was*. Who else would break into my house to steal a picture of the two of us together?"

"Someone who wants us to believe that Donny's still alive?"

"No." She whispered it first, then repeated it in a stronger voice. "No."

"It's a possibility, Lindsey. I know you want Donny to be alive—damn it, so do I—but you have to be prepared for the possibility that he isn't." He knew what it had cost her to lose Donny eighteen months ago. If she became convinced beyond all doubt that her brother was still alive, then found out that he wasn't, that this was simply someone's cruel joke, how would she cope? How could she handle such deception without letting it destroy her?

"Don't come to me, giving me hope that my brother might have survived that fall," she whispered, her eyes glittering with tears, "then destroy that hope by telling me that I have to be prepared for the possibility that he didn't. What about the fingerprints on the money? What about the Mother's Day card? What about this?" She flung out one hand to indicate the room behind him.

"Lindsey—"

She backed away so suddenly that she almost stumbled when she bumped into the wall. Thad was bewildered by her movement until he realized that he had unconsciously, instinctively, reached for her. His need to touch her, to give to her, to comfort her, hadn't diminished in the last eighteen months, he realized bitterly, and neither had her need to avoid his touch.

He stared at her for a long moment, weary and hurt and immeasurably sad. "I would never hurt you, either, Lindsey," he said quietly, referring to her earlier remark about Donny. "If I could protect you from ever being hurt again, I would. That's why I want you to be careful. I want you to remember that just as we have no proof that Donny is dead, we don't have any proof that he's alive, either. Losing him once was terrible. Losing him a second time..."

Could be devastating, she finished to herself as several of the agents came down the hall. Hugging her arms to her chest, she moved out of the doorway and walked the few feet to the window seat at the end of the hall. "I can't give up hope," she said in a low, trembling voice. "That's all I have left."

Thad slowly approached her. Afraid that she would rush away again? she wondered with a bleak smile. It had been fear, not hatred or disgust, that had sent her backing away from his outstretched hand a moment ago. Fear that he might touch her gently, that he might offer her the warm intimacy of his embrace, that he might hold and comfort her the way no other man ever had. And, worse, fear that she would accept whatever he offered. That she would forget the sorrow, the sadness and the grief he had caused her and remember only the love and happiness he'd given her.

It had been only Tuesday morning that she had wondered why, if she had to remember anything at all, it couldn't be the good times between them. It seemed as if her lament had opened the door on memories she had long ago locked away. Since then, every time her mind was idle, they had slipped in. Memories of the first time they'd met, the first time they'd made love, the first time they had fought and the first time they'd made up. The slow understanding that she had fallen in love with this man and the recognition that he had loved her, too. His willingness to accept that, like a single mother, she came with the baggage of a younger brother who depended entirely too much on her. His patience with Donny, who had rarely been as polite, as tolerant or as respectful as he should have been, who had often, like a naughty child, done things for no other reason than to get on Thad's nerves.

She had remembered lasts, too. The last time she'd told him, "I love you." The last time he'd held her. The last time they'd sat quietly, neither of them speaking because they needed no words between them.

And she had remembered the last time they'd made love. The power of that memory had made her tremble. It had made her want, need, hunger.

He sat down at the opposite end of the window seat, facing her, looking more handsome than she wanted him to with his silky brown hair falling across his forehead and his deep brown eyes and his wise, solemn, owlish look. "I'm not asking you to give up hope, Lindsey. Just don't let it blind you to the other possibilities. If Donny is alive, we'll find him."

"And if he's not?"

His expression changed from concerned to grim. "Then we'll find whoever's behind this. I know you don't have much faith in the way we do our job, but—"

"That's not fair." For a moment, she didn't know why she'd interrupted him, but then she realized that, for reasons she couldn't look at too closely, she didn't want him to believe that she'd meant all the horrible things she'd said to him in the past. "I know you're good at what you do. I just think you made a mistake." She sounded grudging, but she couldn't help that. Just getting the words out had been difficult enough. Getting them out in a congenial tone would have been impossible.

He turned away from her then, directing his gaze down the hall instead. "What would you have had me do differently?"

Now she turned to face him, leaning forward so she could keep her voice low. "Why didn't you ever tell me what was going on, what you suspected?"

"I couldn't do that."

"Why not?"

"Because that's not the way we work, Lindsey," he said flatly. "We don't discuss the details of our cases with outsiders."

Echoing his last word, she leaned back. That was one of the things she'd hated, one of the reasons she'd felt so betrayed. Because, when it came to his job, she always had been and always would have been an outsider. Where other men discussed their work, their successes and their failures with their wives or lovers, Thad had rarely mentioned his job to *her*. Because she was an outsider. Because that part of his life was off-limits to her. It was private, confidential and none of her business, not even when it concerned her brother. Not even when it had almost cost Donny his life, when it *had* cost them their love.

"If you had told me what he'd done, I could have convinced Donny to turn himself in."

Thad stood up and looked down at her. "You don't know that, Lindsey. Oh, you would have told him to surrender himself, but you don't know what he would have done. You don't know if he would have obeyed you or if he would have taken that money and run like hell."

"He was my brother! I *knew* him!"

"Did you? Did you know that he was capable of kidnapping a seventy-year-old woman? Did you know that he could threaten to kill her if her family didn't give him two hundred and fifty thousand dollars? Did you know that he could quit his job and live on that two hundred and fifty thousand dollars, buying whatever caught his eye, without feeling so much as a twinge of guilt?"

The silence in the hallway was deafening. Lindsey stared at him in shock and saw the same intensity in his eyes. After a long, breathless moment, he continued. "You didn't know Donny at all, Lindsey, and that's something you've got to keep in mind. If this is Donny, if he is alive, maybe he hasn't come back here because he loves and misses his big sister. Maybe he wants to frighten her. Maybe he wants to hurt her. Maybe he wants to punish her for going to the FBI about him in the first place.''

"That's ridiculous," she whispered weakly. "I *didn't* go to the FBI—I went to *you*. Donny knows that!"

Thad shrugged wearily. "What Donny *knows* doesn't determine what he *believes*. Look at yourself. You know I didn't make Donny kidnap that woman. I didn't make him take the ransom. I didn't make him fall off that bridge. You know all that...but you still believe it was my fault. You still believe I'm guilty.''

She watched him walk away, listening to his steps on the stairs when he was out of sight. He was wrong about Donny, she silently insisted. Even if her brother blamed her in the same way she had blamed Thad, Donny would never physically hurt her, and the only punishment he could even remotely be capable of was staying away from her—letting her know that he was alive, but that he had no place for her in his life.

But he *had* planned and executed a complex, near-perfect kidnapping. He had threatened that poor old lady, had claimed he would kill her if her children didn't meet his demands. Of course, the ransom had been paid and the woman returned safely to her family, but what if they hadn't paid? Would he have carried out his threats? Would he have killed her?

It hurt Lindsey more than she could bear to admit that maybe Thad was right. Maybe she hadn't really known Donny and what he was capable of, because she honestly didn't know if he would have killed that woman. The brother that she had thought she'd known better than she knew herself had kept a part of his life as private, as confidential, as secret, as Thad had. Only Thad hadn't been hiding anything—privacy and confidentiality were essential to his job—while Donny...

Donny had been hiding everything.

She came down the stairs slowly, one hand gliding along the polished rail, and Thad watched her. She was so damn beautiful, he thought with an ache, and he wished briefly that she wasn't. But such a wish was futile. It wouldn't change anything, because it hadn't been her beauty he'd fallen in love with. No matter how the outward package looked, the woman inside would remain the same—beautiful, gentle, fragile, loving. And unreachable. Untouchable.

Their eyes met for a moment, and she paused only a few steps from the bottom. It was Thad who broke the contact, who finally looked away. The men would be done upstairs soon, and everything was finished downstairs—the doorknobs and jambs, both front and back, had been dusted for prints, the process repeated on the stereo, the angel, the frame, the vase and the stair rail that Lindsey still gripped. In a few minutes they would be ready to leave, and this time he had reminded Clint Roberts to give Lindsey one of his own business cards. If anything else happened, Thad wanted to be left out of it. These meetings were too painful, too draining.

Roberts heard Lindsey's return, and he came out of the living room. "We're almost done here, Ms. Phillips."

Thad heard her murmur a response, but he didn't try to make it out. He was already on his way outside.

It was warmer than inside, and the air was heavy with dampness, but he didn't mind. He breathed deeply, and the heavy scents of the flowers chased away the delicate vanilla that flavored the house. A light wind caused the flag that hung on the center column to flutter and lift, and he felt the same breeze ripple through his hair.

This porch was peaceful. He'd spent a lot of evenings here, sitting beside Lindsey on the love seat or swaying back and forth with her on the swing. They had watched the neighborhood children play, and she had known every one of them, from the shy toddler across the street to the teenage boy from the next block with his first serious crush. Sometimes they had talked, and sometimes they had simply sat here, content to touch each other and say nothing.

The door behind him opened, and he knew immediately from the tension radiating through him that it was Lindsey who had followed him out. She came to stand beside the next column, leaving ten feet of white railing between them.

She looked as cool and elegant as always, as if their conversation upstairs had never taken place. As if nothing between them had ever taken place—not the friendship, the caring, the loving or the hating. For a moment he considered jarring that cool, distant look from her face. It would be easy enough to do—an innocent reference to the wicker chair behind her to remind her of that weekend so long ago when they had made love for the first—hell, for the tenth time before it was over.

They had been dating for months, had known each other months longer, and he'd already been in love with her, although he hadn't told her so. He'd already made up his mind that when the time was right, he would marry no one but her. He would spend the rest of his life with no one but her. He would love no one but her.

And so far, he hadn't broken those foolish, romantic vows. There had been other women since Lindsey had forced him out of her life. He'd had frequent dates and had even gone to bed with the ones he'd been most attracted to. But he hadn't wanted to marry any of them, hadn't considered spending the rest of his life with them, hadn't even imagined loving one of them.

When she finally broke the silence, she took up the conversation that had ended upstairs when he'd walked away. "The only thing I think you're guilty of is poor judgment. If you had told me—"

He stopped her with a hard, sharp look. "If I had gone up on that bridge to arrest someone else, someone you didn't know, someone you didn't practically raise, and it had ended in the same way, you wouldn't say I had used poor judgment. You wouldn't say I should have informed the suspect's parents that he was in trouble and facing arrest. You would say, 'That's too bad, Thad, but you're not responsible. You can't blame yourself for someone else's actions.'"

"But it wasn't someone else. It was *my* brother. Shouldn't that count for something?"

"I can't break the rules, Lindsey—not for Donny and not for you. If that's what it takes to earn your respect, then I don't want it, because I would lose my own." He broke off and shifted his gaze to the bed of flowers in front of him, separating the sweet fragrance from all the other scents around him, unemotionally admiring the delicate shadings of color.

Finally he continued in an unforgiving voice. "You run a gift shop, Lindsey. It's not what you are, but what you do from ten to seven, six days a week. I'm an FBI agent. That's not what I do. It's what I *am* twenty-four hours a day seven days a week. Your responsibilities end when you walk out of that store. Mine never end. I couldn't have handled Donny's case any differently, although God knows I wanted to. I wanted to hand it over to someone else. I wanted to help him. I wanted to sweep the whole thing under the rug. But in the end I had no choice. I did what I had to do, and I prayed that you would understand, that you could accept it."

And she had let him down. She acknowledged that with a guilty flush.

Slowly he faced her, closing the distance between them until he was so near that he could see the shadows in her dark eyes. "Would it have made a difference, Lindsey, if Donny hadn't fallen from the bridge? If the arrest had gone the way it was planned, if he'd gone to jail, to trial, to prison...would you still have blamed me?"

She touched him for the first time in eighteen months, a simple touch, just the brush of her fingertips on his hand. "I wish I could say of course not, that I could deal with Donny going to prison far more easily than I could deal with his death. But the truth is I don't know." Meeting his eyes, she withdrew her hand, then shrugged. "I just don't know."

There was more he wanted to say, but the front door was opening again and the team of agents, led by Clint Roberts, was filing out. Roberts thanked Lindsey for calling and reminded her that she had his business card, then went to the car—to Thad's car—to wait. Thad glanced at him, then at

Lindsey, and selected the most important of the things he wanted to say. "There was nothing I could do to help Donny," he said quietly. "By the time I found out what he was doing, he was already in too deep. But I could have helped you, Lindsey. I could have helped you deal with losing him if you had trusted me. If you'd had faith in me."

He left her with that, standing alone on the porch, her fingers wrapped tightly around the railing, and went to his car. But long after he'd started the engine and driven away, long after the house had disappeared from sight, he continued to see her in his mind, sad and lost, and he felt the same way she had looked.

Sad. Lost.

Lindsey spent the weekend as she normally did: working in the shop all day Saturday and around the house most of Sunday. It was a quiet time alone, quiet that she told herself she needed, time alone that she insisted she wanted.

But she lied.

There had been a time when she'd never spent an entire weekend alone, when Thad or Donny or Tess or one of her cousins had come over or invited her to their houses, when she had never been bored or dissatisfied or lonely. Now she spent every weekend alone, and most weeknights, too, and she was often bored, usually dissatisfied and always lonely.

Now she drew her feet up onto the wicker love seat, listening to the woven wood creak as she resettled. The yard work was done for another week, the grass mown, the clippings raked, the flower beds weeded and the sidewalk swept. The house was spotless inside, and even her car had been washed and waxed. She had completed every chore on her list and then some, and it was only three o'clock. What could she possibly do to fill the rest of the afternoon and the evening?

One thing she *wouldn't* do was think about Thad. She would not remember his parting words to her Friday about lack of trust and loss of faith. About *her* lack of trust. *Her* loss of faith. Hadn't she trusted him enough to turn to him for help when Donny needed it? Hadn't she had enough faith in him to believe he *would* help, that he would do whatever would help Donny the most?

And what would that have been? she wondered as she tucked a loose strand of hair behind her ear. What would have helped Donny most? Letting him go? Giving him special treatment because the investigating agent was having an affair with his sister?

Or making him accept responsibility for his actions? Making him grow up, making him see that he'd done a horrible thing and that now he had to pay the penalty?

As much as she wanted to, she couldn't hide from the answer. Letting Donny get away with what he'd done would have been, in his eyes, a seal of approval. It would have meant he would break the law again and again. Special treatment because of her relationship with Thad would have sent him a different message: he could do whatever he wanted, and, just as she'd been doing most of his life, big sister would somehow make it right.

No, Thad had been right. There'd been no other choice. What he'd done had been no more than the law required—than his conscience required—and it had been no less than Donny needed. If anyone was to blame for the scene on the bridge that day, it was Donny—and maybe her, too, for raising him the way that she had—and the FBI for handling the case the way they had. But not Thad himself.

Now if only her heart could accept that as easily as her head did!

"Don't you look as pretty as a picture, sitting there all surrounded by flowers?"

She focused her eyes on the steps and saw Shawn standing there, watching her. "Oh, yes, I'm grubby and sweaty and my hair's falling down. I'm sure I'm just as pretty as can be," she teased. "What are you all dressed up for?"

He pushed his hands into the pockets of his suit coat as he came up the steps and seated himself across from her. "I had a date."

"In the middle of the afternoon? Or is this last night's date just ending?"

"We went out for brunch."

His manner said the date wasn't important, which didn't surprise Lindsey. Shawn had bigger things on his mind than women. They were pleasant company, but nothing was going to divert him from reaching his goal of becoming one of the best comics the South had ever produced. When he had achieved success, then he would look for that special woman. She hoped he would have no trouble finding her, because she knew from her own minor success with her shop and her cards that having no one to share it with dimmed the glow and diminished much of the satisfaction.

"How has your weekend been?"

Lindsey smiled vaguely. "Productive."

He glanced around at the manicured lawn and the hundreds of flowers that showed not a single wilted bud. "I can see that. You know, weekends are traditionally a time to rest, to relax."

"Maybe for men," she retorted. "For women they're a time to catch up on everything they can't cram into the week."

"No sexist remarks, please, unless it's something I can use in my act tonight. So... what is it you're trying to avoid thinking about this time?"

She gave him a puzzled look.

"Whenever you don't want to think about something, you keep really busy and cram three days' work into one. What is it this time?"

Lindsey sat in silence for a long moment, then told him about the incident at the house Friday afternoon. She couldn't bring herself to use the word "burglar" or "intruder," as Thad had. Wasn't it bad enough that her brother was a kidnapper without adding common thief? Nor did she let herself say for certain that it had—or hadn't—been Donny.

"You believe it was him, don't you?" Shawn asked when she was finished.

She remembered Thad's warning that they had no proof Donny was alive, that she had to consider other possibilities, that Donny might have had a partner who now wanted them to believe he was alive. She remembered, as well, that she'd accused him of trying to destroy the hope that was all she had left and the sad, wounded look in his eyes that had caused. A lack of trust and a loss of faith. Yes, she'd shown him both eighteen months ago and, again, only two days ago.

Her sigh was troubled. "Yes, I believe it was Donny. He had a key. He knew what he was looking for and where to find it."

"And what does McNally think?" Shawn smiled gently when she glanced at him. "You have that look."

"What look?"

"Like Donny isn't the only ghost you're dealing with. McNally was here Friday, wasn't he?"

"Yes." She had to force the whisper out.

"And you talked to him, didn't you?"

"Yes." This time her voice was so low that the only sound was a soft hiss, but it was enough. She knew Shawn would have guessed the answer even if she'd said nothing at all.

"Does it hurt so much to see him?"

Lindsey stared past him, but saw nothing of the vibrant pinks and lavenders of the flowers or the dozen shades of green in the grass, the trees and bushes. She saw nothing but the emptiness and loneliness of the last eighteen months, and it was reflected in her voice when she finally spoke. "When Thad tried to see me, to talk to me, after Donny's fall, I was cold to him. I said some things that can't be forgiven. I knew that he was hurting, too, that he hated what had happened, but I didn't care. My brother was dead, and it was all his fault. *I* was the one who truly grieved. *I* was the one whose suffering mattered."

She closed her eyes, sighed deeply, then met Shawn's concerned gaze. "He has a lot of anger and a lot of bitterness. And you know what? He's entitled. Tess was right all those months ago. I wasn't fair to Thad. I should have understood. I should have trusted him. I should have..." She let the sentence trail off. She could finish it any of a dozen different ways. She should have loved him better, should have had faith in him, should have known how hard the case had been for him, should have seen the toll it had taken on him, should have realized that he'd needed her, should have admitted that *she* had needed *him*.

"You'd just seen your brother fall a hundred feet and disappear into an ice-cold river. No one expected you to be totally rational and forgiving."

"No one expected me to blame Thad, either," she said with a sad smile. Deke had been impatient with her, and Tess had been dismayed. And Thad . . . She could still recall the look in his eyes when she had struggled to get away from him, when she had screamed at him that he had murdered her brother. Pain, so raw, so relentless, and all the more cutting because it was so unexpected.

"And no one expects you to blame yourself now," Shawn said quietly. "The things you said and did back then were driven by grief. That's one of the most powerful emotions known to man. It can destroy people. You had such a special relationship with Donny that your grief almost destroyed you, and it did destroy your relationship with McNally . . . but maybe not completely."

It took her a long time to ask the obvious question. She delayed by bending down to pluck a droopy leaf from the pot of geraniums next to her chair, then settling once more on the cushion. She wasn't sure she wanted to hear what Shawn had to say, wasn't sure she wanted to face whatever conclusion he had reached. But she had too much respect for him to ignore him, and she had been ignoring what she didn't want to know for far too long now. "What do you mean?"

"I asked you Monday night if you were still in love with McNally, and you said no. How could you be after what he'd done? Now you're starting to see that he didn't do anything bad. He wasn't to blame for what happened. He was as much a victim of Donny's irresponsibility and greed as you were, as Mrs. Heinreid was."

"So . . . am I also starting to see that I still love him?" Her voice quavered. After so many months of blaming him, of hating him, of pretending that he didn't exist and had never existed, she was almost surprised at how badly it hurt to think of Thad and love. But even if she did love him, even if by some miracle he still loved her, how could they ever go back to the way they'd been before? How could she ever quit hating his job? How could she ever accept that his loyalty to that job would always be greater than his loyalty to her?

How could she ever be sure that she wouldn't, in some secret part of her heart, continue to blame him because it was easier than blaming Donny, than blaming herself? How could she know that the first time they argued, she wouldn't pull out those same accusations, not just to hurt him but because some part of her still insisted that he could have handled the case differently?

And how could she be happy with a man who, eventually, would be responsible for sending her brother to prison for a lifetime? Because she wasn't kidding herself about Donny. He wasn't the smartest crook in the world. He was too immature, too childlike, to avoid detection for long, and now that the FBI knew he was back in Atlanta, it would merely be a matter of time before they caught him. How could she consider loving and maybe marrying and making a future with the man whose investigative work and testimony would send her brother away forever?

How could any love survive all the handicaps theirs would face?

She smiled sadly. "I won't deny that in some ways, I still care for Thad. He was the only man I'd ever loved. I *have* to still feel something. But love?" She shook her head. "There just wouldn't be any hope for it."

"How do you know that?" he asked stubbornly.

"Too much has happened, Shawn. I can say I understand that Thad wasn't to blame, that he was just doing his job, but you'll never convince me that there wasn't a better way to do it. Never." She sat there quietly for a moment, then looked up and smiled. It wasn't a happy smile, she knew, but at least her lower lip didn't tremble with impending tears. "So...what time is your show at the club tonight?"

"Nine o'clock. And I expect to see you there." When she started to protest, he raised his hand to stop her. "You've turned me down the last couple of times I've asked, so I'm not taking no for an answer today. You need to get out and spend a few hours with other people. And who knows? You might even find something to smile about, *really* smile. So I'll pick you up at eight, okay?"

She gave it a moment's thought, then nodded. "I'd like that, Shawn. Thanks for asking." She stood up and walked to the top of the steps with him, where he bent to kiss her cheek before he left.

For a long while she leaned against the pillar there, her arms folded across her chest. Maybe Shawn was right and she *did* need to spend some time with other people. Her daily contacts were limited to Cassie and the customers in the shop, small talk with the clerks in the grocery store and hellos exchanged over the fence with neighbors. Maybe a few hours listening to Shawn's act, then sharing a table with his friends—also comics—was just what she needed. Maybe it would help her relax.

And maybe, she thought wistfully, it would help her forget about Thad.

Chapter 4

Thad sat at the big, dark desk that filled one corner of his bedroom. It was rarely cluttered—even when he worked, he kept things neatly ordered—but today the surface was covered with photographs tossed carelessly about. Photographs of Lindsey—alone, with Donny, with Tess and Deke and a few with Thad himself. Photographs of things they'd done—picnics, 10K runs, afternoons at the lake—and of places they'd been: the mountains surrounding Asheville, the beaches of Kiawah Island and the historic streets of Savannah.

He had loved taking pictures of Lindsey—formal portraits, such as the one that for months had sat on the corner of this desk, until the woman he'd been seeing at the time had asked him to put it away, and casual snapshots, capturing her gentle smiles forever on film. He had put his camera away not long after Donny's fall and had gotten it out only occasionally since, for Christmas pictures with his parents last year in Massachusetts and infrequent photos of Andrew Ramsey as he grew from helpless infant to toddling terror. He had no photographs of the women he'd dated since Lindsey, not even a single one of Carole, who'd dropped him after five months when her increasingly less than subtle hints of marriage and commitment had fallen on deaf ears.

He nudged aside several pictures to pick up one beneath. It was one of the rare photos of him, Lindsey and Donny together. He didn't remember who had taken it or what the occasion had been—they were all dressed for something special—but he remembered why he'd enlarged it. Because that was the day he'd realized that he wanted to marry her.

So many things had changed since then, but not his feelings. If he was given the chance to erase Lindsey from his memories, to erase the happiness and the love and the misery, and to fall in love forever and ever with someone else, he wouldn't take it. He wouldn't give up the memory of the good times between them, not even to get rid of the bad, not even if it meant going on like this—lonely and alone—for the rest of his life. He wouldn't accept that the only love he'd ever known, the only one he'd ever wanted, was lost to him for all time.

He studied the photo a while longer. Lindsey stood in the middle, one arm around Donny's waist, the other around his own, and she was laughing. Happy. Carefree. And why shouldn't she have been? She was with the two men she'd claimed to love most. Who would have guessed that her love for Thad would disappear so quickly, so permanently, while her love for Donny—for her brother, a criminal, a kidnapper who had terrorized a defenseless old lady—would live on forever?

If she'd ever shown *him* that kind of loyalty, that kind of faith, they could have overcome any odds, he thought with a sigh. Like Deke and Tess, nothing could have hurt them. Nothing could have torn them apart.

With another weary sigh, he began gathering the photographs. Some went back into the albums from which he had removed them, and others were stacked neatly in folders and returned to a shelf in the back of the closet. They ought to go into the garbage, all of them, he thought, as a sudden anger surged through him. But how could he throw them away? Along with his memories, they were all he had of Lindsey.

Seated at the desk once again, he reached for the phone and began dialing. He was acting like a fool, he, who had never done anything foolish in his life. But he couldn't forget the vulnerability in her eyes each time he'd seen her last week. He couldn't forget the light touch of her fingers on his hand Friday night. He couldn't forget that he had loved her more than anything else in his world. He couldn't forget that once they'd had a bright, promising future ahead of them, and he couldn't stop hoping that maybe some part of it remained, buried under months of hurt, anger and bitterness, but there all the same.

She answered on the third ring—a cool, polite hello. He almost hated to speak to her, hated to hear that cold, hostile tone creep into her voice, but he forced himself to say hello, to identify himself to her. "Lindsey, it's Thad."

Lindsey, it's Thad. How many times had he greeted her that way, whether speaking to her personally or to her answering machine? Five hundred? A thousand? Even before they'd begun dating, when they'd been merely friends and running partners, they had talked on the phone for a few minutes virtually every day, and the habit hadn't stopped after they'd started dating, after they'd become lovers. It had been one of the hardest habits to break after Donny's disappearance, that routine of automatically reaching for the phone when he got home from work, when he had a few minutes to spare, when he was lonely for the sound of her voice.

At first she was quiet, as he'd known she would be, then she sighed softly. "Hello, Thad."

That part had changed. "Hello, Thad," was a far cry from her old standard, "Hey, sweetheart," or "I was just thinking about you." What did he expect? He should be grateful that she hadn't slammed the phone down the instant she'd recognized his voice. Hadn't she made it clear that she wanted nothing further to do with him?

But she hadn't hung up. She was waiting silently, patiently, at the other end of the line for him to speak, and suddenly he realized he had nothing to say, nothing, at least, that she would want to hear.

That being the case, he cleared his throat, took a deep breath and plunged in. "I'd like to see you tonight."

The silence seemed heavier, more ominous for a moment, then Lindsey cautiously asked, "Have you learned something new about Donny?"

Donny. The only subject she would discuss with him, he thought bitterly. "No. This isn't business, Lindsey. I want to see you."

"I can't."

Before she could say anything more, he gave a low, harsh chuckle. "Of course not. I should have known—"

"I told Shawn I would go to the Comedy Spot with him tonight," she interrupted him. "He's trying out a new routine, and I'd like to see it." She paused, then her voice turned bleak. "I could use a good laugh."

Couldn't we all? he thought, equally as bleak. "Well, have a good time," he said, then abruptly he hung up.

Damn Shawn Howard. He was grateful to the younger man for remaining friends with Lindsey after their only real tie—Donny—was gone, but damn, how he resented him! Shawn had undoubtedly taken Thad's place in Lindsey's life. *He* was the one she turned to now for comfort, the one whose shoulder she cried on, the one she counted on to get her through the bad days.

Was he also there to help her through the lonely nights? Thad wondered, bitterly, savagely jealous. What else did she accept from Shawn? What else did she give him?

He pulled his glasses off and rubbed his eyes with the heels of his hands. He was tired, mentally drained from a weekend of thinking about nothing but Lindsey. Well, enough was enough. He might be a lovesick fool, but he wasn't going to act like one any longer. This part of his life was over. Done with.

It was finished.

So how the hell did he find himself walking into the Comedy Spot a few hours later?

A single phone call had given him all the information he'd needed: Shawn Howard was scheduled to do a twenty-minute routine beginning at nine o'clock. He hadn't needed to check the address since he'd taken Lindsey to the club before. He knew where she would be sitting—a quick glance assured him that she was—and that she would be alone once Shawn went onstage. Since that would be any moment now, he went to the bar and ordered a beer, then waited there for Shawn's introduction.

When it came, Thad picked up the long-necked bottle and made his way through the crowded tables to one in the middle. For a moment, while the applause faded and the lights dimmed, he simply stood there, waiting to be noticed.

It didn't take Lindsey long to realize she was no longer alone. Maybe some invisible antenna had picked up the danger signals, or her sixth sense had warned her of impending doom. Whatever, she slowly shifted her gaze to him, and for just an instant, he thought she was going to smile.

He was wrong.

With his free hand he gestured to the chair beside her, and after a moment, she nodded. "Sit down, please."

So formal and polite. There were times when he preferred her hysterical outbursts over this coolly impersonal behavior she acted out so well. Painful as they'd been to endure, at least her screaming insults and curses had acknowledged the relationship between them. He found that preferable to being treated like a total stranger.

Resisting the urge to remind her that he knew her intimately, more intimately than any man alive with the possible exception of Shawn, Thad slid the chair out and sat down. He made no pretense of watching Shawn or listening to his routine; nor did he bother to laugh at the appropriate times. Instead he watched Lindsey.

She shifted uneasily under his scrutiny. Why had he come? she wondered, sneaking a covert glance at him before directing her gaze to the stage again. Was whatever he'd called her about important enough to bring him here? If he hadn't hung up so quickly, she would have invited him to come along tonight...or at least, she thought she would have. She'd been debating the question when he had so sarcastically told her to have a good time and ended the call.

Well, now he was here, solemnly staring at her, and her palms were sweaty and her cheeks were flushed and her legs felt unsteady, as if they would collapse if she tried to stand. And she could think of absolutely nothing to say to him.

He'd chosen his seat well. He wasn't directly in her line of sight, but right there on the edge, where the only way she could avoid him was to deliberately turn away. She kept her eyes focused on the stage, but she didn't really see Shawn, and his jokes, a set about the eternal ineptitude of Atlanta's professional baseball team, went right over her head. All she could see, all she could think about, was Thad.

Finally she turned in her seat to face him head-on. "I didn't know you had developed a liking for comedy."

"I haven't."

"Then why are you here?"

He took a long drink, then set the bottle down. "Isn't that obvious? Or do you just want to hear me say it?" He shrugged carelessly. "I'm here because you are. I wanted to see you."

"Why?" she whispered.

"Isn't that obvious, too?"

She looked away to pick up her glass and take a drink of the dark liquid it held. Iced tea, Thad bet. For the same reason that ruled so many other areas in her life, Lindsey didn't drink much. She needed to be in control, and loss of control—her parents' death, Donny's disappearance, even the mild loss that came with intoxication—frightened her.

Although the direction the conversation had taken apparently disturbed her, Thad didn't relent. He simply waited until she was looking at him again before he continued. "I wasn't the one who ended this relationship, Lindsey. I wasn't ready for it to end. I don't believe I ever would have been ready."

"So you want to pick up where we left off. You think that because we've seen each other three times in the last week, and all for business, that—"

"Four times," he interrupted her, "and this one's not business."

She stared at him blankly, unable to continue her argument.

"I've missed you, Lindsey," he said quietly. "I've missed you so damn much." He saw that the words surprised her. The intensity surprised *him*. "I'll accept all your blame for what happened with Donny, but I won't accept being shut out of your life. We had something special, something that could have lasted forever, but we—I blew it. Now I want another chance—just a chance, Lindsey, to make things right."

The audience around them burst into laughter, but Thad hardly noticed. His heart was thudding audibly, and his muscles had grown so taut that he was sure if he tried to speak again, his voice would be little more than a croak. He'd blurted it all out—something he'd done too much with Lindsey lately. Had he said too much too soon? Should he have used less force, made less of a demand and more of a request or even a plea? Hell, he would beg if that was what she wanted, if it would get him that second chance.

Lindsey sat motionless, unaware of anything around her. *I've missed you.* The words were so simple, but powerful. How long had it been since anyone had missed her, since anyone had needed or wanted her? The emptiness in her life after Donny's disappearance had been so complete. There had been no one to love her, no one to need her. No one to worry if she made it home safely, no one to care if she was hurting or sick or dying of loneliness. Shawn had done his best to fill the void, but he was only one man, and she had lost too much—her brother, her lover, her closest friends.

Another chance. Just this afternoon she had explained to herself all the reasons a reconciliation with Thad wouldn't work. Too much had happened. She'd said things that he surely couldn't forgive, and she still believed he'd handled the case badly. There were too many negative forces working against them. Love—if any measure of it had survived the past eighteen months—would surely die beneath the burdens it would have to bear if they tried again.

So why did she want so much to say yes? Why did she want to grab this chance with both hands and never let go?

Thad caught her attention as he set the now-empty beer bottle on the table again. "Lindsey, I'm not talking about picking up where we left off," he said patiently. "'Where we left off' was about three weeks from a marriage proposal. I don't think either of us is quite ready for that. No, I'm talking about trying again. Starting over. Resolving the problems of the past year and a half and finding out if there's anything left to build a future on."

Her eyes had widened at his mention of marriage. Three weeks from the time of Donny's disappearance would have been Christmas. Had he planned to propose to her at Christmas? It was the sort of touchingly romantic gesture she would have loved... almost as much as she had loved *him*.

And she *had* loved him. She had loved him more than anything, even Donny. Just a few days ago, hadn't she finally admitted that losing Thad had been more painful and more difficult to accept than losing Donny? If they could love like that again, wouldn't it be wrong to turn her back on it?

But love wasn't a miracle worker. No matter how much she might love Thad, that love could never make her forget or forgive everything. It could never sway her from her belief that Donny could have been saved if Thad had come to her instead of following FBI procedure. It could never convince her that Thad hadn't, in some small way, been responsible for what had happened.

Could they agree to disagree and go on from there? She didn't know. Part of her balked at the idea of getting into a relationship when she knew from the start that she couldn't commit one hundred percent to it. That wasn't fair to Thad or herself.

But the other part of her, the stronger part, wanted more than she'd had these last months. That part of her remembered the loving far too easily, and missed it far too much. That part ached for the quiet evenings together, the long nights, the security of knowing that someone cared, someone needed her, someone was there for her. That part longed for the gentle lovemaking that she'd never experienced with anyone but Thad. That part urged her to say yes, to try, to make an effort at being happy again instead of drifting along month after month, alone and unhappy and doomed to stay that way.

After all, that was all he was asking, wasn't it? That she *try*. Try to work out their problems. Try to salvage whatever was left of something that *had* been very special. If she gave it her best shot, made her best effort, and failed, that didn't mean she'd been unfair to Thad once again. It simply meant that there was nothing left to salvage. That the months and the circumstances had cost them too much. That, as she'd told Shawn this afternoon, there simply wasn't any hope for them.

"What about Donny?"

He shrugged. "Nothing's changed there, Lindsey. If he's alive, he's wanted for kidnapping. If he comes around, he's got to be turned in."

Meaning he would do it if she didn't. But that was no problem for Lindsey. Much as she loved him, her days of protecting her little brother and correcting his mistakes and righting his wrongs were over. Perhaps if she'd reached this decision two or three years ago, it would have forced Donny to grow up. Perhaps it would have prevented the kidnapping and all the awful things that had followed.

"And if he's turned in," she continued softly, "he'll go to prison. And your testimony will make sure of it."

He seemed unsure of how to respond to that. She suspected that he didn't want to say yes, he would testify and send her brother to prison, and maybe lose this second chance before it ever started. But he wouldn't lie to her.

"We have a lot of evidence against Donny," he said at last, carefully choosing his words. "There are fingerprints, handwriting samples, the victim's identification, recordings of his phone calls and his confession on the bridge. But yes, if he goes to trial, I'll have to testify. It was my case. I couldn't get out of it even if I wanted to."

"And you wouldn't want to because it's your job."

"I know you wouldn't be so reluctant if I was an engineer or an accountant or a used car salesman, but I'm not. You knew that from the beginning."

She gave him a small, bitter smile. "If you were an engineer or an accountant or a used car salesman, we never would have had this problem in the first place." But he was right; she'd known from the beginning. The day they'd met, he had told her without conceit, without attempting to impress her as so many men would have done, that he was an FBI agent. And knowing that, she had still chosen to become friends with him. She had still fallen in love with him.

She sighed softly. "I just never suspected that someday your job would focus on my brother."

"It was an unusual situation," he acknowledged. In a city the size of Atlanta, what had been the odds that the suspect in his biggest case would just happen to be his future brother-in-law? And because of the circumstances, at the point that his personal involvement came to light and he would have ordinarily been pulled off the case, he'd been forced to continue working it instead, because Donny had insisted on dealing with him and only him.

For months afterward he had wondered about Donny's motives. There was no doubt that he'd known when he arranged the meeting on the bridge that he was going to be arrested. There was also no doubt that he'd gone to that meeting fully intending to kill himself there. Why had he insisted that Thad be there? And why in God's name had he brought Lindsey along to witness it? Had his childish mocking of Thad's job and his ~~friendly derision of Thad~~ himself masked a deeper, darker emotion? Had he somehow wanted to punish Lindsey for her part in his arrest, for not standing by him regardless of what he'd done?

Or had he acted, as Donny had usually acted, without thought, without regard for anyone's feelings or desires except his own?

"You know that if he's caught, he's going to prison," he said flatly. "If I died tomorrow, they would still get a conviction, simply based on the evidence. And I collected most of that evidence myself. So any way you look at it, he's going to prison because of me. Can you deal with that?"

She refused to meet his gaze, but toyed instead with her glass on the table. "I just wish to God you and I weren't involved with this."

His smile was mirthless. "It's far too late for that, sweetheart. We've been involved ever since the day Donny decided to kidnap that woman." Then his smile faded, and his expression turned somber again. "*Can* you deal with that, Lindsey? Knowing that your brother is going to prison because of me?"

"If Donny winds up in prison, he has no one but himself to blame." Shawn sat down across from Thad as he made the pronouncement, then looked from him to Lindsey. "I've never seen people so quick to take the blame for another adult's actions. Donny knew the difference between right and wrong. He knew the risks he was taking, and he thought they were worth the payoff." He gave a disgusted shake of his head. "He wasn't stupid. He was just plain greedy."

Thad was annoyed by Shawn's intrusion—not because he disliked the younger man. He had always preferred Shawn's maturity and responsibility and general good nature to Donny's childish, moody ways. But in this brief moment, already he'd begun to miss the sense of togetherness he'd felt with Lindsey. He missed knowing that her attention was all his, even when she wouldn't look at him, and he felt again the ugly stirrings of jealousy, intensified when Shawn casually reached across to clasp Lindsey's hand.

"I won't even ask how you liked the act," Shawn said to Lindsey, "since your mind has obviously been elsewhere."

She smiled faintly. "I'm sorry, Shawn, but we were . . . talking."

Thad stiffened. They'd been discussing love, getting together again, fixing their problems, making a future, and forever, and she managed to boil it down to merely *talking*? Had their conversation been that unimportant to her? Or had she been intentionally vague, not wanting Shawn to suspect that she was considering a reconciliation with Thad, keeping him close at hand—and in the dark—in case things didn't work out and she needed him again?

"That's okay. You can come by some other time when you've got less on your mind." Shawn glanced at his watch, then turned to Thad. "Can I ask a favor of you?"

He gestured to him with a slight nod to go on.

"My schedule's been changed, and I've got to do the late show tonight. I know Lindsey doesn't like to stay out so late, so would you mind giving her a ride home when you leave?"

She scowled at him. "I'm perfectly capable of making my own arrangements."

"I brought you, and I feel obligated to make sure you get home safely again," he said, pressing a kiss into her palm. "Do you mind, McNally?"

"No, not at all. I'd be glad to take you home, Lindsey." And just maybe, in exchange for this gift of time with her, he would overlook Shawn's kiss and proprietary manner. Maybe.

"Good. I'll talk to you soon, Lindsey." Shawn kissed her cheek, then stood up and extended his hand to Thad. "Come back sometime, McNally. Maybe we can at least get you to crack a smile."

Thad politely stood and shook his hand, then watched him walk away. After a moment, he looked down at Lindsey. "Do you want to stay or go now?"

"Let's go."

He followed her outside, then directed her past a pay phone and a newspaper box to the brightly lit parking lot. His car was parked near the back. It was his own car, Lindsey noticed, and not the government sedan he normally drove. This was the car they had taken on all those weekend trips she had enjoyed so much. The car in which they had once, with much awkward struggle and unrestrained laughter, made love at the end of a shadowy mountain lane somewhere in North Carolina. Just the brief glimpse of memory she allowed herself made her cheeks burn and her throat go dry.

Always the gentleman, Thad opened her door first, waiting until she was settled inside and buckling her seat belt before locking and closing the door. As he slid into the driver's seat, he asked, "Do you see him often?"

"Shawn? A couple of times a week."

"How is his career going?"

She didn't like the way he said "career," as if Shawn's drive to succeed as a stand-up comic was less than admirable. Thad had never been a snob before, had never judged anyone by his work, had never cared about the prestige that accompanied a particular job. If he had, he never would have been interested in her when they'd first met and the unofficial title of "gopher" was the only one she'd had. "He's developed quite a reputation," she said touchily. "He's very good at what he does."

"Is he?" he asked, making no effort to disguise his snide tone as he backed out of the parking space.

Lindsey looked at him, then pointedly turned away.

There was little traffic on the street and nothing to distract her attention from Thad. Even with her head turned away from him, he was all she could see, all she could think about. He still wore the same after-shave, a faint, exotic scent that filled the car and had, on more than one occasion, clung to her clothing and her skin. He still dressed the same, too—tonight in khaki slacks and a navy blue polo shirt—like an ad for the preppie life-style. And he still tolerated uncomfortable silences not one moment longer than necessary.

"I like your shop."

She turned from the view out the side window and faced forward again. "Thank you."

"I like your cards, too. I've bought them for my parents and Andrew and Carole—" He broke off, adjusted his glasses, then shrugged. "But I never connected Lindsey's Blooms to you."

"Who are Andrew and Carole?"

"Andrew is Deke and Tess's son. They also call him Drew. He'll be one next month."

She waited for him to continue, even though his sudden uneasiness made no further explanation necessary. So he had been involved with another woman since they'd broken up. Of course, she hadn't expected him to remain completely alone, pining away for her, even though *she* had spent the past eighteen months utterly alone except for Shawn. But she hadn't wanted proof that he'd gone on to other women, other affairs, either. Even when she had hated him, she hadn't wanted to think of him with another woman, holding a stranger the way he'd once held her, loving anyone else the way he'd once loved *her*.

Jealousy was a new emotion to her. Before Thad, she had never cared enough about the men she'd dated to waste energy on jealousy, and Thad himself had never given her cause to be jealous. He had always treated her as if she were the only woman in his life. He had never flirted with other women, had never done anything to attract their attention, had never returned their interest.

He'd been entitled to his affair with this woman named Carole, she reminded herself. As he'd pointed out at the club, *he* wasn't the one who had ended their relationship. It hadn't been a mutual agreement to go their separate ways; he'd had no choice in the matter. And if he'd found comfort with Carole, it was certainly none of Lindsey's business.

And all the rational, logical thinking in the world couldn't ease that little twinge of hurt at the thought of him sharing his life and his bed with another woman.

"The cards have done well," she said, forcing herself to speak politely about business instead of shrewishly demanding all the details of all his affairs. "They supplement my income, give me a creative outlet and keep me busy."

"And that's important, isn't it? You have no people in your life, so you fill it with work—and, of course, Shawn Howard. Can't forget him, can we?"

Again his tone stung, and again she turned away. What was going on? At the club, he'd been determined to convince her to try to mend their relationship. Now he seemed equally determined to make her angry. Why?

He was doing it again, Thad realized—making a fool of himself, when he had prided himself for years on never playing the fool. He couldn't help it, though, when she spoke to him in that cool, polite, formal voice, as if he were someone she had just met and would never see again, as if he *weren't* someone who knew the soft, sweet secrets of her body better than she knew them herself. He wanted to pull into the next parking lot, find the darkest corner and drag her across the center console onto his lap. He wanted to kiss her, touch her, stroke her until she trembled, until her blood was hot and her body was moist, until she would die if she tried one more time to deny what had been between them. He wanted to fill her so deeply that she couldn't tell where *he* stopped and *she* began. He wanted—

More than she could give. Pressing his fist against his mouth, he swallowed back a groan. Technically, all Lindsey had accepted from him tonight was a ride home. Not a chance to patch up their relationship. Not an offer to resume their affair. Not a hope of rediscovering their love. She had never given him an answer to that, but instead had asked him about Donny; then Shawn had interrupted and they had left. And all she had taken from him was this ride that would be over in less than a mile.

They spoke at the same time, their words jumbling. She politely let him go first. "I'm sorry," he said quietly, not looking at her.

"You never disliked Shawn before. Why now?"

He turned onto her block, parked in front of her house and shut off the engine before answering her. When he did, he looked across at her. Her face, solemn and gentle and beautiful, was illuminated by the streetlight. His was in shadow. It was easier that way. "I don't dislike him," he admitted, "but I do envy him."

"Why?"

He smiled faintly. "Because he has what I want. You."

She swallowed hard, looked away, then back at him.

"When Shawn comes over, you're glad to see him. You open the door to him because you want to, not because you feel obligated. When he calls, you're happy to talk to him. When he kisses you…" He took her hand and lifted it to his mouth, placing a kiss in the center of her palm as Shawn had done earlier. She sat utterly motionless for an instant, then snatched her hand free and clenched it tightly in her lap.

He smiled sadly. "When Shawn kisses you, you don't jerk away as if you've been burned . . . or worse."

Lindsey picked up her purse and opened the door. She started to get out, but hesitated and turned back to him. "When Shawn kisses me," she said in a low, unsteady voice, "I don't do anything . . . because I don't feel anything."

Business at Lindsey's Gifts was often busy and sometimes hectic, but disastrous only on occasion. Of course, today had to be that occasion, Lindsey grumbled to herself as she sank wearily into one of the rockers.

First, she'd come to work to find that an accident in front of the shopping center had caused a power outage in all the stores. Next, a particularly difficult customer who always demanded Lindsey's personal attention had come in for her monthly shopping. She'd left after nearly an hour with almost a hundred dollars' worth of merchandise and a good portion of Lindsey's patience.

Then she'd gotten so busy that she couldn't find a spare minute to eat the sandwich she'd bought at the deli three stores down, so her stomach had growled all afternoon.

One customer had come in after school with her three young hoodlums-in-training, and they had proceeded to reorganize the entire store. The oldest one, maybe six, had managed to climb to a precarious perch on top of a display case, where he had then dropped two very fragile and expensive figurines to the floor. Of course, the mother had refused to pay for the breakage since Lindsey had been foolish enough to leave the items within the child's reach in the first place. Since when, Lindsey had wondered, had five feet off the floor been considered within a three-foot-tall child's reach?

To top it all off, Cassie had called to say that she couldn't come in today; her mother was sick and needed her to babysit the younger children.

The day had been perfectly awful. She couldn't think of anything else that could have gone wrong. And she still had to get through dinner. With Thad.

His call this afternoon had been the only bright spot in a dark day, and she worried about *how* bright. The sound of his voice over the phone had made her smile, even after sweeping up eighty-five dollars' worth of glass shards. She shouldn't be looking forward to this so much. She shouldn't be thinking about how comfortable, how *right*, it felt to be planning an evening out with Thad. She certainly shouldn't be remembering how, in the past, those evenings had usually ended.

But last night's little kiss made it hard to forget. It shouldn't have been sexy or sensuous or erotic or anything more than Shawn's identical kiss had been: a casual, friendly gesture. But it had had none of Shawn's casual flavor and all too much of the friendliness. It had made her skin burn, on her palm where his mouth had touched her, on her wrist where his fingers had held her, in other places where no one had touched her for all too long. It had made her heart rate increase unevenly—she wondered if he'd noticed that in the brief moment he'd held her wrist—and had made her nerves tingle and heat gather and hunger rise.

After jerking back the way she had, she'd felt incredibly foolish for a moment. She had overreacted; after all, it was just a simple kiss.

But then she knew she *hadn't* overreacted. Eighteen months had passed since she'd been kissed—not the brotherly pecks Shawn gave her, but *really* kissed, with passion and tongues and need and satisfaction. Eighteen months since she'd been held. Eighteen months since she'd made love. She could go for weeks without thinking about it, only to suddenly awaken in the middle of the night from a dream so vivid, so steamy, that sleep became impossible.

And those dreams always involved Thad.

And last night, with just a little coaxing, those dreams could have become reality. The funny thing, the frightening thing, was that she didn't know who would have had to do the coaxing: Thad...or her. That simple kiss had aroused long-unsatisfied physical needs. It had reawakened long-buried emotional needs. It had, in that one brief moment his mouth was against her skin, made her incredibly careless and greedy. Forget the past, forget the future, just take care of the present. Get satisfaction *now*.

And pay for it later. Pay for it with her heart and her soul. Pay for it with sorrow if things didn't work out. Pay for it with what little hope she had if she rushed into intimacy with this man she had once loved—this man who had loved her—and discovered that the love wasn't there any longer, the relationship irreparable, the past unforgivable.

No, if they stood a chance this time, they had to take it slowly. Things had changed. *They* had changed. Before, they had already been friends. All that had been left to do was fall in love; it had been simple and easy and wonderful. Now they had to get to know each other again. They had to decide if they could accept and live with the way the other had changed. They had to discover how much they could forgive and how much they could forget. They had to determine a way to deal with the subject of Donny. They had to find out if the love was still there, if it had survived, if it could be rekindled.

And they had to decide if it was worth the cost.

It wouldn't be so simple this time or so easy. She couldn't be sure it would be wonderful. She couldn't even guess whether it would be successful. They might be making the worst mistake of their lives. There was so much working against them and so little in their favor—only Thad's belief that there was still something worth having between them.

A clock high on the wall chimed as its little door opened and a wooden bird on a perch slid out. Its head and beak moved from side to side as its wings fluttered, and it chirped seven times. Closing time, Lindsey thought with a sigh of relief.

It took her only a few minutes to balance the cash register drawer and prepare the daily deposit. Now a quick walk to the bank at the end of the shopping center, then she'd be ready to go home and get ready for her date.

Lindsey turned off the overhead lights, leaving a single lamp burning in each corner, then locked up. She went first to the bank and then to her car, making the drive home in record time. When she had accepted Thad's dinner invitation, she hadn't known Cassie would take the afternoon off. Originally, she had planned to leave the shop in her assistant's capable hands and come home early and have plenty of time for a long, relaxing bath and for a careful inspection of all the clothes in her closet, all the jewelry in her drawer, all the shoes lined up on the rack. She had planned on looking as close to perfect for tonight's date as was possible.

But she'd been wrong. Thad was picking her up at eight, and she knew he wouldn't be late. If she hurried, she could manage a quick shower, but she wouldn't have time to do anything with her hair and she would have to wear whatever outfit she could manage to put together in five minutes. And she would start out the evening frazzled and rushed and neither looking nor feeling her best.

But she didn't consider for one moment the possibility of calling Thad to cancel.

Tucking her hair under a plastic cap, Lindsey stepped into the shower, sighing when the stream of hot water hit the taut muscles in her neck. After a day like today the only thing better than this would be a massage—and Thad gave such good ones. His fingers were long and sensitive and strong, and he knew just where to rub and how hard. And once the offending muscles were relaxed, his hands had always found others to tighten with his skilled caresses and gentle strokes.

She bit her lip in frustration and reached for the washcloth, rubbing the soapy fabric roughly over her skin in an effort to chase away the exquisitely shocky sensations that had flooded over her with the mere thought of Thad's hands. She rubbed until she was squeaky-clean and her skin was red and only a faint tingling deep in her belly remained.

She was just stepping out of the shower when the doorbell rang. For an instant she stood motionless, then pulled off the shower cap and began drying herself. By the second peal she was dry enough to slip into her robe, tying the belt as she hurried down the hall and the stairs. She caught a glimpse of disheveled hair and a face scrubbed clean of makeup. This wasn't how she had wanted the evening to start out, she lamented with a heavy sigh.

When she opened the door, Thad, of course, looked perfect. He wore a dove gray suit, white shirt and burgundy tie. Not a hair was out of place, and not a fold of fabric fell the wrong way. He looked gorgeous, relaxed and at ease, while *she* was none of those things.

He knew her too well, Thad thought as his gaze moved slowly over her. That tiny frown that drew her brows together meant she was dismayed at not being ready on time, and the way her fingers were knotted together meant that the stress which had filled her on each previous meeting hadn't lessened. He suspected that it wouldn't for quite a while.

He gave her another long look, starting with her hair, which fell in soft waves down her back. She usually wore it in some sophisticated style that kept it off her shoulders, or wore an intricate braid or ponytail. The only times he'd seen it down like this were in bed, spread like a silken web across the pillow, or tumbling down to brush his cheek and throat when she had leaned over him. He liked it in all the up-swept, controlled styles, but he liked it even better like this—soft and free.

Her robe looked like satin, but he couldn't be sure without touching it, and that, he thought as a band tightened around his chest, wouldn't be a good idea. After her response to last night's kiss, it would be a long time before he risked anything similar.

The robe was black with bright flowers in crimson, royal blue and cream, and leaves in muted forest green. Only a thin belt of matching fabric held it together. A simple tug, and he could see her, all of her, soft and beautiful and sexy as hell, because it was obvious she wore nothing beneath it.

Swallowing reflexively, he pulled his gaze away from the gentle curve of her breasts and the narrow line of her waist and focused on her face again. Without makeup, with her hair loose, she looked so young, so innocent. The cool elegance, the formality and the impersonal politeness were all gone, and nothing remained except the woman he had fallen in love with so long ago.

She tugged the robe tighter, then folded her arms across her breasts. "I—I'm running late. Come in and sit down, I'll be ready in ten minutes."

He had to clear his throat to answer, and his voice still came out thick and unsteady. "Take your time." He closed the door behind him, watched her hurry up the stairs, then went into the living room. He didn't sit down, but wandered around instead, looking without touching at all the items she had displayed in the room.

Nothing had been chosen merely for its looks. Each item, each book, each figurine, each picture, was here because of its personal meaning to her. There were the angel and the vase that had been gifts from Donny. The sand dollar that she'd found on their trip to Kiawah Island. A woven basket bought from a street vendor when they'd driven down to Charleston. A collection of miniature oil lamps that had belonged to her mother, and her grandmother before that. A wooden vase filled with wooden flowers and beside it a corn husk doll that he'd bought for her in Asheville.

He was surprised to see the wooden flowers and the doll still on the shelves. He had assumed that she'd packed up or gotten rid of anything that might remind her of him. The book of poetry that he'd once given her was nowhere in sight, and the photograph of the two of them that had sat on the corner table was gone, too.

Stopping in front of the fireplace, he pushed his hands into his pockets and gazed around. Once he had felt more comfortable in this room than in his own apartment. He'd built countless fires in this fireplace, had worked at that rolltop desk, had spent hours lying on that big sofa, watching television, reading, listening to the stereo or making love to Lindsey. Although they had usually wound up in bed, their lovemaking had almost always begun right there on the sofa, starting with an absentminded embrace, then proceeding to a more deliberate seduction that sometimes moved upstairs to the bedroom but sometimes ended right here in a passionate tangle.

There were times when he wasn't sure which he missed more: Lindsey's lovemaking or just having her in his life. Sex with her had been more intense, more emotional, more explosive, than with any other woman he'd ever known. If he hadn't already been in love with her the first time he'd taken her to bed, he would have been shortly thereafter. It had been an incredible experience, one he knew he could never duplicate with any other woman.

But as much as he missed that, as much as he wanted it back in his life, he missed Lindsey herself more. He missed talking to her, whether in person or on the phone. He missed those long hours out on the front porch when they hadn't bothered to talk at all. He missed the feel of her in his arms when he slept at night, missed her cold feet against his, missed waking up in the mornings to the soft tickle of her hair and the softer sounds of her breathing. He missed the meaning she'd brought to his life.

"Sorry I'm late."

Looking up, he saw her standing in the broad doorway. In her white silk dress and heels, with her makeup subtly and expertly applied and her hair smoothed into a forties-style roll, she was beautiful. Utterly and untouchably beautiful.

He thought rather sadly that he preferred the young, innocent face and the unrestrained hair, the thin robe. *That* woman he could someday seduce. *This* one had all her defenses in place.

They left the house in silence and drove to the restaurant he'd chosen. There they were shown to their table in a quiet corner, where Lindsey finally spoke. "I've never been here before."

He glanced around the dining room, knowing as he did that she approved. It was all dark woods, subdued lighting, snowy white linens and sparkling crystal. It was romantic, and she loved romance. "It opened about six months ago. I've been here several times, and I like it."

"With Carole?"

He looked at her, wondering why she'd asked, then shrugged. "Yes."

"Are you still seeing her?"

"You know me better than that, Lindsey."

Her cheeks turning pink at his rebuke, she reached for the napkin and spread it across her lap. She took a sip of water, then studied the silver lined up beside the plate.

"Lindsey."

Reluctantly she looked at him.

"We weren't this awkward with each other the first time we met. We used to be fellow runners, friends, lov—" Now it was his turn to flush.

"That's part of the problem," she pointed out. "If this were our first date, we wouldn't feel awkward. We would only be concerned with the present and the future—the very near future. But this *isn't* our first date, and the past behind us is much stronger and more certain than the future ahead of us."

"We could always pretend," he suggested halfheartedly.

"Pretend what? That we don't know each other? That I don't know you come from a wealthy family in Boston and the only reason you don't have the accent is because they sent you to private schools all over the country? That I don't know that when you run too much, your left heel gets bruised and sore or that the reason you don't wear contacts is because you have an aversion to putting them in? That I don't know you like to sleep on your left side, that you take up more than your share of the bed and that you like to make love in the middle of the night?"

He studied her solemnly for a long time before quietly asking, "Do you know that I'd like to make love to you right now?"

She wet her lips, then swallowed but said nothing.

"It's been a long time, Lindsey."

"You've had Carole." It wasn't a simple point, but more of an accusation, and she made it in a trembling whisper of a voice.

"But I wanted *you*. I've always wanted you."

She clumsily pushed her chair back and stood up, her napkin falling to the floor. "I—I'll be back. Will you order...?" She gestured helplessly in the direction of the menu, then whirled and walked away, making a beeline for the ladies' room.

Thad didn't bother picking up the menu. He knew it, knew which dishes she would prefer. From the first time he'd brought Carole here, he'd known exactly what Lindsey would order. But he'd never known that someday she would come here with him.

He'd come on a little strong there. All his warnings to himself to take it slow, to give her time, had been totally forgotten the moment she had referred to the nights they'd spent together. Did she have any idea what her reminder of all those times they'd made love in the middle of the night, slow and sleepy and lazy, had done to him? Suffice it to say that it would be a long time before he could give up the privacy afforded by the long, white tablecloth.

He wondered briefly if she would take advantage of her time away from the table to slip out, then immediately rejected the idea. That was the coward's way out, and Lindsey had never been a coward. No matter how uncomfortable he'd made her, she would come back, and she would endure the rest of the evening. Then, when they were alone in the car or on her porch, she just might tell him that she never wanted to see him again.

But he didn't think she would. Eighteen months ago she had loved him—he'd been as sure of that as he'd been of his own love for her—and nothing that had happened since then could change that fact. Maybe she didn't love him now—all right, he admitted, *obviously* she didn't—but he refused to believe that she didn't feel *something*. Tenderness. Friendship. Desire. He would settle for any of those things—or all of them.

But he wouldn't settle for nothing.

Chapter 5

In the ladies' room Lindsey sank down on one of the low, padded stools in front of the mirror and took a deep breath. She was shaking like a frightened virgin. How could he sit there and so calmly say something like that to her? *Do you know that I'd like to make love to you right now?* Merely hearing it echo again in her mind made her tremble. While he knew that, like most women, she normally preferred the subtle approach—romance, seduction, one kiss leading to another—he knew, too, that sometimes the quickest way into her bed was the direct route. And his question had most definitely been direct.

Her cheeks were burning, though her reflection in the mirror showed only the faintest blush. This was more than she could comfortably bear, after her own errant thoughts in the shower and the way he had looked at her when she'd answered the door wearing nothing but that satin robe. It was as if her body had endured all the months of abstinence it was capable of and was now rebelling.

It hadn't been so bad before. Of course there had been times when she had literally ached for a man's touch—no, only for Thad's touch—but since there had been absolutely no chance of finding satisfaction, those episodes had been easier to ignore. How could she hope to ignore them now, when Thad had sat right there across from her so plainly and bluntly telling her that he wanted her in his bed again?

She wasn't even sure what was going on between them. Was it the old attraction, the old friendship, maybe even the old love gradually regaining strength? Or was it lust, pure and simple? There was no denying that they had never encountered a single problem in the bedroom. Their sex drives, their likes and dislikes, all had been equally matched. She hadn't had many lovers, but there had been enough for her to know how rare such perfection was. Thad could do more for her with one simple stroke of his tongue in her mouth than any other man could achieve with a full-scale seduction.

Was desire blinding her to the reality of the situation? She wasn't sure. All she knew was that she wanted him more than he could imagine ... and that she couldn't accept him until she knew they had a chance, at least a slim chance, of salvaging their old relationship. Without that proof, that hope, she simply couldn't risk it.

Her hands steady now, she touched up her lipstick, then smoothed a stray strand of her hair. She had seen the way Thad had looked at it when it hung in undisciplined waves down her back, and she had remembered that he'd liked it that way, that he had often played with it when they'd made love, that afterward he had lain beside her and stroked it, tangling his fingers in it. And so, to discourage such thoughts, she had deliberately put it up in this old-fashioned style.

But he'd thought them anyway.

When she returned to the table, she knew she appeared calm and cool and controlled. She also knew it was the best act she'd put on in years. She sat down across from Thad, sipped the wine that he'd ordered in her absence and gave him a long, level look. He returned her steady gaze with what she had always considered his wise, old owl look. His glasses contributed to the effect, she knew, but it was mostly his eyes, big, dark and unblinkingly solemn, that did it.

"I take it your sudden departure means you're not going to bed with me tonight."

The one small part of her that remained under control both admired and was gently amused by his straightforwardness. How in the world could she have fallen in love with a rigid, humorless, uptight G-man? Donny had asked her numerous times. This was part of the answer right here. Behind that serious, strict, by-the-book facade, there was one wickedly sexy man who could be devastatingly blunt... and breathtakingly gentle.

"Did you really expect me to?" she asked.

He shook his head. "I haven't been that lucky in a long time. But did I really want you to?" His rueful smile was the only answer she needed. It almost made her regret her decision.

"How is business?"

It took her a moment to shift gears from contemplating the pleasure she would have found if she'd accepted his offer and the frustration she was sure to face alone in her bed tonight. "It's fine," she said with a shrug. "How is it for you?"

He blinked, reminding her once again of an owl. She had learned early in their affair not to question him about his work, but that had to be one of those problems he had talked about resolving. She wouldn't be shut so completely out of such a major part of his life.

"It's okay," he replied, the surprise echoed in his voice. "There's never any shortage of crooks in Atlanta."

"Any news about *my* crook?"

His mouth thinned, and his eyes darkened before he looked away. "Lindsey—"

"Don't treat me like an outsider," she interrupted him, her voice clear and quiet and chilling. "If you trust me enough to sleep with me, then trust me enough to talk to me."

He sat in silence for a long time. Outsider. He had used the word Friday evening without thinking of how it would make her feel. Since her parents' death, she had always felt like an outsider, shut out of the small world of her aunt's family, allowed to exist on the edges only because her aunt had felt bound by duty. Then *he* had shut her out of the part of his life that was his job, because he, too, had been bound by duty.

Was she really asking for so much? To know if her brother was really alive, if they were any closer to catching him? After all, it wasn't as if she could do anything at this point to protect Donny, even if she were willing—and he believed with all his heart that she wasn't. Eventually they *would* catch him. He wasn't smart enough to elude them for long.

"There were a lot of prints on the cards, but his weren't among them," he said quietly. "As far as the note on the last card, our handwriting experts compared it to the ransom note, but they can't make a determination either way. The fact that both notes were printed instead of written makes it harder to tell. The way you print usually isn't as distinctive as the way you write."

She looked very calm. He wondered if she felt that way. "And the money at the bank?"

"It was part of the ransom."

After a thoughtful silence, she looked up at him and smiled. "Thank you. Now...what are we having for dinner?"

It was after ten when they arrived back at her house. Lindsey pulled her keys from her purse as she climbed the steps to the porch. Thad was right behind her. A perfect gentleman, he always walked a lady to her door—more often than not, to her *bedroom* door, and beyond.

She sighed silently. She knew he would stay if she asked him to, knew he wanted to, knew *she* wanted him to. But she didn't have the courage. Intimacy was harder the second time around, when the pain was still powerful, the hurts still raw.

She fitted the key into the lock, then turned to face him. He was closer than she had expected, and even as she realized that, he moved closer still. She took a step back into the slight recess of the door, and waited for his next move.

He made it slowly, placing first one hand on the door frame only inches above her head, then the other. Unless she wanted to brush against him intimately, she was his prisoner now. But she didn't feel threatened or trapped or afraid. No, what she mostly felt was hot. Skin-crawling, nerve-tingling hot.

He bent his head close to hers, but didn't touch her, didn't kiss her as she'd thought he was going to. "Do you know that all I have to do is look at you and I get hard?" he asked, his voice mesmerizingly low and husky. "But of course you do. That was one of your powers. You enjoyed it. You used to tease me about it."

She pressed her hands together behind her back. To protect her white dress from the door when she leaned against it. To stop herself from pushing him away, unlocking the door and rushing inside to safety. To keep from grabbing him and dragging him inside with her.

"Do you remember what I used to do to retaliate?"

He was doing it *now,* she thought, nearly in a panic. Making her breasts ache, her muscles weak, her body tremble. Making her throb with hot, damp, burning need. Making her hunger. And doing it all with only his voice, his words. "Thad," she whispered, helplessly protesting, pleading, begging.

"Yes?"

He was so close that his breath brushed her lips, that his heat reached out and wrapped around her. She tried to breathe but her lungs were constricted, tried to swallow but her mouth was too dry, tried to speak but found she had no voice.

He laughed softly—a rare sound in the best of times and the sweetest, dearest sound she'd heard in ages. That, more than anything, would have been her undoing if he hadn't moved away to the top of the steps, pushed his hands into his pockets and asked in a totally normal voice, "How about tomorrow night?"

All she could do was nod.

"I'll call you."

She watched him walk away, her lips compressed to stop herself from calling him back, from asking him to stay, from pleading with him to make love to her. When he closed the gate behind him, she finally unlocked the door and went inside, standing for a long time in the cool, quiet darkness.

Things had changed. *They* had changed. She had told herself that before, had tried to warn herself not to rush into anything, not to risk too much, not to lose it all. And logically she knew she was right. They *had* changed. It would have been impossible to go through that whole experience involving Donny and still come out of it the same person. She had lost so much—her brother, her lover, her friends. And she had lost a part of herself—the innocent, trusting part.

But one thing hadn't changed: the desire—no, the *need*—to put herself in Thad's care, to throw herself into his arms, pour out her problems and ask him, as she had so many times before, to take care of them. To take care of *her*. She had never felt as safe, as protected, as she'd always been in his arms.

And resisting that desire, that need, was going to be almost as impossible as resisting the man himself.

With a sigh she put her purse away, dropped her keys in the porcelain dish, then started up the stairs. She was halfway up when the phone began ringing. Kicking off her heels and scooping them up, she hurried to her bedroom and picked up the receiver with a breathless greeting.

The hum on the line almost masked the slow, even breathing at the other end. Lindsey repeated her greeting in a sharper voice, then scowled when the only response was the continued measured breaths. She could do without crank calls, she decided as she hung up and turned toward the closet. She had more important things to think about.

Such as getting to bed so she could get up early enough in the morning to run and make up for missing it tonight. Such as turning off the desire Thad had so easily kindled. Such as falling asleep alone in her big bed when she knew he would have gladly shared it with her.

Such as wondering whether she was already falling in love with Thad again. And whether she could risk the possibility of losing him again. And whether she could ever face living without him again.

Tuesday evening's dinner date was the complete opposite of the night before. Instead of white linens and crystal, they had paper napkins and plastic tumblers; instead of quiet elegance and flamed duck, there was loud music on the jukebox and platters of spicy barbecued ribs.

Lindsey licked the sauce from her fingers, then finished the job with a napkin, grimacing when the paper stuck to her skin. With a small laugh, she accepted the moist towelette Thad offered and cleaned away the last remnants of sauce.

"Want some dessert?"

She considered the dishes in front of her. She'd already eaten a helping of coleslaw, a plate of greasy French fries and half a rack of ribs. One more bite, and she would be forced to run at least ten miles the next time to work off the calories. "No thanks," she said with a contented smile.

"They have a pecan brownie served warm with vanilla ice cream and about a gallon of fudge sauce," Thad said coaxingly.

It sounded like the kind of sinfully rich and gooey concoction they'd often shared in bed after their middle-of-the-night lovemaking. Their chocolate-flavored kisses had invariably led to further loving. And that—calories aside—was reason enough to turn it down. "No thanks."

He rested his elbows on the red plastic cloth that covered the picnic-style table and studied her. "You look more relaxed tonight," he finally decided.

She smiled again, a little shyly this time. It was easier to relax when he was being charming and not seductive. With the noise around them and strangers sharing the other end of their table, it had been impossible for him to make any remarks of a sexual nature.

Not that it had been necessary for him to make the remarks for her to know he was thinking them. She had watched him watch her lick her fingers, had seen the muscles in his jaw tighten and the smoky look come into his eyes. Power, he had called it last night. The power to arouse him by doing virtually nothing. It made her feel special. Lucky. And needy as hell.

She shifted uncomfortably on the bench. With Cassie to handle the store, she had left early this evening. They had eaten earlier than last night, and they would get home early enough for her to invite him in. What would happen then? Quiet time? Conversation? Or more?

Suddenly she realized that a photograph had appeared in front of her. She stared at it briefly, blankly, before taking it from Thad and studying it more closely. It was a baby, big but not chubby, all long legs and arms, with a mass of brown curls and big brown eyes, an angelic smile and a devilish gleam. He was dressed in an immaculate sailor suit, and his hair was combed as neatly as it was ever going to get.

"That's Andrew, Deke and Tess's son," Thad said. "He stayed that way for about as long as it took me to snap the picture. He's into everything. He runs both of them ragged."

"He has his mother's smile and his father's eyes." Lindsey looked at it a moment longer. She was genuinely happy that Tess's fierce desire for a baby had been fulfilled . . . and briefly sorry that her own wish for a child had so far gone unanswered. She would be a good mother—she *knew* it. Her failures with Donny notwithstanding, she knew she could be the best mother in the world for some little brown-haired, brown-eyed charmer.

Well, she was still young, and there was still hope. As long as she lived, she had hope.

Reluctantly she handed the photo back to him, and he replaced it in his wallet. "So you're still creating masterpieces with the camera," she remarked with a forced note of cheer in her voice.

"Occasionally. I kind of lost interest after I lost my favorite subject."

She busied herself with bringing order to the mess on the table. "That's too bad. You're too good a photographer to give it up."

"Maybe I can get started again."

The husky, suggestive note in his voice sent shivers down her spine. In the beginning she'd felt awkward in front of his camera; then she'd grown used to it. Most of the time it had been fun. Other times it had been a prelude to some of the steamiest—

She squeezed her eyes shut and shook that memory away. Lately she'd found it next to impossible to get her thoughts out of the bedroom. Their lovemaking had always been so intense, so fierce and so fulfilling. Practically everything he said or did reminded her of it, and it had been so damned long. If the yearning didn't kill her, the frustration of constantly wanting—and being afraid to take—would.

Thad's smile was slow and secretly satisfied. He knew exactly what memories had made her react that way, remembered the times when he'd set out to take some simple shots of her and they'd wound up naked and hot and wildly aroused. Of course they had often wound up that way, regardless of what they had initially planned.

And they would wind up that way again. They had to. He was betting his future on it.

He picked up the bill the waitress had left on the table and pulled a few bills from his pocket for a tip. "It's still early," he said as he stood up. "Do you want to go someplace—to a movie, for a walk?"

"A walk? At night? In Atlanta?"

He pointedly looked down at her shoes. "You have on tennis shoes. We could probably outrun any muggers. And if we couldn't, I'm sure I could outshoot them."

She waited until he had paid the bill and they were outside to answer. "I got my exercise before work this morning, and I'm not in the mood to see a movie or anything."

"Then show me your shop."

She gave him a sidelong glance. "Now?"

"Now. When it's closed and no one will disturb us."

It took her a moment to answer, but finally she agreed.
''All right.''

On the drive to the shopping center, he wondered why she
had hesitated. Had she wanted an early end to the evening?
Had she had enough of his company for one day? Had she
disliked the idea of being alone with him in the empty shop?
Had she thought he was intruding in the first thing in her life
that was wholly hers?

He smiled grimly. Determining a person's motives for any
particular action was a part of his job, and he was usually
good at it, but it had never been necessary with Lindsey. She
had always been so open, so honest and forthright. There
had been no secrets between them, no hedging, no subter-
fuge. She had been easy to read and easier to understand.

Until Donny.

Now that there was so little openness between them, now
that their easy, loving relationship had been replaced by this
tense, mistrustful wariness, he found himself second-
guessing everything she said and did, searching for motives. For truth. For hope.

So far, he hadn't found much.

The shopping center parking lot was empty except in front
of the grocery and video stores. Thad parked in the space
closest to Lindsey's Gifts, and together they went into the
dimly lit store. ''I like the name of this place,'' he remarked as she turned on a few more lights.

She laughed softly. ''I think it sounds sort of egotistical
myself. Lindsey's Gifts, Lindsey's Blooms. The advertising
firm that I used when I got started suggested them. Since I
couldn't think of anything else, I agreed.''

''But I like them. They fit.''

She glanced around, then gestured with one hand. ''Well,
here it is. My home away from home.''

He wandered up and down the aisles, taking a more
thorough look than his brief visit last week had allowed. He
could see Lindsey's very definite stamp on everything—not
just in the homey decor, but also on the selection of gift
items, the stationery, the cards. There was nothing tacky or

tawdry here, as could be found these days in most card shops. Everything was quality, classy, elegant.

"How do you choose what to sell?" he asked, stroking the fur of a soft, stuffed bear.

Lindsey came to stand beside him. "I buy what I like. My taste seems to agree with the customers. All these things are handmade, so they tend to be a little unusual, and the workmanship is excellent, the prices reasonable." She tugged gently at the bear's ear. "I get these stuffed animals from a lady in Dahlonega. The blown glass is done by a man in Macon, and the dolls are made by a woman in the Blue Ridge Mountains. Those vine wreaths and baskets come from a woman in Tennessee, and her husband does most of my pottery. No two items are ever exactly alike, so they don't have an assembly-line look. People like that."

"And the cards come from you." He replaced the bear in its spot on the low bench, then turned toward the cards. "You create your own masterpieces."

"I wouldn't call them that. The drawings are very simple, and the verses are very sweet. There's nothing very skillful about either one."

"Simple and sweet is what's selling these days. All the store owners and clerks Clint Roberts has interviewed say your cards are very popular. They sell too many, they say, to remember if a man matching Donny's description bought those particular cards."

She was standing very still, and the expression she wore was an odd one. Surprised. Startled. She probably couldn't believe that he had actually offered her information about the case without being prompted first, he thought with a grin.

"Does that mean the cards are a dead end?" she asked quietly.

"No. They haven't spoken to everyone on your list yet. It takes time." He picked up an anniversary card, studied it, then replaced it and took down a sympathy card. "Do you do all the work yourself?"

"Yes."

"Along with running the store, that must keep you busy."

She smiled bleakly. "As you so kindly pointed out Sunday night, I have no people in my life, so I fill it with work."

He'd been angry when he'd made that comment, angered by her polite, impersonal manner, but he hadn't meant to cause her pain. He hadn't meant to remind her of the emptiness of the past eighteen months of her life. "Lindsey—"

She stopped him with a gentler smile. "What you said was nothing less than the truth. After Donny's disappearance, I shut out everyone else—you, Tess and Deke, the people I worked with, my cousins, my aunt. I didn't want anyone around me. I just wanted to hide away and grieve, and that's exactly what I did for months."

She broke off for a moment and rubbed her finger over a glass shelf as if testing it for dust. Of course there was none. "Then one day Shawn brought me here to a card shop that was going out of business. On a desperate impulse I bought the inventory and took over the lease. I had always wanted a business of my own. I had been saving for it since I was eighteen. And the opportunity couldn't have come at a better time. It forced me to get on with my life, to deal with people, to deal with living. Donny was dead, and you were gone, and as much as I wanted to change those things, I couldn't. This shop saved me."

"You say that as if I abandoned you," Thad said sharply. "That's not true, Lindsey. I gave up only after you made it painfully clear that you didn't want me around."

"I couldn't bear the sight of you." She sat down in the nearest chair and picked up a yellow-haired, blue-eyed doll from the washtub beside it. Was it coincidence, Thad wondered numbly, that she'd chosen that particular doll, when Donny had been a blue-eyed blonde?

"I know that's a horrible thing to say, especially considering that I had loved you," she continued, her voice low and emotional and distant. "But every time I looked at you, I saw you fighting with him on the bridge. And every time I talked with you, I heard your shout and his screams when he fell, and I couldn't stand it."

He pulled a low stool over and sat in front of her. "I could have helped you, Lindsey, if you had only let me."

Slowly she wrapped a strand of yellow yarn doll's hair around her index finger, then let it unwind. "No, I don't think you could have. I blamed you, Thad, and I blamed myself. And if we had stayed together, I think my anger and guilt and hatred would have destroyed both of us."

He reached out and took her hand. Her fingers were cold and limp, and she didn't even seem to notice that he was holding them. "What did you blame yourself for?" he asked gently. "Telling me that something was wrong?" He paused, but she didn't speak. "Saying nothing wouldn't have made a difference, Lindsey. He was careless, and he left enough clues behind. Eventually, we would have caught him. Even if you'd never said a word to me, it wouldn't have changed the outcome. We still would have arrested him, and he still would have fallen."

Finally she met his eyes. Hers were dark, sad, haunted. "How can you be so sure of that?"

He knew she wasn't asking about the arrest, but the fall. How could he be so sure Donny would have fallen from that bridge? Because he knew that Donny hadn't fallen but had deliberately jumped. And he couldn't tell her that. Not now. Suicide was always hard on the survivors. It was harder to accept than accidental death, and the victim's family invariably blamed themselves. Lindsey already blamed herself for Donny's death, even believing that it was an accident. How much worse would that blame be if she knew the truth?

"I *am* sure," he replied. "How we reached that point—Donny and me and the rest of the team on that bridge that afternoon—doesn't matter. It didn't affect what happened there. Whether you had come to me with your concerns or whether we had uncovered him completely on our own, nothing would have changed what happened on that bridge."

With a sigh, she turned her hand over so that her fingers were twined with his. "I'd like to believe that, for my sake, for *our* sake. But I just don't know...."

"You can't blame yourself for any of this. You didn't do anything wrong. You gave Donny everything a kid needed."

"And maybe that was part of the problem. I *gave* him everything. He never had to earn anything. When he wanted money or help, I gave it to him. When he got into trouble, I handled it for him. When he'd done something wrong, I took care of it. Maybe if I hadn't babied him, if I had made him accept some responsibility for himself, if I'd made him earn what he needed and handle his own problems, maybe he wouldn't have gotten into such trouble."

Stubbornly Thad shook his head. "I don't believe that."

"Don't you? You always said I was too easy on him."

"It's more complicated than that, Lindsey. You can't trace his decision to kidnap that old lady back to a single instance in his life. For years psychologists have been studying why one person becomes a criminal when another doesn't, and they still don't have an answer." He sighed softly. "Donny was your brother—not your son, not your puppet, not your creation. You didn't mold him into what he became. You didn't determine what direction his life would take. You *know* you didn't, or he would have been more like you—mature, responsible, reliable. I doubt that Donny himself could tell you what made him do the things he did."

She wasn't totally convinced, though she wanted to be. Wouldn't it be nice, she thought wistfully, to finally be free of the guilt she'd carried for so long? But she doubted that it would ever happen, not completely. The same inconsistency that allowed her head to know Thad wasn't guilty, yet still let her heart blame him was at work here. Logically, she knew she wasn't at fault. Emotionally, she couldn't quite forgive herself.

Wearily she took a deep breath, gently removed her hand from Thad's, put the doll away and gestured around them. "Well, you've seen everything except the workroom and the storeroom, and they're no different from any other workrooms or storerooms. Ready to go?"

He nodded and followed her through the store as she shut off the extra lights, leaving the main room once more in the dim glow of the four lamps. Once she'd locked up, she paused on the sidewalk and breathed deeply. "I love spring evenings. Fall and winter are nice, but spring is like... starting new. The leaves are back and the flowers are blooming and everything is fresh and alive again—" She broke off abruptly. *She* felt alive again. Maybe it was a good omen that their love, lost in winter, was being given this second chance in spring, the season of rebirth.

At Thad's patient prompting, she walked to the car with him, and they drove to her house in silence. There, she turned in the seat to look at him. "Don't come to the door with me, please," she said softly. "I'd rather say good-night here."

Thad looked as if he wanted to protest, but in the end he simply shrugged and said nothing.

Lindsey hesitated, then leaned over and brushed a kiss against his cheek. It wasn't intimate, wasn't even particularly personal, but it was enough. It was almost, for those few seconds she was close to him, for that instant her lips were in contact with his skin, too much. Then she got out of the car and started up the walk.

"Lindsey."

She stopped and looked back. Thad had gotten out and was standing beside his car, one hand resting on the roof.

"I have to go to Savannah tomorrow afternoon. I won't be back until Friday."

She nodded once.

"Will you have dinner with me then?"

She didn't hesitate, didn't give it a moment's thought, didn't warn herself that she was coming to need these evenings together. She simply nodded again.

"I'll pick you up at eight."

After one more nod, she turned and took a few steps, then turned back. "Call me?"

Slowly he smiled, one of those rare, treasured smiles that transformed his entire face. "Yes," he said quietly. "I'll call you."

She went inside the house, locking the door behind her and listening as the sound of his car faded away in the distance. She was smiling, too, she realized when she dropped her keys into the dish beneath the mirror—a silly, sweet, foolish smile that reminded her of better times. A better life.

Upstairs she showered and changed into her nightgown, then she returned to the living room and flipped the television on while she sorted through the day's mail. Bills and junk, she saw, and she set them in their place on the desk. Then she lay down on the sofa.

There was a lawyer show on, and she halfheartedly watched it. She liked the miracles of television, she decided as the cops on the show solved the crime in the first half hour and the prosecutors got the conviction in the second half. Everything was so neatly wrapped up. There were no loose ends, no shattered lives, no sorrow. If only real life could imitate art.

When the phone rang at the end of the show, she automatically glanced at the clock. When she had asked Thad to call, she hadn't meant he should go straight home and call her, but maybe tomorrow before he left town or tomorrow night from Savannah. Still, she wouldn't mind another good-night, especially a safe one over the phone.

But when she answered on the second ring, it wasn't Thad on the line. It wasn't anyone at all—at least, no one who wanted to talk to her. There was just the sound of slow, even breathing. Annoyed, she hung up after her second hello brought no response.

She rarely got nuisance calls or wrong numbers, and she couldn't remember ever getting an obscene call. Now she'd had two strange calls on two consecutive nights... immediately following dates with Thad... only a week after finding out that Donny was back in Atlanta. Could it be...?

She refused to let herself get excited. Why would Donny call and say nothing? He couldn't be so lonely for the sound of her voice that he would call just to hear her say hello and nothing more. He wouldn't deliberately call and say nothing; he would know that because she lived alone, such calls would disturb her. He wouldn't be so cruel.

Then one of Thad's warnings came back to her. Maybe Donny had come back to Atlanta because he wanted to hurt her, to punish her for her role in his arrest. She had refused to believe him, had insisted that the idea was ridiculous... but was it? She had finally acknowledged that her own feelings of guilt were illogical, that her blaming Thad was irrational. Wasn't it possible that Donny could behave just as illogically and irrationally? Even though he *knew* that she wasn't responsible for his arrest, his fall and the horrifying injuries he must have suffered, wasn't it possible that he blamed her anyway?

No. Donny was her brother, and he loved her. He would never blame her for the bad things in his life.

But Thad had been her lover, and she had loved him, a small voice reminded her. Yet she had also blamed him. She had destroyed what was between them, what they were now trying cautiously to rebuild. Maybe Donny wanted to destroy her.

Shivering, she reached for the lacy afghan on the back of the sofa and wrapped it around her. She just couldn't imagine Donny as vengeful, no matter how hard she tried. If that had been him on the phone—and that was a major *if*—then there had to be other reasons why he hadn't spoken. Maybe he knew she was seeing Thad again. Maybe he thought that Thad was even in the room with her. Maybe he was afraid that the phone was tapped, that if he spoke, the call might give away his location.

But not vengeance. Not Donny. Not ever.

Wednesday afternoon Thad showed his credentials to the security personnel at Hartsfield International, Atlanta's airport, then walked through the metal detector, listening to the alarm sound as it registered his gun. He waited for the suit bag he'd laid on the conveyor belt, then picked it up and started down the corridor.

Waiting a short distance ahead was Deke Ramsey, a similar garment bag slung over his shoulder. They didn't often get to work together, but Thad always enjoyed it when they did. He'd never been the type to make particularly close friends—his personality, serious and too often aloof, had made it difficult, and the rootlessness of too many boarding schools when he was growing up had compounded the problem—but Deke was the best friend he'd ever had.

They were unlikely candidates for good friends. Deke was nearly eleven years older than Thad. He had grown up tough, the oldest of five kids who had helped support his family following his father's unexpected death, while Thad had led a privileged life, with money to pay for every need and servants to provide them. After high school, Deke had joined the Marine Corps and fought in Vietnam, then put himself through college on the G.I. Bill and a lot of hard work, while Thad had gone straight from his exclusive private high school to an exclusive private college, all expenses paid by his family. Deke liked country music, faded jeans and worn-out boots, while Thad liked classical music and didn't own a pair of jeans or boots and wasn't sure if he ever had.

But on the important things, they agreed. Deke was a dedicated husband and family man, a role that Thad was more than willing to take on himself if Lindsey ever gave him a chance. And corny as it sounded, they both loved their country, when patriotism was in style and when it wasn't. Neither of them had ever considered using their hard-earned college degrees for anything other than government service. They both held a deep pride and respect for their jobs and their responsibilities.

And they were both damned good poker players.

"How's Tess?" Thad asked as they started toward the gate together. Over the past couple of years it had practically become his standard greeting whenever he saw Deke without his wife. He'd been a frequent guest in the Ramsey home, particularly while he'd been with Lindsey, and he'd become very fond of Tess. And Andrew—well, it went without saying that he loved Andrew, exhausting, unruly, hyperactive child that he was.

"The doctor says she's fine. She says she feels wonderful." Deke's smile had lost the strain of last week. Thad could tell that he felt better about this pregnancy, probably thanks to Tess. She was one very persuasive woman, and there was no doubt that she wanted this baby. Thad had no doubt that Deke wanted the baby, too, and that, added to Tess's determination, had helped him relax.

After a moment, Deke asked, "How's Lindsey?"

Thad simply looked at him. He had run with his friend every evening since last Monday, except for the weekend—that was family time, Deke insisted—and there had been no further mention of Lindsey or the Phillips/Heinreid case. So how did Deke know he'd been seeing her?

"One of the guys at work tried a new barbecue place last night," Deke explained without being asked. "He saw you there and described a woman who couldn't possibly be anyone other than Lindsey."

Thad turned to look out the plate-glass window. The Atlanta airport was always busy. There were two planes landing simultaneously, and he could see another four awaiting their turn. He watched them while he considered the question. How was Lindsey? She was sorrowful, sad, torn by guilt, wary, frustrated, angry, bitter and trying to make the best of it all. She was beautiful, sweet and gentle. She was sexy as hell, and still the only woman in the world with whom he wanted to spend his life.

Finally he settled on a variation of Deke's answer about Tess. "She's all right." It was a far cry from fine, but it beat most of the alternatives. "The past year and a half has been really tough on her."

"It's been tough on you."

Still watching the planes, Thad nodded.

"How much time have you spent with her?"

"Her house was broken into Friday evening, and I went over with the team then. I also saw her Sunday, Monday and last night."

"Is this serious?"

He smiled. "The first time I laid eyes on her, it was serious." Slowly he turned from the window to face Deke. "Do you remember right after the kidnapping happened when I told you I had bought a ring and was going to ask Lindsey to marry me?"

Deke nodded.

"I still have the ring. And I still intend to ask her. The only difference is then I knew what her answer would be. Now I don't."

But there was one other difference: then he'd known that she loved him.

Now he knew that she didn't.

Chapter 6

Lindsey sat cross-legged on the sofa, a sketch pad propped on her lap and a hanging basket of delicate lavender petunias sitting on the coffee table in front of her. She'd been trying for more than two hours now to master the simple lines and lacy edges and gracefully curving vines, but her efforts had all been stiff. Lifeless. Substandard.

With a sigh, she leaned back and rolled her neck from side to side. She could work for hours at a time, satisfied with even a smidgen of progress, but when each sketch was worse than the preceding one, frustration made her tense. Stiff, like her renderings.

And when she was already tense to start with, she didn't stand a chance in the world of succeeding. And she had been tense all day. Because Thad hadn't called.

She knew he'd gone to Savannah yesterday on business, and she knew his hours when he was out of town tended to be long and unpredictable. He may not have finished working until late last night. He might not have found an opportunity today when he had both the time and the privacy to call her. Or maybe he had misunderstood and thought she'd meant call before their date tomorrow night and not while he was gone. After all, she hadn't made herself very clear. *Call me* didn't exactly explain that she'd meant tomorrow night and the next night and Friday, too.

Still, she had waited all last evening and again all day today to hear from him. She was disappointed that she hadn't, and was worried by just how disappointed she felt.

She set her sketching materials aside and unfolded her legs, stretching out the kinks in her knees. There was no rush on the petunias, but she did hate to admit defeat, and by a bunch of common lavender posies, no less. She considered what other flowers in her yard could be brought inside. Short of cutting a branch off the pink dogwood in the corner of the backyard, she couldn't think of anything she hadn't used already or was in the mood to tackle tonight.

The ringing of the telephone sounded loud in the house. She didn't work with the television or stereo on, and the bell shattered the quiet. Automatically she reached for it, then she paused and checked the time. It was ten-forty-five. The other two calls, she couldn't help remembering, had come between ten-thirty and eleven.

Before the second ring finished, she answered, offering a cautious hello.

"Lindsey, it's Thad."

She breathed a sigh of relief—both that it wasn't her mysterious silent caller and that Thad had finally called as he'd said he would. "Hi. How's Savannah?"

"Well, we just finished work for the day, and dinner was cold fast-food hamburgers. All things considered, I'd rather be with you."

Smiling shyly, she settled into the deep cushions of the couch, propping her feet on the back. "Then you've had a long day."

"Yeah. I wanted to call you last night, but it was after midnight when we got back to the hotel."

"We?" she echoed, her hated jealousy sensors going on full alert. "I thought you were going alone."

"I'm the only one from my office, but Deke's here, too. He's in the next room."

"Oh. What kind of business requires both an FBI agent and a marshal?"

"We're conducting some interviews, and when we're finished, Deke is escorting a prisoner back to Atlanta. We've been after this guy a long time, and he finally showed up at his mother's house."

"And she turned him in?"

"Does that surprise you?"

"A little."

"If Donny walked into your house right now, you would call Clint Roberts and tell him."

She waited for him to add a doubtful, "wouldn't you?" But he didn't go on. "Are you sure of that?"

"Yes. I *know* you would, because that's the kind of person you are. Because it's the right thing to do, not only in the eyes of the law but in terms of what's right for Donny. When faced with a choice between right and wrong, good people tend to do the right thing."

"And I'm good people, huh?"

"The best."

She gave that a moment's bleak thought, then shook her head. She didn't want to talk about Donny, about right and wrong or good and bad anymore. With a weary sigh, she asked, "When are you coming home?"

"Tomorrow afternoon. Are we still having dinner?"

"Sure, if you feel like it."

"I will. Do you want casual or dressy?"

She considered it a moment, then chose dressy. She always enjoyed getting all dressed up. It made a date seem like such a special event—not that all her dates with Thad hadn't been special, whether they had included dinner at Atlanta's classiest restaurants or a picnic on the beach at Kiawah Island or hot dogs at a Braves game.

"I'll make the reservations. How about that place we went to with Deke and Tess on her birthday?"

"That's fine." She was silent for a moment before hesitantly asking, "Does Deke know that we're...?" She couldn't bring herself to finish the question. It sounded too secretive, as if she might want to keep their relationship that

way when that wasn't the case at all. She didn't care who
knew that she was seeing Thad again. She simply felt shame
when it came to the Ramseys. They had been good friends,
and she'd treated them as badly as she had treated Thad.

"Yes." He paused. "I doubt that there's anything about
me worth knowing that Deke doesn't know. He was the only
one who knew that I was going to ask you to marry me before Donny..."

The mention of marriage saddened her, and it showed in
her voice when she softly asked, "Do you ever think how
different our lives would be if he had never kidnapped that
poor woman?" Thad would have proposed to her, and of
course she would have said yes. They would have had a
spring wedding and an unbearably romantic honeymoon,
and he would have moved into this house. By now they
would have been parents, settled into the routine of night-
time feedings, first steps and first words. They would have
missed out on all the tragedy, all the sorrow, and right now,
instead of might-have-beens, they would be exchanging
words of longing, of missing and needing and loving.

"We can't change the past, Lindsey," he said quietly.
"We can only change the future."

"Sometimes I get so angry with him. What he did was so
unfair. To that woman, to himself, to us. I gave him everything I could, and he repaid me by taking away everything I
valued. And I know it's wrong to be angry—"

"No, it's not," Thad interrupted her. "It's a perfectly
normal response. Someone you loved and trusted let you
down. Of course you're angry."

She was silent for a long time, then she defensively admitted, "I want this whole thing over with. Even if it means
seeing Donny in prison. I want this to end, and I want to put
it behind me, and I want to start living again. I want to have
a future again."

"Soon, Lindsey," he promised. "It'll be over soon."

"Want to hear a Braves joke?" Shawn paused exactly
long enough to lend impact to his punch line. "*That's* a re-
dundancy. The Braves *are* a joke."

Lindsey gave him a long, solemn look.

"Okay." Not the least bit unnerved by her response, he thought for a moment, then asked, "Do you know who the Braves are playing tonight?"

She dryly fed him his line. "Who?"

"The winners."

This time she smiled. "I like that one," she admitted. "Tell me, Shawn, do you get your worst jokes out of your system with me so you won't be tempted to use them in your act?"

"Sometimes. Hey, what are friends for?" He gave the swing a push with one foot, then gave her a measuring look. "Got a date tonight? Is that why you took off work so early?"

"As a matter of fact, it is."

"With McNally?"

She nodded.

"Getting serious?" he asked, then grinned. "As if the two of you know any other way to be."

She paused in opening her mail. "What do you mean?"

"Maybe that you and McNally take life so damn seriously all the time. You don't take much time out for fun." Then he grinned again. "Or maybe I meant that you two are so damn perfect for each other that you can't help but be serious about each other. For whatever it's worth, Lindsey, I'm glad he's back in your life."

She gazed down at the phone bill she held without really seeing it. "For whatever it's worth, Shawn..." She looked at him then and smiled solemnly. "So am I."

"Does this mean you've settled everything?"

"No. There are still things I resent and things he must resent. Donny's still a sore point. I can't talk about him without feeling such bitterness, yet I can't seem to keep him out of our conversation."

"Any news about him?" he asked quietly.

She shook her head. "His fingerprints weren't on the cards, but they didn't seem surprised by that. The writing on the card wasn't conclusive. It might be his or it might not.

But the money deposited into my bank account was definitely ransom money."

"This Roberts guy came to interview me at work this week. Needless to say, my boss was not thrilled, but once I'd explained it to him, he didn't mind. I understand they're talking to several of Donny's old friends."

"Part of me wants to believe that if he got in touch with anyone from his past, it would be me," she said, her voice low and thick with emotion. "And part of me wants to believe that if he got in touch with any of his old friends that I knew that they would be decent enough to tell me."

"And what would you do with that information?"

"I would give it to the FBI. And maybe that's why Donny has refused to contact me."

"Maybe," Shawn agreed. "Wherever he's been, you know the past eighteen months couldn't have been easy for him. He had to have been badly hurt when he fell, and he couldn't turn for help to the one person he'd relied on all his life—you. What he'd done had cut him off from everybody—all his friends, all his family. He had nothing."

"Oh, he had something, Shawn," she said bitterly. "He had over two hundred and twenty thousand dollars of ransom money. I imagine that if you care about money as much as Donny apparently did, that could ease a lot of pain."

He left the swing and crouched in front of her chair. "I'd better be going. If you need anything—"

Smiling, she brushed her fingers through his thick blond hair. "In the past eighteen months I've relied on you almost as much as Donny used to rely on me. You've been a good friend, Shawn. You'll never know how much I appreciate everything you've done for me."

"That sounds almost like a brush-off, Lindsey," he teased, taking both her hands in his.

"No, of course it isn't. I'll always treasure your friendship, and I'll always need you in my life."

"But McNally is back, and you can rely on him in ways that you and I never even considered."

"Thad has always filled a number of roles in my life, but he could never take your place, Shawn."

He kissed her cheek, then stood up. "Bring him to the club sometime. I *will* get a laugh out of him yet." At the top of the steps, he stopped and looked back at her. "Or maybe I won't. He doesn't even look capable of it."

Lindsey stood up, too, and saw the blue government sedan with its conspicuous antenna parked in front of her house. Standing beside it, one hand on the roof and the other in a fist on his hip, was Thad. No, she silently agreed with Shawn, at this moment he didn't look capable of laughing. "I think he's jealous of you," she remarked softly.

Shawn looked down at her. "Of *me*? Good old Shawn? The kid you knew when he had braces and pimples and a life-threatening crush on Mary Kay Hampton?" He glanced at Thad again, then said, "I'd give him something to be jealous of, except that my daddy taught me not to mess around with a woman whose man carries a gun."

She walked down the steps with him and out to the sidewalk. "I'm glad you stopped by, Shawn. Have a good weekend."

"I'll see you." He grinned as he passed Thad on the way to his car. "McNally."

Intensely aware of Thad's scowl, Lindsey remained just inside the gate, her hands clasped loosely, her smile barely under control. She waited until Shawn had driven away before meeting Thad's gaze. He *was* jealous. She could read it in every stiff line of his body.

After a moment, she turned back toward the house. At the bottom of the steps, she looked over her shoulder at him. "Are you coming?"

He pushed himself away from the car and followed her up the steps and into the cool, dim quiet of the house. As soon as he closed the door behind him, he asked, "Are you sleeping with him?"

Lindsey turned to face him. Her expression was so blank that he couldn't read anything in it—not anger, annoyance, embarrassment or guilt. Nothing. After a long, shimmering silence, she replied, "If I were having an affair with Shawn, *you* wouldn't be here now. And if I had had an affair with him in the past, it wouldn't be any of your business.''

None of his business. As impossible as it seemed, she was right. Nothing in her life in those eighteen months they had been apart was any of his business. Even though he had loved her, even though he had longed to be with her again, he had no right to know what she'd felt, what she'd done and who she might have done it with.

This wasn't the homecoming he had envisioned. Tuesday night when she had kissed him good-night, then asked him to call her, he'd thought they had reached a turning point in their relationship. Just like old times, she had wanted to talk to him when they couldn't be together. And last night on the phone he'd gotten the distinct impression that she'd missed him, that she had been waiting for him to call. Now the jealousy he couldn't quite control had spoiled everything.

It wasn't even that she and Shawn had done anything wrong. He simply hated the way she had stroked Shawn's hair so gently, the way he'd taken her hands and later kissed her. As if he'd had the right . . . when Thad himself didn't. If *he* touched her so casually or kissed her so easily, she would stiffen and endure or pull away.

And the differences in her behavior hurt.

He turned away, tracing the outline etched into the frosted glass pane in the door. ''I'm sorry,'' he said flatly. ''I just . . .'' He just couldn't stand the idea of another man touching her, kissing her, making love to her. Just couldn't bear to think that she could share herself with another man in the same way she'd given herself to him.

Lindsey cleared her throat. ''Did you just get back from Savannah?''

''Yeah. I dropped Deke and the prisoner off downtown, then came here.''

''What is this prisoner wanted for?''

''Making threats against the judge who sent his brother to prison.'' He turned to face her and smiled uneasily. ''Now he's added Deke and me to his hit list.''

She didn't smile back. Instead she seemed to grow paler. Concern for him? he wondered. "Then be careful," she whispered.

"I am sorry, Lindsey. I had no right to ask you that. But it's hard to see you look at him and smile at him and touch him that way when I want..." His words faded away when she approached him, stopping only inches away. She lightly rested both hands on his shoulders and leaned forward for a gentle, soft, sweet kiss.

It lasted only a moment but went on forever. It wasn't intimate, but it touched his heart and his soul. It wasn't sexy, but it made him hungry and hard and hot. And just as he reached for her, it ended.

She took a few steps back and smiled gently. "Apology accepted. Now go home, so I can get ready for dinner."

Feeling a little dazed, he opened the door and stepped onto the porch. Then she called his name.

"For whatever it's worth, there hasn't been anyone else," she said evenly. "Not Shawn. Not anyone." Then she closed the door.

Now that she'd admitted it, he felt ashamed that he'd made it necessary. Deep in his heart he'd known she wouldn't have an affair with Shawn, who'd been like a second brother to her. He'd known that simply surviving the past year and a half had been difficult enough for her; where would she have found the time and the energy to get emotionally involved with another man? And he'd known that it would be impossible for her to go to bed with a man she wasn't emotionally involved with.

Then the shame was swept away by a rush of relief. Of arousal. Of gratitude. She wasn't angry with him. She had kissed him. She still wanted to see him. She was still willing to give him a second chance.

Now it was up to him to make certain she didn't regret it.

Lindsey was waiting on the porch in her running clothes when Thad arrived Saturday morning. She propped one leg on the railing and bent over it, stretching the muscles, then repeated the process with the other leg as he climbed the steps.

"Good morning."

She turned her head sideways and smiled at him. It *was* a good morning so far. For the first time since opening her shop, she had taken a Saturday off, so the entire weekend stretched pleasantly empty and unplanned ahead of them. She had slept well after their date last night, and this morning she had the energy to run an easy ten miles—well, maybe seven, she amended—instead of her usual five.

When she straightened, she gave him a long look. While no one wore a suit as well as Thad did—he seemed made for formal attire—she had to admit that few men looked as good as he did in more casual clothes. His cotton gym shorts and T-shirt were identical to the outfits that most joggers wore, but they somehow looked so much better on him. Of course, there was the fact that he was in superb condition—body fat kept to a bare minimum and every muscle well-defined and rock hard. He had gorgeous legs—long, lean and muscular—the kind of legs women admired.

And, of course, she admitted with a small smile, the fact that he was so darned handsome didn't hurt the image any.

"Do you still run over to the park and pick up the trail there?" he asked as he tightened the laces on his left shoe.

She nodded. There was a park exactly a mile away with a lake, tennis and basketball courts, playground equipment and a jogging trail that wound through the pines. It was her usual route unless it was too late in the evening; then she had to be satisfied with a few miles around the neighborhood.

When she started down the steps, Thad stopped her with his hand on her arm. "I had a good time last night," he said quietly.

After a moment, she smiled again. "So did I." It had been like old times—a quiet restaurant, an excellent meal and easy conversation. There'd been no mention of his job or Donny or the months they'd been apart. It had been pleasant. Comfortable. Right.

But the similarity to old times had ended when he'd brought her home. He had walked her to the door, touched her hair so lightly that she'd barely felt it, said good-night and abruptly walked away. And she had gone inside to find that her answering machine had picked up a call while she was out. There had been no message, no greeting, just a fifteen-second tape of silence before the caller had hung up. A wrong number? A caller who hated machines?

Or Donny?

When they reached the sidewalk, they set out at an easy pace, slowing only slightly before they crossed each street. Lindsey could hear the jingle of her house keys in her pocket and the fainter sound of Thad's in his own pocket. It was still early enough to be cool, and the humidity was heavy in the air, but they both ran often enough to be used to it.

She hated this first mile. She had jogged five miles practically every day for the past ten years, and she still hated the first mile. It seemed that her bones were jarred and her muscles were tight and her lungs were constricted. It didn't help that at her side Thad was completely unaffected by the initial exertion. He could run forever and never feel the same discomfort.

But by the time they reached the park, her stride was smoother and longer and her muscles were warmed up and stretching easily and her breath came more easily, too. She set a moderately fast pace, not because she wanted to be able to run quickly but because she had always, until recently, run with men—acquaintances, friends, Thad. She had learned early that it was easier to adapt her rhythm to theirs than ask them to slow to the pace that came more naturally to her.

"Deke and Tess would like to get together sometime," Thad remarked as they rounded the first bend in the trail. It took them out of the weak morning sun and into the shade of the tall pines. It was cooler there, and the air was rich with the woodsy fragrance.

Lindsey remained silent for the next eighth of a mile. She could feel the slap of her ponytail against her back with each step, and tiny beads of sweat were forming across her forehead. There was a bandanna, the same shade of pale blue as her shorts, folded and tucked into her waistband. When the sweat began stinging her eyes, she would put it on, she decided, but that wouldn't happen for another half mile.

"I take it your silence means you don't want to see them."

She glanced at Thad, then back at the path ahead. "No, that's not what it means. Do you know why Tess and I quit being friends?"

"Yes."

She grimaced at his brusque reply. Of course he knew. How had he phrased it when he'd told her about Andrew's birth? Oh, yes, that she had dumped Tess and Deke at the same time she'd dumped him. "I treated her badly—I treated both of them badly. I don't quite know how to apologize."

"They're not looking for an apology, Lindsey. Tess just wants her old friend back."

She wondered if he had singled out Tess because her friendship had been stronger with her or because Tess was the one interested in renewing it. Probably the latter. Deke had been a good friend, too, but his loyalties, first and foremost, belonged to his wife. He wouldn't easily forgive anyone for hurting her, and, as much as she hated to admit it, Lindsey *had* hurt Tess. She had hurt everybody.

"I would like to see her," she admitted. "But I just don't know what to say to her."

It was Thad's turn now to be quiet. Lindsey risked a look at him as they began a circuit around the small lake. He looked so serious. Was he disappointed in her? She didn't want him to be, but she couldn't just agree to what he wanted. This wasn't a casual meeting with casual friends that he had suggested, but a reunion with a very special couple who had stood by her through the worst time in her life, whose friendship she had repaid with bitter anger.

When he finally spoke there was no disappointment in his voice, only concern. "Don't keep punishing yourself, Lindsey. You went through a bad time when Donny disappeared. You did some things, said some things, that maybe weren't fair. But they're in the past now. You don't have to keep paying for them."

"I'd like to believe that," she said wistfully. "But some things can't be forgiven."

Thad stopped in the middle of the path, not hearing another runner's curse when he had to swerve around him. Lindsey jogged on a few yards before stopping and turning back. "We're talking about people who love you," he said, studiedly keeping his voice patient even though his patience was strained. "There's precious little that you can't forgive when you love someone."

Precious little. She veered off the path and walked to the water's edge. They called it a lake, but it was really nothing more than a pond, shallow and muddy and home to a greedy family of ducks who loved day-old bread and crackers.

Precious little. Then why couldn't she forgive Thad for not giving her the chance to intervene with Donny? Did that mean her love was flawed, that she didn't love as well as he did, as Tess and Deke did? Did that mean that *she* was flawed?

Thad stepped to the side of the path, then waited, his hands on his hips, his heart thudding, his breath thunderous in his ears. What was she thinking? Of all the things that *she* couldn't forgive? All the things she still blamed him for?

Finally, when she'd stood there without moving for several long moments, he went to her. He gave no thought to keeping his distance, to not rushing her, to not asking for more than she was ready to give. He simply walked up behind her, slid his arm around her and pulled her back against him. "You've punished yourself long enough, Lindsey—too long," he murmured in her ear. "You need Tess and Deke back in your life. You need friends. You need to be loved." He paused, and his voice was even lower when he went on. "You need me."

She raised both hands to his forearm, but not to push it away. Instead she held on with a painful grip.

He settled his other arm around her waist and simply held her. He could feel her ragged breathing and the occasional shudder that rippled through her, and he heard the slight catch in her voice when she finally whispered, "I do need you. But God help me, I can't..."

"Forget what happened?" he prompted when she didn't go on. "Forgive my role in it?"

Another delicate shudder was her only response.

"So hate me for it, Lindsey. But don't shut me out of your life. Don't push me away again."

Tears in her eyes, she twisted in his arms then and grasped a handful of his T-shirt. "I can't hate you, and I can't totally forgive you, and I can't—" She caught her breath in a trembling gulp before continuing. "I can't go on this way."

Would it help her to know the truth about that day on the bridge? To know that Donny hadn't fallen but had deliberately jumped? That Thad hadn't been struggling to subdue him but to save him, to keep him from going over the edge? That instead of causing Donny's fall, Thad had risked his life to stop it?

Part of him said yes. Her emotions were pulling her in opposite directions, and sooner or later something would have to give—her condemnation of him, their future or her reason. If telling her the truth would ease that conflict, if it would make her understand that nothing Thad could have done, nothing *she* could have done, would have saved Donny that day, wasn't it worth the disillusionment it would cause?

And part of him said that was a selfish answer. Did he want to make things easier for her...or for himself? How could he possibly justify telling her that her brother had tried to commit suicide, that Donny had taken her with him that day so she could be there when he died? How could *any* benefits outweigh the harm?

So in the end, he said nothing. He simply stood there and held her until the shivering stopped, until the tears dried from her eyes, until she took a long, deep breath and gently pushed away from him. Avoiding his eyes, she took out a sky blue bandanna, shook it loose and wiped her face. Then, finally, she looked at him. "I would like to see Tess and Deke," she said quietly. "When can you arrange it?"

"Are you sure?"

She nodded.

"I'll call them when we get back to your house."

She started back toward the path, then stopped and lightly touched his arm. "You're right, Thad. I need you. Regardless of everything else . . . I do need *you.*"

When they got home Lindsey went to shower while Thad went to the phone. She came downstairs twenty minutes later, dressed in shorts and a comfortable shirt, her damp hair gathered loosely at the nape of her neck.

"I invited them over here for lunch," Thad said, reaching for the gym bag he'd brought in from his car. "Nothing fancy—just sandwiches or burgers in the backyard. Okay?"

She nodded apprehensively.

Sliding his fingers beneath her hair and getting a gentle grip on her neck, he pulled her closer. "Don't worry about it, Lindsey. It's just friends." Then he released her—sooner than she was ready to be freed, she realized—and started up the stairs. "As soon as I get out of the shower, we'll go to the grocery store, okay? So be thinking about what you want for lunch."

She sat down on the step as he disappeared into her bedroom. A moment later she heard the water come on. He was taking a shower in *her* bathroom, using the soap she had just used, the shampoo she had just washed her hair with, and in a few minutes he would dry himself with *her* towel. She tried to tell herself that it was no big deal—he'd taken hundreds of showers at her house before—but it wasn't hard to remember that she'd found the idea achingly erotic each and every time. She had stayed often in the bathroom with him, putting on makeup or drying her hair or just sitting on the counter beside the sink and talking. Other times she had gotten into the shower with him, and on those occasions they had always made love, wet and slick with soap, under the hot spray.

The water upstairs shut off, but that didn't pull her from her long-ago memories. It didn't lessen the tingling in her breasts or the need between her thighs. It didn't chase away the unbearable emptiness that suddenly overwhelmed her—

emotional emptiness because she was alone, and physical emptiness because she'd been alone too long. I do need you, she'd told Thad a short while ago, and at the time she hadn't been thinking about making love, about being joined so intimately, filled so deeply. But she missed him in that way, too. She needed him in that way, as well.

He came downstairs, neatly dressed as always in oatmeal-colored trousers and an emerald green shirt. His hair, like hers, was still wet and was slicked back. He looked gorgeous, she thought as he stepped around her and sat down on the step below her. "Are you ready?"

She breathed in deeply of his scent, clean and sensual. What would he think if she said yes, that she was ready—not for shopping, but to go to bed, to make love, to end this awful loneliness and fill this awful emptiness? Would *he* say yes? Or would he think they needed more time? Would he feel used?

Using the stair railing, she pulled herself to her feet. "Yes, I'm ready."

They went to the grocery store near her shop. Lindsey resisted the irrational urge to stop in and make sure Cassie was all right. She trusted her assistant completely and knew that she wouldn't have any problems. She knew, too, that her desire to stop there was born of a desire to delay the meeting with Tess and Deke.

They decided to cook hamburgers on the grill, and filled their cart with meat, buns, tomatoes and sweet Vidalia onions. Indulging her taste for junk food, Lindsey added a box of chocolate-iced brownies from the bakery, two bags of potato chips and a package of cookies. After picking up a six-pack of beer and several bottles of soda, she surveyed the contents of the cart, making sure they hadn't forgotten a thing. "I guess Tess will bring Andrew's food," she remarked.

"I'm sure she will. Don't worry about it. Andrew's not picky. The kid will eat dirt."

She smiled faintly—the first smile she'd managed in too long, Thad realized.

"You think I'm teasing, don't you?" He guided the cart into the shortest checkout line, then reached casually for Lindsey's hand. "I'm not. I've seen that child eat dirt. And a penny. And a dusty old cookie that he found under the couch, where he no doubt hid it earlier for just that purpose. There are teeth marks on everything in their house, from the coffee table to the telephone to the television remote control."

"Sounds like Tess has her hands full. Is she still working?"

"No. Personally, I don't think she could pay someone enough to keep Andrew for her. Whatever the going rate for baby-sitters is, they'd have to charge double for him. He's a full-time job."

"I'm glad she can stay home with him. That's one of the nice things about having my own shop. Being the boss, I could take a baby to work with me, at least until he started walking." Then she flushed uncomfortably. "That is, if I ever have any children."

Thad raised her hand to his mouth. Her shiver when his tongue touched her palm traveled into him through that small contact. "You will," he replied without hesitation. "You'll have three or four, and you'll be the best mother any man could want for his children."

"I didn't do such a great job with Donny."

He controlled his annoyance at that. "Donny was not your son—he was your brother. You were only six years older than him, Lindsey, and you were his sister—not his mother, not his guardian, not his conscience. When you have a baby, you'll see what a big difference there is between being a mother and a mothering sister."

"You sound so sure that I will have kids of my own, when I don't even know myself."

"I am sure. I know you want them . . . and I know I do, too."

And so he believed they would have them together. Lindsey skittered away from the intense pleasure such thoughts brought her. Babies—Thad's babies—were a dream she'd had too long, had wanted too much, to think about now with such certainty. When she had no idea what her future held—years with Thad or a lifetime alone—she couldn't let herself imagine kids in it. It would hurt too much if the dream turned out to be just that—a dream. A fantasy. An illusion.

"This is certainly interesting conversation for the check-out line," she said with a lightness she didn't feel as she began unloading the groceries onto the conveyor belt. When Thad came forward to help her, she pulled her checkbook from her purse and began filling out a check.

"I'll pay for this," he protested. "I'm the one who invited company over."

"I asked you to, and it's my house. Besides, it's my turn." She watched as the clerk totaled the final purchases, then finished writing the check and handed it over.

They carried the groceries to the car themselves, then returned to her house. Once everything was put away Lindsey suggested that they sit outside. She chose to sit on the wooden swing, and Thad joined her at the opposite end. "Why aren't you assigned to this case again?" she asked unexpectedly, surprising both Thad and, to some extent, herself.

He pulled his glasses off to clean them—an old habit, she remembered, that as often as not had been a delaying tactic rather than a genuine need for cleaning. When he finally replaced them he looked very solemn. "I could have been, but I didn't want it," he admitted. "I didn't want to be spending my days working on something that would remind me constantly of you. Besides, I had always wanted a second chance with you, but had never found the courage to try. If I were assigned to this case, I wouldn't be able to see you. I couldn't have dinner with you. I couldn't even talk to you on the phone unless it was regarding business."

"When you found out the last time about Donny, why didn't you turn it over to somebody else? Don't you have rules against working on cases you're personally involved in?"

"By the time I found out for sure that it was Donny, he already knew that I knew. He insisted on dealing with me and nobody else. I didn't have any choice, Lindsey. He didn't *give* me a choice."

She turned to face him and drew her feet onto the bench between them. "When he's caught, he'll go to trial and then to prison. Once he's been convicted and locked up, won't your boss frown on your relationship with me?"

"Does it matter?"

"If your job destroys us a second time? If you get into trouble because of me? Yes, that matters. It matters a lot."

Thad's smile held a hint of satisfaction. They were definitely making progress. Not only was she concerned about their future, but the blame for their past had shifted subtly from *him* to his job. Definite progress.

He set the swing in motion and for a moment watched her gently sway with it. "If Donny were already in prison and I had just met you, maybe they wouldn't like that so much in the office. But he's not in prison yet, and I've known you a long time, and I was in love with you a long time. They know the facts. They know that you and I were involved long before Donny committed his crime. They wouldn't care, Lindsey, and even if they did, *I* wouldn't care. I haven't done anything wrong. You can't compromise me or the way I do my job. The incident with Donny proves that."

She tilted her head back to stare up at the ceiling. "I don't blame him for staying away so long. The thought of prison must terrify him."

Thad shook his head. "Knowing Donny, I doubt he's admitted to himself yet that he's going there. Recognizing the seriousness of his own actions was never one of his strong points. Neither was accepting responsibility for them."

Lindsey was silent for a long time, staring out across the yard, her expression distant and sad. Was she offended by what he'd said? he wondered. Still blaming herself for Donny's shortcomings? He waited edgily for her to say something, to give him some hint of what she was thinking, feeling.

She sighed heavily before she spoke, and Thad prepared himself for the worst. It didn't come. "I need to weed the flower beds," she said lazily. "And mow the grass. And mulch around the azaleas again."

He laughed as he got up from the swing and went to stand behind it. Resting his arms along the back, he leaned down close to her ear. "Invite me over tomorrow, and I'll help you."

"All right. Would you come over tomorrow and help me work?"

"And what would I get in return?"

She pretended to consider it a moment. "I'll fix dinner for you."

"What else?"

"The satisfaction of a job well-done." She swung her feet to the floor, then glanced back at him. "Or you could spend the entire day alone in your empty apartment watching the Braves on TV. Is that dismal enough for you?"

Before he could answer a familiar car caught Lindsey's attention. She looked at Thad, who came around the swing and took her hand, pulling her with him to the top of the steps. "Maybe this isn't such a good idea," she whispered as Tess Ramsey got out of the car.

"You weren't this nervous about seeing *me* again for the first time," Thad whispered back. "I think my feelings are hurt."

"Yes, I was. I was just angry enough to hide it." She watched Tess sling a big yellow bag over her shoulder while Deke leaned into the back of the car to unbuckle their son from his safety seat. Her first glimpse of the baby was an immaculate white playsuit and a head of soft, silken curls.

Taking a deep breath, Lindsey reminded herself of what Thad had said this morning. *There's precious little that you can't forgive when you love someone.* She had loved these people. They had been her closest friends and had seen her through such bad times. And she had missed this couple almost as much as she had missed Thad—Tess, in particular. This was her chance to make up to them for what she had done, to apologize, to hope that they would forgive her.

Releasing Thad's hand, she moved slowly down the steps, saying a prayer as she went. Please, she silently whispered, let Thad be right.

Tess set the bag on the sidewalk, wrapped her arms around Lindsey and hugged her tightly. The moment was broken only seconds later, though, by a cranky cry. Tess released her and turned to take her son from Deke. The boy was big, Lindsey noticed, and made his mother, who was all of five foot four, look smaller in comparison.

"Lindsey, this is Deacon Andrew, Jr.," she said with a proud smile. "We call him Andrew or Drew. He answers to whatever strikes his fancy."

"He's pretty," Lindsey said, patting his chubby knee gently. She would have liked to hold him, to feel for the first time in longer than she could remember the weight of a baby's body in her arms. But the child was giving her a wary look, reminding her that she was a stranger and should keep her distance. "He looks like both of you."

"Actually, I think he gets his looks from my side of the family," Tess confided. "And he gets his size and his behavior from the Ramseys. His grandmother raised five of the biggest and rowdiest boys I've ever seen." Shifting Andrew to her other hip, she called, "Hi, Thad. Nice seeing you again, too."

He came down the steps to join them as Lindsey turned to Deke, extending her hand. He hesitated only an instant before accepting it. "Thank you for coming over," she said softly.

He simply nodded. He was reserving judgment, she thought, waiting to see if she deserved to be forgiven for hurting his best friend and his wife. She didn't blame him at all.

They returned to the porch, Lindsey taking a seat again on the swing. Thad sat beside her, and after a moment Andrew joined them. He pulled himself up, using the wooden slats as handholds until he was finally seated between them. He grinned triumphantly first at his parents, then at Thad. When he looked at Lindsey, though, the grin faded and the wary look returned. He immediately rolled onto his stomach and wiggled to the floor, gave her another long look, then went off to explore.

Conversation was stilted those first few moments. Lindsey was too self-conscious to make more than awkward responses to Tess's questions. Finally Thad stood up. "You take care of things in the kitchen, Lindsey, and I'll light the fire."

"Are we eating outside, too?" Tess asked, standing up and prying a bruised geranium blossom from Andrew's fingers. "I hate the thought of turning this child loose in your house."

"He couldn't do any harm," Lindsey protested, only to be laughed down by the other three.

"We don't keep anything that's important lower than four feet," Deke explained. "He's lost the stereo remote control. He put the cordless phone in with the laundry, and, needless to say, it didn't work properly after a hot-water rinse. Tess's cat went to live with her parents when we couldn't stop Drew from eating its food. And we never did find the message tape that he took out of the answering machine."

"We think he ate that, too," Tess said matter-of-factly.

"You're exaggerating," Lindsey said, looking from her to her husband, then at their sweet, angelic child. Their angelic child who was, at that very moment, chewing thoughtfully on a white-painted twig. A twig broken off one of the wicker chairs. "Or maybe not."

Tess calmly took away the twig and stuck her finger in Drew's mouth and cleaned out the pieces there, then swept him up and into his father's arms. "You watch him. I'm helping Lindsey in the kitchen."

Once in the kitchen Lindsey gave Tess her choice of chores: shaping the ground beef into patties or slicing the tomatoes and onions. Washing her hands at the sink, Tess replied, "With Drew, I'm used to messy things. I'll do the patties."

Lindsey took the package of meat from the refrigerator and turned toward the counter, then simply stood there holding it. "I feel so awkward," she confessed, feeling every bit as distraught as she sounded. "We were friends, and I—"

Tess took the meat from her. "You did what was necessary for you at that time. It's okay, Lindsey. It doesn't matter anymore."

"I was so angry with the entire world then. I just couldn't be friends with Thad's friends. I felt so..."

"Betrayed?" Tess suggested. "I remember the first occasion after we were married that Deke was assigned to a sensitive case. He was preoccupied all the time and not paying enough attention to me, I thought, so I figured if he wouldn't talk to me about anything else, at least we could talk about his case. But when I tried to, he looked at me and said, 'I can't discuss that with you.' It was as if I were some casual acquaintance and not his *wife*. My feelings were hurt, and they stayed hurt until the case was over—and that case didn't even involve me or anyone I knew. So I know how you felt."

Lindsey gave her a sidelong glance as she took a bowl from the cabinet and handed it to her. "Does he still do that?"

"From time to time. He tells me about most of his cases, but he won't open his mouth about the others."

"Does it still bother you?"

"I wish I could say no, of course not. I understand. It's his job. And I *do* understand that it's his job. But I do feel shut out sometimes when he's spending so much of his time on something that he can't discuss with me."

"Thad called me an outsider," Lindsey admitted. "He said he couldn't discuss the details of his cases with an outsider."

"Yeah, that's how it feels sometimes. But..." Tess sighed, then smiled. "We can't say we weren't warned. You knew what Thad was, and I knew what Deke was, before we got involved with them."

Lindsey washed and dried the tomatoes, then began slicing them as she changed to a happier subject. "Thad said that you're staying home with Andrew."

Up to her wrists in a mixture of ground beef, spices and raw egg, Tess laughed. "What Thad *probably* said was that Drew is such a brat, we couldn't find anyone crazy enough to stay with him, and he's right." After another laugh, she sobered. "Before he was born, I intended to continue working part-time—a marshal's salary isn't overly generous, you know—but he was five weeks premature. He didn't get to leave the hospital until he was four weeks old. Deke and I talked it over and decided that it would be best if I stayed home with him. We could get by financially, and it was what I really wanted. I'd had some problems while I was pregnant and had come close to losing him a couple of times, so... I really wanted to stay with him."

"I'm sorry," Lindsey said. "I didn't know."

"So far, it's been better. My mom and Deke's mom take turns helping out with Drew, and I'm more relaxed about it this time around, and that seems to help."

"This time?"

"Thad didn't tell you?" Tess smiled one of the happiest smiles Lindsey had ever seen. "I'm pregnant again—about two and a half months."

"Oh, Tess, that's wonderful!" But even as she spoke Lindsey couldn't help but feel jealous. She hoped it didn't show on her face, but assumed that it did when Tess looked out the window at the men, then back at her and said quietly, "Your turn's coming, Lindsey. And Thad is really good with Drew. He doesn't overwhelm him the way Deke's brothers tend to. Drew adores him."

Lindsey stopped working a moment to look outside for herself. The flames on the grill near the detached garage were slowly burning down. A safe distance away, Thad and Deke were both on the ground, tossing a big yellow ball back and forth with Andrew. Thad *was* good with the baby, Lindsey thought, when she saw Andrew topple over and watched Thad pick him up, dust him off and kiss his scraped knee. She watched him place a second kiss on the finger the boy offered him. Then he accepted a kiss, sloppy and wet, from Andrew in return.

"So how are you two getting along?"

Lindsey turned away from the window and began peeling a big yellow onion. When the juice dripped onto her thumb, she raised it to her mouth, savoring the sweet flavor. "We're..." She thought for a moment before settling on a word. "Trying. Actually, I can't help but feel that Thad's trying a lot harder than I am. He's so much more forgiving, so much more willing to forget the past and face the future."

"It wasn't his brother who died, or almost died, on that bridge. He has a lot less to forget."

"You don't know the things I said to him that day."

Tess sighed as she formed the last thick patty, then began scrubbing her hands again. "Lindsey, you feel so guilty that you've punished yourself far more than anyone else would have, and Thad knows that. If he no longer cares about what you said to him, why should you?" She didn't wait long enough for an answer, but went on. "Other than that, how do you feel about him?"

"I've really missed him. I've missed the time we could have spent together and the things we could have done together. I miss knowing that, if not for Donny, we would have been married now, maybe with a baby of our own. I miss what could have been—what *should* have been."

"Do you still love him?"

She concentrated for a long while on arranging the tomato and onion slices on a platter, carefully leaving a place in the center for pickles. When she couldn't dawdle anymore, she looked up and met Tess's gaze. Her friend— heavens, she liked the sound of that!—was smiling knowingly.

"I haven't answered that question for myself yet," Lindsey said as a blush turned her cheeks red. Was she embarrassed because she was discussing such an intimate subject with a friend she hadn't spoken to in eighteen months... or because she was lying? She knew the answer to her own question, just as she knew the answer to Tess's. She just wasn't ready to admit either one yet.

Tess stuck the hamburger patties in the freezer to harden, then tore open the bag of cookies and took one out to munch on. "All right," she conceded. "No more interrogation. Is there anything else for me to do?"

Chapter 7

Insisting she needed no help, Lindsey took a handful of dirty dishes into the kitchen, the screen door closing with a bang behind her. She scraped the leftovers into the sink and rinsed the plates, stacking them on the counter while watching the scene outside.

Tess was sitting on the glider underneath the giant oak, and Thad and Andrew were on a quilt spread over the grass nearby. The baby had been stripped down to his disposable diaper after spilling a combination of catsup, mustard and soda on his white clothes. Now he was asleep in Thad's arms with a chocolate cookie stain around his mouth and down his stomach.

The screen door opened, and Deke came inside. After helping himself to the last two beers in the refrigerator, he came to lean against the counter. Lindsey handed him a bottle opener, then remarked, "You have a beautiful family."

"I know."

"Congratulations on the new one."

"Thanks."

She shut off the water and dried her hands, then faced him. "I'm sorry about everything."

"I don't want an apology, Lindsey. I just have a favor to ask."

"What's that?"

"Be careful this time. Tess doesn't need the stress, and Thad doesn't need the pain of another breakup."

She felt the sting of his censure, even though she knew she deserved it. She *had* caused a lot of problems for everyone. "I wish I could say that I would never hurt either of them again and that you could bank on that, but we both know that wouldn't be true. All I can say is I'll do my best."

Deke nodded once in acceptance, then quietly stated, "He's still half in love with you, you know."

She smiled tremulously, but said nothing. Just as she wasn't yet ready to deal with the question of her own love, she couldn't deal with the possibility of Thad's, either.

He opened both bottles of beer, then gestured for her to precede him out the door. As she stepped onto the small back porch, he spoke again. "I have one other favor to ask."

"What's that?" she asked warily.

"Get him to start jogging with you again. When he had to find another partner, I was the only one available, and I'm not into this the way you two are. He's about to kill me."

Her laughter, clear and filled with delight, carried across the yard to Thad. He turned to look at her, envious that it was his friend she had laughed for instead of him, but grateful to hear it just the same.

"You two belong together," Tess said softly as they approached.

"I know," Thad agreed. "I'm just trying to convince her."

Lindsey took one of the beers from Deke and sat down next to Thad, offering it to him. When he freed one hand to take it, she leaned close to gently stroke Andrew's hair. "He's so precious."

"He usually doesn't nap during the day," Tess said, sliding to one side to make room for Deke. "He sleeps twelve hours straight at night."

"Yeah, storing up energy so he can run for twelve hours straight the next day," Deke added dryly.

"I envy you," Lindsey murmured.

"Wait until you have yours." Tess grinned slyly. "Maybe you'll have twins. They run in Thad's family, you know."

Two years ago the comment would have been insignificant; everyone had assumed then that he and Lindsey would eventually get married and have half a dozen children. Even two hours ago, Thad suspected, if Tess had said the same thing privately, Lindsey wouldn't have minded. But now, because she was sitting here beside him and knew that he'd heard, she was blushing a delicate pink.

"She's right," he said, leaning forward to gently ease Andrew onto the quilt. The baby's arms twitched and he sighed, then settled once again into a deep sleep. "My younger brothers are twins, and so's my mother. What about your family?"

"None that I know of," Lindsey replied uncomfortably.

"Well, that just lessens the chances. It doesn't negate them." Then, because he knew she really was uneasy with the direction of the conversation, he turned it into something less personal, less embarrassing for Lindsey. But all the while they talked, he couldn't rid himself of the image of Lindsey pregnant—and with his child. Although he thought he could love any child of Lindsey's, simply because of his feelings for her, in his fantasies it was important that the baby be his, too. Maybe it had something to do with his masculinity, or maybe it was pride.

Or maybe it was simply jealousy. He could not, would not, imagine Lindsey making love with another man. Any child she might have would *have* to be *his*.

It was late afternoon when the Ramseys left. After seeing them off Thad and Lindsey returned to the backyard for a little last-minute cleanup. The picnic table and benches were returned to their spot under the tree and the grill, its fire now out, was emptied and replaced in the garage.

When that was done Thad companionably slipped his arm around her shoulders. "That wasn't so bad, was it?"

She smiled at him. "I had a good time."

"Even with the talk about babies?"

Her smile faltered but only a bit. "Even with that."

He reached down to brush a strand of her hair back. It was a simple gesture, yet it made her tremble. "Have you seen enough of me for one day, or would you like to go to a movie tonight?"

"I'd rather rent one and stay here," she suggested. She felt his gaze on her, steady and thoughtful, and knew what he was thinking. That in all the time they'd spent together this past week, they hadn't spent a single evening at her home, the way they had so often in the past. That it was too intimate, too close, too private. That restaurants were safer in the evening hours—the waiters and other diners provided a buffer and removed a great deal of pressure from them. They were alone, but not alone. They had privacy for talk, but not for anything else.

Who would provide the buffer if they stayed here alone this evening?

"Okay," he slowly agreed. "I need to go home and change." He smelled smoky from cooking the hamburgers, Lindsey noticed, and there were chocolate stains, courtesy of Andrew, on his shirt and grass stains on his slacks. "Why don't you come with me? I'll shower and change, then we can stop at the video store on the way back."

She went inside to get her purse and lock up; then they left in Thad's car. When they reached his apartment he left her alone to look around while he went to shower.

The apartment filled one half of the first floor of one of Atlanta's historic old homes. It was at the other end of the universe from the clusters of cramped apartment complexes that blanketed the entire metropolitan Atlanta area. There was no gym, no pool, no clubhouse. No tennis courts, racquetball courts, computer rooms or weekly get-togethers.

Just a piece of history, and privacy from the other three neighbors who lived there and valued it as much as he did.

It had been so long since she'd been to this place that had once been a second home to her. She had missed it, she realized—the big rooms and the high ceilings, the cool, masculine colors and the sleek, modern furniture that somehow didn't look out of place with the ornate moldings and the elaborate marble fireplace.

Unlike her own house, which she liked to think of as being filled with controlled clutter, there was nothing unnecessary here—no knickknacks, no souvenirs, no treasured little gifts. The only decorations were photographs: of majestic maples with their yellow autumn leaves, of the Great Smoky Mountains wreathed in hazy blue, of waves hitting a South Carolina beach, of waterfalls and spring blooms and winter snows. She remembered each occasion, each trip, and regretted that they'd ended so long ago.

Of all the photographs only two contained people: an endearingly casual shot of Tess, Deke and Andrew, and a larger, more formal portrait of the McNally family—Thad's parents, the twins and their wives, their baby sister and Thad himself. All the people he loved.

Once, she remembered sadly, there had been a picture of her here, too.

He came out of the bedroom, wearing a pair of gray trousers and a towel around his neck. His hair was wet and slicked back the way he usually combed it, and his eyes, hazy and brown, were squinted. He looked so harmless, she thought, and so dangerous. Soft, yet bone-crushingly strong. Innocent, yet seductive.

"I'll be ready in a couple of minutes," he said on his way into the kitchen. When he returned with a small container of bottled water, he detoured to join her. "The rogues' gallery," he teased.

"You have a nice family."

"They seem to be," he agreed. "I don't really know them that well."

She stared at the photo a moment longer, then asked, "If your parents didn't want children, why did they have four?"

"What makes you think they didn't want us?"

"They sent you all to boarding school, didn't they?"

He opened the bottle and took a long drink. "It was easier that way. My parents traveled a lot, and even when they were home they had other obligations. Instead of leaving us in the care of servants who always quit soon after experiencing my father's legendary temper, they put us in boarding schools. It provided a more stable environment for us."

She gave him an unblinking look. "What obligations could be more important than your own children?"

"None that you can think of, I know." He shrugged expressively. "It's just the way things were done, Lindsey. All their friends' children were in boarding school, too. It was normal to us."

"You weren't lonely?"

"Sometimes. But I think I would have been lonelier at home. Overall, I enjoyed boarding school. I got an excellent education, I met a lot of people and saw a lot of places and I learned to take care of myself."

"And you don't resent your mother and father for it?"

He shook his head. "They did what they thought was best, and it probably was. It's not a choice I would ever make for my own children, but for theirs—for us—it was okay."

"You never missed having a traditional family? Where the father worked and, if they could afford it, the mother stayed home and took care of the children? Where even if she had to work, one of them was always available when the kids needed them?"

He grinned patiently. "I never knew that kind of family, Lindsey. Living in that kind of household is just as foreign to me as the way I grew up is to you. All I know about that type of family is what I've learned from you and Deke and Tess and some of the people at work."

"It just seems so lonely," she murmured.

Thad brushed her hair back, then rested his hand lightly on her shoulder. "I turned out okay, don't you think?" When she didn't agree right away, he tickled along her jaw with one fingertip.

Smiling reluctantly, she pushed his hand away, then caught it in hers. "You turned out fine," she agreed. "You're a good man, Thad."

For a long time he looked at her, soft and hazy and blurred. He was bending forward, intending to kiss her and maybe never stop, when she released his hand and stepped away. "Finish getting dressed," she whispered. "Or we'll never find a decent movie on a Saturday night."

He wanted to ask her to forget about getting dressed, to forget about the movie and to spend the evening—the night—with him here making love, making up for old times, making a future. But she'd put too much distance between them, both physically and emotionally, so he was left with no choice but to do what she'd asked. He went into the bedroom and got dressed.

Monday night was cool and quiet, the kind of evening they had often spent on the front porch. Though the swing looked inviting, Lindsey didn't turn toward it when they reached the top of the steps. Instead, she unlocked the door, then glanced back at Thad. "Will you come in?"

He seemed to consider his options. Did he wonder, as she did herself, exactly what her invitation included? Coffee, conversation, a kiss or two or maybe a whole lot more? She honestly didn't know. She just knew that she didn't want him to leave. Not yet.

They'd been virtually inseparable the entire weekend. They had spent Saturday here, alone and with the Ramseys. Sunday they had jogged, done yard work, passed a lazy afternoon and cooked dinner together. Today—Memorial Day—they had gone running early and had a picnic lunch at the park and dressed up for an elegant dinner out. Now it was after nine, but she didn't want him to go. She didn't want to be alone.

Then she silently corrected that thought. She didn't want to be *without him*.

"Sure," he replied with a faint smile, gesturing for her to lead the way.

She pulled the key from the lock as she pushed the door inward. Only a few feet inside, though, she came to a stop so suddenly that Thad bumped against her.

Something was wrong. She couldn't pinpoint what it was—there was no sound out of place, no smell that didn't belong. Just a feeling. A disturbing feeling of intrusion. Violation. Danger.

They noticed the thin glow of light from the end of the hallway at the same time, and Lindsey reached for Thad just as he reached for his gun. He shook her hand free, pulled the pistol from its holster beneath his jacket and took a single step before the darkness erupted in a flurry of movement and noise. A table toppled over, the porcelain bowl it held shattering to the floor, and a shadowy figure rushed along the hallway, colliding with Thad and shoving him against Lindsey before gaining the freedom of the open door.

Lindsey fell to the floor beneath Thad's weight, but almost instantly Thad was on his feet again. "Stay here!" he ordered as he raced out the door in pursuit of the intruder.

She slowly sat up, rubbing the shoulder she'd banged when she'd fallen. Her hands were trembling, she realized, and she felt an incredible urge to cry.

Had it been Donny? God help her, she didn't know. How could she have been that close—close enough to touch—to her brother and not know if it was him? But all she'd seen was a shadow, a tall, slender shadow. A shadow who'd found it easy enough to move about her house in the dark.

A shadow who could have been any of thousands of men in Atlanta, she sternly reminded herself. For all she'd seen, it could have just as easily been a woman. It could have been anyone in the world.

Or it could have been Donny.

Why? Why would he come to her house a second time? Why would he be waiting in the dark for her to come home? Why would he frighten her like this? Why would he run away without speaking to her, without letting her see his face?

She got to her feet and held on to the door frame for a moment until the shaking in her legs stopped. Then with halting steps she went out onto the porch, looking in both directions down the street. She had no idea which way they had gone, Thad and the other man—Thad and Donny?— and the street gave her no clue. It was quiet and empty of traffic, well lit under the street lamps and shadowy under the trees.

She was shivering uncontrollably. Reaction, she thought numbly. Fear. Anger. Frustration. She wanted to cry and scream and stamp her feet. She wanted to beg her brother to stop hiding, to end his cruel games and come forward. She wanted to curse him for letting her believe he was dead all these months, and she wanted to tell him how glad she was that he was alive.

When she reached the top step, her foot struck something, and the item clattered and bounced onto the next step. She automatically looked down, then sank onto the step, unable to stand any longer, unable to hold back the tears.

It was a pocketknife—small and inexpensive. The engraved plastic handle, meant to resemble ivory, had once been white, but now it was yellowed and the ridges were filled with dirt from years of use. Unlike fancier knives, this one had only two blades, but they were more than enough to do the many jobs required—to cut fishing wire and knotted shoelaces. To remove chewing gum from a little girl's hair. To scrape out bee stingers left behind or to sharpen a pointed stick for a wiener roast. To peel an orange shared by father and daughter, and years later the same task for brother and sister.

How many times had she seen that knife—not one like it, but *that* particular knife—in her father's hands? In her brother's hands? How many hours had she and Donny spent as children, legs spread wide around a circle scratched into the ground, playing mumblety-peg, flipping the knife through the air so that its blade became imbedded in the dirt? How many times had she borrowed it to cut a tag from a new blouse or scrape gum from the bottom of her shoe or open a box?

For years Donny had carried that knife with him everywhere he'd gone. It had been his good-luck charm, his talisman, all he'd had left of the father he could hardly remember. She hadn't seen it in months, hadn't found it when she packed his things and moved them from the apartment he'd shared with Shawn and into the upstairs bedroom. She had assumed that, as usual, he'd had it with him that day on the bridge.

And now he'd dropped it here.

She didn't touch it, didn't pick it up and clasp it tightly in both hands. She merely sat there, arms crossed over her chest, tearstains on her cheeks, and looked at it.

That was how Thad found her when he returned a few moments later, out of breath and carrying his coat over his shoulder. Restricted by his clothing and hampered by the other man's head start, he'd chased the man four blocks before losing him in the shadows. Only an instant later the squeal of tires as a car pulled away from the curb half a block ahead had confirmed that he had, indeed, lost this chase.

All the way back he'd asked himself the same question over and over: Had it been Donny? And each time he'd given himself the same grim answer: He didn't know. He hadn't seen the man well enough to be sure one way or the other. He knew the man was tall and thin—like Donny. He knew he had blond hair—like Donny. He knew he'd been wearing a brown leather jacket—like the expensive leather jacket Donny had bought before he'd disappeared. The same jacket that had been stolen from Lindsey's house little more than a week ago.

But was it Donny?

He saw Lindsey sitting on the steps and quickened his stride, crouching in front of her. "Are you okay?" he asked, grasping both her arms and giving her a little shake.

She nodded mutely, then gestured toward the step. Thad looked and recognized the knife immediately. "Have you touched it?"

She shook her head.

"I'm going to call Clint Roberts. Wait here." He went inside the house, flipped on the desk lamp, and called the other agent at home. When he hung up, he looked around the living room and what he could see of the sitting room. That was where the man had been hiding, and when he'd come out, he had knocked over the hall table. The dish where Lindsey always kept her keys and a tall, graceful, glass flower vase lay in pieces on the floor along with the arrangement of dried flowers it had held, some now crumpled and broken.

Had it been Donny, he wondered grimly, and if so, what had he wanted this time? Had they come home earlier than he'd expected, before he'd had a chance to make his escape, or had he been waiting for Lindsey? Had he been watching them long enough to know that after most of their dates, Thad had said good-night at the door? Had he merely wanted to talk to her, then, frightened by Thad's presence, changed his mind and run away? Or had he had something more sinister, more threatening, than talk in mind for his sister?

He went back outside, sat down behind Lindsey and pulled her back against him. He felt the trembling that shivered through her body and swore that if Donny was alive, he would pay for putting her through this. Thad would make sure of that.

She let her head rest against his shoulder. "Do you think he meant to hurt me?"

"No," he said with more certainty than he really possessed. "Maybe he wanted to talk to you and was just surprised to see me, too."

"Maybe." But she didn't sound too convinced. She reached up to clasp his wrists with both hands. "What can I do, Thad?"

"About what?"

"I want to see him. I want to talk to him. I want to find out if he's all right and if he blames me and why he's doing this. I want—" Her voice grew choked and thick. "Damn it, I want him to stop!"

"Honey, you can't do anything," he whispered. "You just have to wait until he decides to reveal himself . . . or until he gets caught."

"You know what?" She didn't wait for him to respond. "I'm afraid. For the first time in my life, I'm afraid of my own brother! I love him, and I've always believed in him and tried to protect him and take care of him and make excuses for him, and now I'm afraid of him! Why is he doing this? Why doesn't he just call me or come to the door and ring the bell? Why doesn't he turn himself in? Why—"

Thad hushed her with a kiss. "We don't have any answers yet, Lindsey, but we'll find them. We'll find *him*, I promise."

She shifted, snuggling closer to him, then fell silent. He didn't need to look, though, to know that she was staring at the knife. He didn't need to ask to know that she was thinking about Donny, repeating the million and one questions in her mind. He didn't need to reflect to know that she could drive herself crazy with unanswered questions if he let her.

But he had no chance to distract her once Clint Roberts arrived. They were joined over the next few minutes by four other agents. The first thing they did was place the pocketknife in an evidence bag. Then, leaving Lindsey on the porch, Thad went inside with them, describing how the light burning behind the closed kitchen door had alerted them to the intruder and the events that had followed.

"The guy fell a hundred feet into a shallow, rocky river and eighteen months later manages to outrun you?" Roberts asked, shaking his head. "You must be slowing down."

"You try running all out in a suit and dress shoes," Thad retorted.

"Did you notice any sign of a handicap? A limp? Maybe he favored one leg?" Roberts paused. "The man had to have some serious injuries—broken legs, at the very least."

"If he did, they healed just fine. He was in good shape."

The lone female agent joined them. "There's no sign of a forced entry, although there are what appear to be some fresh scratches on the back door knob—as if he fumbled with the key in the dark.''

"Does the same key fit both the front and the back door locks?" Roberts asked.

Thad shook his head. "And Donny's key *was* to the back door." He remembered that because he'd had Lindsey's only extra key to the front door himself.

Out on the porch, Lindsey finally stood up from where Thad had left her and moved toward the door. She stopped just out of sight of the agents in the hallway, just out of sight of the broken glass and porcelain and the table, still lying on its side. She didn't want to go any closer. She didn't want to go inside and be afraid.

She didn't know how long she stood there, trembling and trying to control her breathing. Until the agents were done with their work. Until they'd left and Thad was the only one left in the house. Until he came out to find her.

"Where are your keys?"

She looked blankly at him. "I don't know."

He slid his fingers beneath his glasses and rubbed the bridge of his nose. Was he surprised? she wondered. There'd never been a time when she hadn't known precisely where everything in her house was. He had teased her about it, calling her compulsive. But she would bet he preferred such precision over this shock-induced incomprehension that had blanked her mind.

"I'll find them," he said. "And I'll get some clothes for you, too. You're spending the night at my apartment, and tomorrow we'll change the locks here, okay?"

She nodded. She couldn't argue if she'd wanted to, and she didn't want to. She wanted Thad to stay close, close enough to whisper to, close enough to touch, close enough to make her feel safe again.

He went back inside, and a moment later she heard the jingle of her keys as he picked them up off the floor. Next she heard the scraping of wood against wood as he set the table upright, then the sound of his footsteps climbing the stairs. She didn't offer to go inside and help him. He knew his way around her bedroom, knew where she kept her cosmetics, which drawer held her lingerie, where her hose and shoes and nightgowns all were. He even knew where to find the small leather bag she had to pack the things in.

When he came out again a few minutes later, the bag over his shoulder and a slim white skirt and a blue silk blouse hanging from one finger, he turned off the lights and locked the door. It was a feeble attempt at securing the house, Lindsey thought miserably. The one man they were worried about had his own key, and no qualms whatsoever about using it or about scaring her half to death in the process.

They walked to the car together. Thad opened Lindsey's door for her, then went around to the other side and draped her clothes on the back seat. Her bag went back there, too.

It was a short drive to his apartment, made shorter still by the absence of traffic on this late holiday evening. Thad parked in the small lot that he shared with the three other tenants, got Lindsey's things from the back and followed her onto the porch and to his door. She held the bag while he opened the door, then reached inside and turned the lights on.

She went inside, past the kitchen and into the living room, letting the bag slide from her hand to the floor without watching. She walked to the empty fireplace as if seeking warmth from it, shuddered, then turned and faced him.

For the first time in all the years she'd known him, he looked awkward. Bringing her home with him had probably been his first and only thought. He hadn't looked ahead to what he would do with her once they got here. Being the gentleman that he was, she suspected he would tell her that she'd undergone a shock and needed to go straight to bed. In his bed. Alone.

But she knew what she wanted, knew what she needed, and it wasn't that.

He hung her clothes in the coat closet, then retrieved the bag from the floor where she'd dropped it and set it on the sofa. "It's been a long day."

She nodded.

"You need to get some sleep."

She nodded again. How did she tell him, she wondered, without sounding forward or silly or overly emotional that sleep was the last thing she needed? How did she tell him, "I want you to make love to me"? And how did she know if he was at all interested in the same thing?

Thad drew his fingers through his hair, wondering if she had remembered yet that the apartment had only one bedroom, if she'd given any thought yet to where he would sleep. If she had, she certainly didn't show it. If she hadn't, well, *he* had. He wanted nothing more than to share his bed with her—just that, no more. He wanted to hold her all night. He wanted to listen to her slow, even breathing and know that she was safe, that nothing could harm her.

But she'd done nothing to indicate that she wanted him there, so he would sleep here on the sofa. He'd done it a time or two before. He could do it again tonight.

He picked up her bag by the strap, then crossed the room to her and took her hand in his, guiding her into the bedroom. She wandered over to the window to gaze out while he folded back the covers on the bed, automatically choosing the right side where she had always slept. He laid one of the extra pillows on the desk, then added a sheet and blanket from the closet.

Finally he went to her, touching her shoulder gently. She winced and shrugged away. "Are you all right?"

"I hit my shoulder when I fell at the house. It's okay."

"Let me see."

"It's just tender, that's all."

"Let me see," he repeated.

She gave him a sidelong glance, but made no move to obey him.

For a long moment Thad simply looked at her. He loved the way she looked all dressed up—elegant, beautiful, untouchable. So distant and aloof. So perfect. And so stubborn.

Then he shifted his gaze downward, finding and unfastening the single button that closed her jacket. The jacket was pale green and had long sleeves and was incredibly soft when he touched it to slide it down her arms. With its matching skirt, narrow and close fitted, the outfit was perfectly demure and proper.

But underneath the jacket, he discovered as he drew it away, was a camisole in the same delicate shade, and it was anything but demure. The silk draped over her breasts, obscuring the gentle curves but clearly defining the crests of her nipples. Thin straps crossed her shoulders, which were already bronzed from Atlanta's warm spring sun, and dipped low down her back before connecting once again with the silk mere inches above her waist.

And underneath one of those straps was a bruise—ugly and puffy and painful. Gently he lifted the strap and let it slide off her shoulder, then even more gently probed the edges of the bruise. The swelling wasn't extensive, the injury not severe.

Lindsey caught her breath when he touched her, then forced it out again. She tilted her head to the opposite side and fixed her gaze on the windowpane, trying to pretend that she didn't ache for this touch, trying to pretend that she wasn't hungry for this caress. But when he touched his mouth to the sore spot, she couldn't pretend any longer. Eyes closed, she reached blindly for him, hooking one hand around the waistband of his trousers, sliding the other into the warmth of his hair.

She didn't know for sure when the soothing kisses had moved away from the bruise and along her throat to her jaw. She didn't know when they had changed from soothing to something more, something stronger, more potent, more erotic. All she knew was that she was trembling with need ignored too long, greedy for pleasure denied too long.

Cupping both hands to his face, she brought her mouth to his. It was the only encouragement he needed. He kissed her then, his tongue seeking and finding entrance to the dark wet warmth of her mouth. Their noses bumped, and his glasses made it awkward, but he couldn't release her, he found, even for the seconds it would take to remove them.

She tasted exactly as he'd remembered—and yet completely different. There was a familiarity gained from thousands of shared kisses, but a newness, as well, as if it were their first time all over again. In a way, he supposed, it was. The past eighteen months had changed them, subtly but permanently. This wasn't the same woman he had loved so long ago, and he wasn't the same man.

But the feelings were the same. The love was the same.

Finally he drew away and breathed in deeply. With one finger he adjusted his glasses, then said in a hoarse voice, "If you want me to leave, Lindsey, tell me now."

After a moment, she smiled, but just barely. She looked so prim with her hair neatly pinned back, not a strand out of place, her makeup perfectly applied—and so wickedly sexy with her lipstick kissed off and that secretive little smile and her camisole falling off one shoulder, revealing the delicate curves of her breast while barely concealing her nipple.

And after a moment, he slowly smiled, too. There was no mistaking the invitation in her soft brown eyes, no mistaking the need, the desire, because he recognized it as the other side of his own.

He moved close enough to touch her again, raising both hands to her hair, his fingers searching out and finding the pins that contained it so smoothly. When her hair fell, it tangled, all soft and silky, around his hands, capturing them, capturing him. For a moment he simply held it, combing through it, rubbing the silken strands between his fingers, letting them sift through his fingers to gently fall across her shoulders, down her back, over her breasts.

Lindsey shivered beneath his fleeting touches. She reached for him, reaching for his glasses, but he evaded her hands.

"I want to look at you while I still can," he murmured. When he took his glasses off, she would be just a blur—a beautiful, soft-edged blur—and right now he wanted details. He wanted to see the pleasing contrast of the pale green silk against her skin. He wanted to see the sweet, erotic way she was looking at him. He wanted to see that there was no fear in her eyes, no anger, no bitterness, no guilt, no regret. Nothing but hunger. Desire. Need. Love.

He wanted to see the rise and fall of her breasts with her swift intake of air as he reached behind her and undid the button on her skirt, slid the zipper down. He wanted to see her eyes grow dark and shadowy, as they always did when she was aroused, as they did right now when he slid the skirt over her hips and to the floor.

She balanced herself with one hand on his shoulder as she stepped out of the skirt, and he took a long moment to lay it aside. Now she wore only the camisole, a slip the color of champagne and hose and heels. He looked at her and swallowed hard. "I've hardly kissed you, hardly touched you," he said in a thick, unsteady voice. "But I want you more than I've ever wanted anything. Just looking at you..." He couldn't finish the sentence and shook his head instead, then murmured, "You're beautiful."

"Kiss me now, Thad," she whispered, pleaded. "Touch me now. It's been too long...."

Obediently he did as she asked, touching her but only with his fingertips. They glided across the smooth silk, making achingly slow caresses over her breasts, around her nipples, across her stomach. Her eyes drifted shut, and her breathing grew erratic, soft gentle sighs mingled with nerve-tingling shudders when finally he cupped her breast in one hand, bringing his palm into contact with her nipple.

She swayed unsteadily as her knees grew weak. Thad ended the intimate caress and knelt in front of her, removing her shoes, laying the spiky heels out of the way. Next he slid his hands along her thighs, underneath the slip to her waist, and removed her hose and panties, leaving her in nothing but silk.

He pulled the camisole free of the slip and brushed a kiss across her midriff, grinning when the muscles there tightened and shimmered. Rising to his feet again, he pulled her close and gave her another kiss, this one hard and hungry and hot, his tongue thrusting, demanding, seeking.

This time it was Lindsey who ended it, Lindsey who was in control. She gave him a series of small, parting kisses before turning her attention to his tie, lazily undoing the Windsor knot, pulling the burgundy-patterned silk free from his collar and dropping it to the floor.

His jacket was next to go. She dropped it, too, carelessly. Finding that the camisole straps draped at her elbows hampered her movements, she paused for a moment to remove it, pulling it over her head, shaking her hair free as the pale green garment drifted down to the floor.

The intensity of Thad's gaze made her shiver. She didn't mind that he was fully clothed, didn't feel self-conscious that she was naked except for her slip. He had that power— to simply look at her and make her feel sexy. To merely touch her and make all her inhibitions disappear.

"Lindsey—"

His voice was a bare whisper, raw with longing. Bracing her hands on his shoulders, she rose onto her toes to kiss him . . . a simple straightforward kiss that promised him everything, in time. The movement brought her close against him, rubbed her breasts against the expensive fabric of his shirt, pressed her silk-clad stomach against the hard, heated length of his arousal. She shifted slowly from side to side, savoring the delicate sensations that tingled in her breasts and the liquid fire that gathered deep in her belly and between her thighs.

"Lindsey—"

His voice was stronger now. A command, a warning. She smiled at the sweetly familiar sound of it and knew that his control was stretched thin, his will too weak to resist much longer. How many times had she taken him this far . . . then pushed him further still? And how many times had she pushed him further, only to pay the price herself with the delicate torture of his caresses, the intimate pleasure of his kisses, the sweet torment of his loving? How many times had he turned the tables and taken the power from her, making her tremble and writhe and plead? And how many times had he answered her pleas with endless, mindless, soul-deep satisfaction?

More than she could count. More than she could remember. And tonight she knew he would do it again.

With an aching tenderness, she brought the intimate body-to-body caress to an end and began pulling his shirt free of his trousers. It was a simple white dress shirt, perfectly tailored of a fine cotton that was as soft as silk beneath her fingers. She unfastened the bottom few buttons, then, impatient for the feel of him, gave up her task and slid her hands underneath, gliding them over his stomach and his chest.

She had always loved the feel of him—the texture of smooth skin and swirling hair and tautly defined muscles. If "sexy" had a feel, she was convinced that this was it. Sexy, silken, sensuous, sinful. Once she had tried to sketch him with his shirt off, and he had good-naturedly sat still for her, but after half a dozen futile tries, she'd put away the pad. How could she capture what she saw better with her fingertips than with her eyes? How could she possibly translate what she felt in her soul into cold—although technically good—but lifeless drawings?

And so they had made love instead. Fast and frantic the first time, then long and slow and lazy the next. So long that her need for release had made her ache and tremble uncontrollably all over. So slow that when he'd finally given her that release with his fingers and his mouth, she had cried. So lazy that she had loved it.

At last she unfastened the remaining buttons. A moment later the shirt followed the path of his other clothes, and she pressed her lips to his chest. In spite of the coolness in the room, his skin was hot, and in spite of the heat, she made him shiver when she touched her tongue to his nipple. She suckled it the way she knew that he liked, drew her tongue over it, gently nipped at it.

When he groaned, she laughed softly, and when she did, he used his hands in her hair to pull her head back, to tilt her face up to his. "Touch me," he demanded, his lips brushing hers with each word. "And you'll know how close I am. You'll know how dangerous your playing is."

Laughing again, she obeyed him, sliding her hands down from his chest, over the narrow leather belt, across the soft fabric of his trousers to the taut swelling there, and her throaty chuckle became a needy moan. He was hot and thick and throbbed beneath the gentle caresses of her fingers. Clumsily she unbuckled his belt and unfastened his trousers, sliding her hand inside, beneath the thin cotton of his briefs to hold him in her hand. "Oh, Thad," she whispered, gasping when he moved his hips, rubbing his flesh against her palm. "Make love to me now."

Such simple words, he thought numbly. Such powerful words. They turned his longing to merciless needing, his wanting into relentless hunger. They started an ache deep inside that throbbed and intensified with every passing second, an ache that he knew could destroy him...or save him.

He wanted to tease her, to torment her, to lovingly caress every inch of her body and fuel every ounce of desire until she burned the way he did, until she begged the way he would if she only asked. But it had been too long. He had waited too long.

He took her hand away, then pulled off his glasses, kicked off his shoes and stripped off his remaining clothing. Then, before Lindsey could even think of removing her slip, he was lowering her to the bed, pushing the silk to her waist, seeking his place within her. For just a moment, he was motionless, then he groaned softly, barely managing to form her name.

"Do you know how empty my life has been without you?" he whispered, nuzzling her ear before outlining it with his tongue and making her shudder.

She knew, because her life, her heart, even her soul had been just as empty.

He moved slowly, testing the tight, perfect fit of their bodies together. Tentatively he withdrew until only the barest of contacts remained, and not at all tentatively she wrapped her legs around his hips and drew him back, deeper this time, snugger, until nothing could have come between them.

Bracing himself on one arm, he rubbed her breast, feeling her nipple pucker and harden, hearing her breath catch when he gently pinched it, feeling her tremble when he lowered his head and suckled it. She stroked his hair with one hand and teased his own nipples with the other until finally he had to stop for a badly needed breath.

As she'd done before, she laughed softly at his slipping control, and just like before, her laughter slowly faded into a low sound of pleasure and pain, hunger and need, satisfaction and demand. "Make love to me, Thad," she commanded.

"I am," he replied, finally beginning a slow, torturous rhythm of deep strokes and long withdrawals.

She shook her head from side to side, her hair tumbling and falling, and her hands moved restlessly at his hips. "This isn't enough," she whispered. "I need more... faster... harder. Let me feel you. Fill me."

He did her bidding, increasing his rhythm, sliding his hands beneath her bottom and lifting her, deepening his thrusts. He felt the demand for release building inside him, growing stronger, more insistent, more savage, and he felt the convulsive tightening of her muscles around him as she reached her own release, heard her mindless whimpers, savored her helpless shudders and let them all combine to push him over the edge into a violently satisfying completion.

For a long while he couldn't think, couldn't move, couldn't do anything but lie there, buried deep inside her. He heard his own breathing, harsh and ragged, and hers, uneven and punctuated by an occasional sob. He remembered that she cried sometimes when the sensations were intense enough, the need great enough, the loving sweet enough. She was the only woman he'd ever made love to who did that, and he loved her for it.

Slowly her quaking subsided, and she raised her hand to stroke his face. She wanted to say so many things, but her voice wouldn't work and the words wouldn't come, so she contented herself with tender caresses and the certainty that, even without words, he understood. He knew how perfect their loving had been. He knew how much it had meant to her.

Gathering strength, he finally left the warmth of her body and settled onto the bed beside her. Out of long-held habit, they moved toward each other, Thad wrapping his arm around her and Lindsey turning onto her side and resting her head on his shoulder, her leg across his thigh. In that position, he was just able to reach the switch on the lamp on the nightstand and turn it off.

Darkness came swiftly, then her eyes adjusted, and the light from the living room and light shining through the window became enough. Slowly she stroked his chest the same way he stroked her hair. But gradually his caresses slowed, and so did his breathing, and she knew he was falling asleep. She felt a panicky flutter in her chest. There were things she needed to tell him before he drifted off, before they faced each other again in the bright light of morning, before this intimacy was lost. Thank you. I've missed you. I've missed *this*. I need you. Stay with me forever.

But he was already asleep, and by the time she awakened him, the intimacy would be gone. It was too late.

But he wasn't completely out yet. He shifted once, drew her nearer and nuzzled her hair from her forehead. He placed a feathery kiss there and murmured in a lazy, drowsy voice, "I love you, Lindsey."

Then he became still, his breathing slow, deep and even, his features relaxed, his grip on her shoulder lessening. *Now* he was asleep. But that was all right, she thought dazedly. Because now she couldn't think of a single thing to say.

Chapter 8

Lindsey lay in Thad's arms, listening to the slow, steady rhythm of his breathing. He was sleeping soundly and had been for the last hour, but thanks to his little bombshell just before he'd drifted off, she was wide-awake. She'd wanted to wake him up and ask him if he really meant it. She had wanted to demand of him how he could possibly make such an announcement then snooze away as if it were of little importance.

But in the end she had merely lain here in his arms, exactly as she was now, and listened to the words echo in her head a thousand times. She had even tried returning them: *I love you, Thad.* They shouldn't have been difficult to get out—she'd said them dozens of times in the past. But they wouldn't come. They couldn't. And frustrated by their refusal, she'd given up trying.

Did she love him? She didn't have to think about it, didn't have to compare the way she felt now with the way she'd felt eighteen months ago. The answer was simple enough. Yes, she loved him.

But there was nothing simple about love the second time around—not *her* love, at least. Loving implied forgetting, forgiving and accepting. It meant forgetting his involvement in Donny's disappearance. It meant forgiving his role in Donny's arrest and forgiving his refusal to confide in her, to warn her about what was going on. It meant accepting that his job had come first in the past and was likely to do so again in the future. It meant accepting that, when it came to his work, she would always, in some way, be an outsider.

Oh, yes, she loved him—more than she wanted to, because she wasn't sure she could do all those things. She wasn't sure she could be an accepting, forgiving person, and she *knew* she couldn't forget.

But she could love him in spite of those things. If she tried, she could go days, even weeks, without thinking about them.

Only love like that was no prize. Not even if he'd been warned beforehand. *So hate me for it, Lindsey,* he'd said Saturday. *But don't shut me out of your life.* But how long could he continue to feel that way? How long before his acceptance turned to resentment, before his love turned to ashes? How long could she continue to blame him for the events leading up to Donny's fall from the bridge without it poisoning all the good between them?

Not long enough. She had to forgive him...or let him go. Let him find someone who would love him the way he deserved to be loved—wholeheartedly, without reservations, without conditions.

Those were her only two options. And she didn't know if she could do either one.

It was still dark out when Thad woke up Tuesday morning. For a moment he lay there on his side, wondering what had disturbed his sleep, why the lights were on in the living room...and why his bed felt so crowded. Then he remembered. Lindsey.

Rolling onto his right side, he found her on the very edge of the bed. She lay on her stomach, her face turned away from him, one arm and a leg dangling off the mattress. Her hair was wound around her neck and under her arm and fell in unruly waves over her face. She had always accused him of taking up more than his fair share of the bed, he remembered, and if she awoke now, clinging to the edge of the bed, she would insist it was his fault.

Smiling, he gently urged her closer to the center, closer to him. She rolled over, sighed and snuggled deeper under the covers. He put on his glasses and lay there, his arm supporting his head, simply looking at her in the dim light.

She was beautiful.

Not that he was biased in his opinion, of course. But he truly couldn't understand how any man could look at her and not see the same gentle beauty he saw. He supposed that was how every man in love felt about the woman he loved.

Thad brushed her hair away from her face, winding a strand of it around his finger, then watching it uncurl. He wished she would wear her hair down always, yet at the same time he didn't want anyone else seeing it like this—wild and untamed and achingly sexy.

Tentatively he eased the covers down an inch or two, then a little bit farther until finally her breasts were bare. He hadn't looked at her enough last night—would he ever see enough of her?—and sound asleep like this, she wasn't likely to get him aroused and distract him from the simple joy of looking.

Her breasts were small, her nipples flat now and marvelously responsive. All it would take was one caress, one kiss, and they would harden and swell and ache to be pleasured. He knew exactly how to do it—how she liked for him to rub her breasts, to coax her nipples into peaks. He knew that she especially liked for him to rub them while she was still dressed, that she found caresses through clothing erotic. He knew how to suckle her nipples, how to gently bite them to increase her arousal without causing her pain, knew which one was more sensitive than the other.

The simple joy of looking, he thought wryly as he cautiously edged the covers a little lower, was turning into something more, evidenced by the need in his belly, by the stiffness of his flesh against her thigh. The response, familiar after so many months, still surprised him. Before he'd met Lindsey, he had been seduced by experts, and not one of them had had as easy a time of arousing him as Lindsey did without even trying—without even being awake!

Now the blankets were bunched around her hips. She still wore the slip from last night, he realized. He had been in too much of a hurry to remove it, and it had added a different sensation to their lovemaking, that of silk warmed by the movements of their bodies, rubbing sensuously back and forth with each thrust.

He wanted to see her naked, wanted to kick off the covers and remove the slip and sit beside her and just look at her narrow waist and slender hips. At her long, lean, runner's legs. At the soft, brown curls that shielded her femininity. But to undress her now, while she slept, while she was defenseless to stop him—

"I know you can arouse me without even touching me," she said, her voice sleepy and husky and erotic. "But it would certainly make me feel much better if you would."

He looked and saw that her eyes were still closed and her nipples were erect and her smile was wickedly inviting. A rush of desire surged through him so quickly that he almost groaned with it.

"But if you don't want to do that, lie back and *I'll* touch *you.*" Her smile grew more wicked when she opened her eyes, and he saw that wickedness reflected there. "I'll kiss you here—" She brushed a kiss across his mouth. "And I'll touch you here—" A feather-light caress across his nipple made him stiffen. "And I'll love you here—" Her fingers gently closed around his hardness.

She didn't give him a chance to decide whether he would prefer to seduce or be seduced. She sat up in bed and pushed him down with both hands on his chest. Then she twisted around until she was between his thighs, and drew her hands down his chest and over his belly, her nails lightly scraping, until once again she cradled his hardness. He filled both of her hands, heavy and straining and smooth as heated satin, and he filled her mouth when she offered him that most intimate of kisses.

Every muscle in his body went taut as he arched his hips against her. She gave him a moment to relax when she ended the kiss, but the tension rushed back as she continued to seduce him, to stroke and tease and rub and tickle and taste and play.

She moved up the bed, up his body, caressing and kissing. At last her hips were pressed against his, nothing separating them but the slip she wore. She lazily moved her hips back and forth along the length of him, intensifying his arousal, sending her own bursting into flames. "I would really like to prolong this," she whispered, her voice breathy and insubstantial because she couldn't breathe, couldn't concentrate on filling her lungs with air but instead could only think of filling herself with *him*. "But I think I've already waited too..."

She tugged the slip over her head and dropped it as she moved into place over his hips and took him, with an agonizing groan, deep inside. He reached for her then, but she caught his hand with both of hers and held it back with surprising strength. "If you touch me..."

Holding on tightly to her hands, he raised his other hand to cover her breast, his palm tormenting her nipple with tantalizingly hard caresses. She gasped, then accepted the inevitable. Instead of holding his other hand away, she brought it to her other breast, pressing it flat over her aching nipple. Instead of sitting perfectly still astride him, she rocked back and forth once, twice, three times. Then shudders rocketed through her, and she cried out in a harsh voice that bore no resemblance to her own.

Thad didn't hold her and soothe her as he normally would have, but continued to stroke her breasts, sending little shivery shocks straight through her body, and he took control, thrusting into her with long, deep strokes. When she tried to push his hands away, he refused to let her. "With me this time, sweetheart," he whispered hoarsely. "You can do it.... You can feel it...."

He moved one hand lower, sliding it between their bodies, between her thighs, and rubbed her in rhythm with his thrusts. She was marvelously responsive there, too, and hot and sensitive and swollen. And just as he'd asked, just when he knew he could wait no longer, just as he began to empty himself into her, she went over the edge, too, quaking and crying and tightening violently around him.

Then he held her. Then he soothed her. He stroked her hair and her face and her spine. He gathered her beneath the covers and chased away her chill with his own warmth. He kissed the single salty tear that escaped. And he whispered one thing over and over.

"I love you, Lindsey."

Instead of trying to sleep, they got out of bed and took their time getting ready for work. Lindsey showered first, then dried her hair and put on her makeup while Thad showered. When he came out of the bathroom, a towel wrapped around his waist, she was sitting on the bed, pulling on her hose. She wore a royal blue robe monogrammed with his initials, a Christmas gift from his mother several years ago. He'd known it was in the closet, but he hadn't seen it in months. Because Lindsey had worn it far more than he ever had, he had pushed it to the back of the closet when they had broken up. Out of sight, out of mind, unlike her. In those eighteen months she'd never been out of his mind.

For a moment, he leaned against the door frame and indulged himself in just watching her. Of course the robe was too big for her—the hem fell closer to her ankles than her knees, and the sleeves were so long that only the tips of her fingers showed—but that was part of its charm. It made her look small and even more delicate than usual.

She stood up and tugged her hose into place. How could she look so damn sexy, he wondered, putting on a garment as awkward as panty hose? Then she looked at him and smiled, and he saw that she hadn't tied the robe's belt, that the rich fabric was merely draped over her breasts, and none too securely at that, and suddenly he no longer wondered how she could look so damn sexy. He was just grateful that she did.

"I found this in the darkest corner of your closet," she said, tugging at the dangling ends of the belt with both hands. "I hope you don't mind."

"It looks better on you than it does on me."

She smiled again. "That's only fair. You look better in a towel than I do."

He went to the closet and began gathering clothing for the day: a plain white shirt, a gray suit, a red-and-black tie, a pair of black shoes. After he dumped those on the bed, he removed socks and briefs from the dresser, then returned to the closet for a belt and a holster, adding them to the pile.

Lindsey scooted up to lean against the headboard. "Accessories for the young successful career man. A gold watch." She dangled it from one finger, then laid it back on the nightstand. "Preppy-style glasses." She gave them a twirl, then put them back, too. "Italian leather shoes. A fine leather belt. A gorgeous silk tie. And a holster." She picked it up by the strap and turned it in her hands, looking at it. "Do you buy these in different colors to match your wardrobe?"

He had pulled on his trousers while she was talking. Now he took the holster and slid it into place on his belt. "I have a black one, a tan one and this brown one. I also have two clip-on holsters and a shoulder holster."

She got to her feet and gave him a slow kiss. "For the well-dressed FBI agent," she teased. "Want me to make some coffee?"

"No thanks. We'll stop somewhere."

"After we get my car."

"Do you need it today?"

"Just to get home from work." She slipped out of his robe and into the bra he'd packed for her. Of course it was the sexiest one she owned—narrow straps and little bits of sheer fabric lavished with lace. Had he taken the time to choose it? Or had he just grabbed from the drawer and come up with this?

"We need to talk about that."

She took the skirt from its hanger and, rather than muss her hair, stepped into it. It was one of her favorites, straight and fitted and lined, and it showed off her legs. And Thad did like her legs, she thought with a satisfied smile as she studied her reflection in the mirror.

"Lindsey."

"What's to talk about? Six days a week, I work. When I'm done, I go home."

"You can't go back to that house until the locks are changed."

"So I'll call a locksmith and meet him there."

He took her blouse from her and held it while she slipped into it. Then he smoothed the thin pads over her shoulders and watched as she fastened the fabric buttons and tucked the tails inside her skirt. "I don't want you doing that alone."

She reached up and caught his hands. "I appreciate your concern, but that's my house, Thad. It's where I live. I can't let anyone, especially Donny, make me afraid to go there."

"He could have come back after we left last night. For all you know, he could be there right now."

"All right."

He blinked. "All right what?"

"All right, I'll let you handle it. All right, I won't go over there alone. All right, I'll wait until you have time to go with me." She broke off and grinned. "Stop me if I'm getting close to whatever you're about to suggest."

He bent to kiss her ear, a shuddering, tingling delight that made her eyes drift shut and her head tilt to one side and her pulse flutter erratically. His tongue circled the outside and dipped inside, bathing the lobe with erotic strokes. Then, deliberately, unexpectedly, he bit it, startling her eyes open, making her yelp in protest.

"You are smug and arrogant and you know me too well," he said with an easy grin as he moved away to finish dressing. "When we get to the shop, you can call a locksmith and find out what time he can make it. Then I'll pick you up and take you over there myself."

"Okay." She buttoned and zipped her skirt, adjusted her blouse, then stepped into her heels and turned to face him. "How do I look?"

"Good enough to undress and take back to bed."

"If we only had time," she said with a mournful sigh. "But here we are, both fully dressed and ready for work."

He approached her as he tied his tie. She backed away one cautious step at a time until she was leaning against the dresser. "Or maybe good enough to take right here," he said, his voice tantalizingly soft as he trapped her with his arms on either side of her hips. "This is a good, solid piece of furniture. I think it could take the abuse. All I'd have to do is slide your skirt up and unzip my pants and—"

She cut off what he was about to say with a kiss, wrapping her arms around his neck, covering his mouth with hers, sliding her tongue between his teeth. It was slow and languid, hinting at pleasure and promising ecstasy. It made his blood hot and his body hard, and made leaving for work less appealing by the second.

When she finally released him, she rubbed her fingertip back and forth over his lips, wiping away the last traces of her lipstick. "Bring some clothes with you when you pick me up at the store," she said in a throaty invitation. "And when the locksmith is done, you can show me instead of telling me."

He opened his mouth and caught the tip of her finger between his teeth, bathing it in a sensual caress.

Her smile was hopelessly erotic. "And when *you're* done, I'll have a little show-and-tell of my own."

Slowly he backed away. If he didn't do it now, he never would, and then neither of them would make it to work today, and the locks wouldn't get changed, and the interviews he'd foolishly scheduled for this morning wouldn't get conducted, and...

He sighed regretfully as he shrugged into his jacket. For the first time in his life, he could fully embrace one of Donny's credos. Responsibility was hell.

"How is Lindsey?"

Thad didn't look up from the report he was typing as Clint Roberts sat down across from him. "Okay. I'm taking her to the house this afternoon to get the locks changed. I don't want a repeat of last night sometime when she's alone."

"I don't blame you. We got the report back on the knife."

That made him stop and turn his full attention to the other agent. "And?"

"The prints on the handle were smudged and useless. But we lifted five prints off the blades. The right thumb is Lindsey's. The other four belong to her brother."

"That doesn't tell us anything we didn't already know. She knew it was his the instant she saw it."

"At least we know for sure now."

"How are you coming on the stores where her cards are sold?"

"We have twelve left, seven in Atlanta and the other five. Two in Savannah, two in Augusta and one in Macon." His smile was little more than a grimace. "We're saving those for last."

"You should have told me about the two in Savannah. I could have gone by while I was down there last week."

Roberts shook his head. "You're dating the suspect's sister. You don't need to be officially involved with this case."

He was right, Thad knew. The belated suggestion had slipped out without thought. There was no problem with Roberts sharing information with him like this, but the moment Thad did get officially involved, Lindsey would once again become off-limits to him. Given a choice of roles—active investigator or on-the-sidelines lover—there was no doubt which one he preferred.

"How's the auto-theft case going?"

He gave a shake of his head. That was his least favorite of his active cases. A group of very experienced and talented thieves was stealing luxury cars in Atlanta and taking them into Florida, where they fraudulently retitled, tagged and sold them. They were making a lot of money, and taking very few risks. And for two months now he and the Georgia Bureau of Investigations at this end, along with the FBI and Florida state officials at the other, had been trying to catch them, but progress was slow. "A BMW and Porsche were stolen last week. That brings them up to seventeen for the month, and they've still got four more days left till the first."

Another agent nearby laughed. "McNally's got a real interest in solving this one," the man said. "He wants to get them before they get to his Audi."

"The campaign to convince American consumers to buy American-made products had little or no effect on this man," another agent joined in. "He wears imported shoes. He drinks imported wine. He drives an imported car. Since he refuses to *buy* American, maybe he can convince the crooks to *steal* American. That way his Audi would be safe."

"Don't worry, McNally," the first man added. "If they steal your car, my kid's got a German import he'll let you borrow." He paused before delivering the punch line. "A '69 Volkswagen Bug."

Thad good-naturedly ignored the ribbing. In his twelve years with the Bureau, it hadn't changed—the teasing about his privileged upbringing, his private school education, his custom-tailored suits and his preference for expensive cars. He'd heard it all before.

As the others wandered away, he turned back to his report, but his concentration had been broken. For a long time all he could think of was Lindsey.

Whatever grudges he had against Donny, he had to thank him for last night. Without his nudge, God only knew how long it would have taken Lindsey to forget all the things she couldn't forgive Thad for and give in to her desire.

But he didn't kid himself that she'd forgotten permanently. He hadn't been so drowsy last night—or so satiated this morning—that he hadn't noticed her silence when he'd told her that he loved her. She hadn't had anything to offer him in return, and so she had said nothing.

That was all right. He knew she'd probably been skeptical, but he'd meant what he had told her at the lake Saturday morning. She could hate him for everything that had happened with Donny. She could think that her brother was totally innocent if she wanted, and that Thad was totally guilty. She could believe until the day she died that Thad had handled the case badly, that it was his fault Donny had fallen.

And he wouldn't care. As long as she didn't force him out of her life again.

He wondered idly if he was shortchanging himself, if he didn't deserve better than the incomplete sort of love that was all she would ever give him. Then he considered the eighteen months they'd been apart, and he knew the answer. Maybe he did deserve better, maybe not, but he wasn't being cheated. Half of something was better than nothing, and nothing was all he'd had those eighteen months.

Nothing was all he would ever have without Lindsey.

Cassie went into the storeroom and crossed over to the far shelves, where Lindsey was unpacking the latest shipment, and set a small ceramic owl in front of her. "You know, I counted once—just out of curiosity—and you had eighteen little owls in the shop. Seeing that they're not particularly pretty or even particularly popular, I wondered why. And now I know."

Lindsey looked from her to the owl, then back again. "What is it you know, Cassie?"

"There's someone here to see you. And he's got these big wide eyes, all serious and dark, just like that owl." The girl gave her a knowing smile. "You never told me that you have a boyfriend."

Lindsey continued unwrapping the miniature vases she'd bought from a potter in South Carolina. "He's thirty-five years old. Isn't that a little too old to call a boyfriend?"

"Would you prefer that I called him your lover?" she asked impertinently.

"Cassandra! Such talk from a sweet young girl," she scolded. Then, trying unsuccessfully to hide her smile, she pushed the box into her assistant's arms. "Here. Finish unpacking these, will you?"

"Oh, yes, ma'am." Cassie executed a curtsy even with her arms full. "Leave the sweet young girl in the back room where she can't see anything interesting." She raised her voice on the last words as Lindsey closed the storeroom door and went through the office into the shop.

Thad was standing in front of the Father's Day cards. Unaware of her, he occasionally picked one up and glanced at it, then returned it to its slot. Lindsey tried, but couldn't get the goofy smile off her face as she approached him. "Can I help you?"

He didn't glance at her. "I need a card for my dad."

"Do you call him that?"

Then he did look at her, his brow furrowed in a frown. "What kind of question is that to ask a customer?"

"Well, it's not exactly as if you're a real customer."

He seemed offended by that. "I have money."

"It shows," she said dryly, giving him a long head-to-toe look. "Seriously, do you call your father Dad?"

"Of course I do. What would you expect me to call him?"

"I don't know. Being raised the way you were, something more formal, I guess. Like Father."

He grinned suddenly. "Well, he did suggest once when we were all home on break at the same time and raising more than a little hell that we call him *Mister* McNally, so people wouldn't know we were related to him. And I tried calling him Patrick once. I never made that mistake again." He picked up another card, a Lindsey's Blooms, and scanned the message inside. "No, he's just plain Dad, and my mother is Mom. My grandmother, though . . . she's Grandmother. No Gran, Granny or Grandma for her."

Lindsey watched him as he read another of her cards. She had missed him all day today and had thought four o'clock would never get here. It was frightening how quickly she'd come to need him again. To think that it was only fifteen days ago when he'd walked through that door with Clint Roberts. And now she couldn't imagine a day without him.

Maybe the need had come so quickly because it had always been there. Maybe, in spite of her months of anger and bitterness, she had never stopped wanting him, had never stopped needing him.

Maybe she had never stopped loving him.

Slowly she became aware of his fingers waving side to side in front of her face. Her eyes followed them to the left, then to the right, then she blinked and looked at him. "Wh-what?"

"I said I'll take this one." He handed her a card, and she numbly looked at it. It was her favorite of the half-dozen Father's Day cards in her line. It was the one she would give her own father if he were still alive.

She took the matching envelope from the rack, slid the card inside and handed it back to him. "Here you go."

He accepted it with a puzzled look. "I think you forgot something here. It's an integral part of doing business, called paying. You know, you go to the cash register and add the tax, I give you the money and you give me my change?" With his fingers on her chin, he gave her head a gentle shake. "Does any of this sound familiar to you?"

"Don't be silly," she said with a gentle smile. "I'm not going to charge you for a card."

"Then take it back. I'll buy it from the store downtown."

She refused to accept it. "That's ridiculous. A two-dollar card is not worth arguing over."

"That's right. It isn't. So either take the money or forget it."

She thought he was behaving like a child. Giving away one single card wasn't going to cost her more than a few cents' profit, and she felt funny about accepting his money. For heaven's sake, this was *Thad.* If he'd told her at home that he'd needed a card for his father, she would have thought nothing of pulling out the small supply she kept in her desk drawer and giving him one, and he would have thought nothing of taking it.

But here in her shop, in her business, he had to make an issue of it. "Some people don't accept gifts graciously," she said in a low, snide voice as she snatched the card from his hand and went to the cash register.

He followed her, withdrawing a five-dollar bill from his wallet as he did. "If you want to give me your time, your attention, your affection, your body or someday, maybe your forgiveness, I'll accept those gifts, and I will be damn gracious. But this is business, Lindsey."

His quiet words stopped her in the act of making change. For a moment, she simply stood there, staring at the cash drawer, then she finished counting and shoved the money into his hand. "I hate it when you're so reasonable," she muttered. "And I hate it when you're right."

"Now business is taken care of." He leaned across the counter, wrapped his fingers around her neck and pulled her close for a kiss—sweet and hot and intense.

"I've missed you," she whispered when he released her.

"Good."

She managed to smile faintly at the satisfaction in his tone. "And how was your day?"

"Fishing for compliments?" He brushed his hand over her hair. "Just let me say that you make it very hard to concentrate on stolen cars. Are you ready to go?"

"Let me tell Cassie and get my purse."

"Yes, by all means, let that poor girl out of that back room."

Lindsey hesitated, her smile a little nervous. "Oh. You heard that."

His smile was broad and amused. "Yes, I did."

"What else did you hear?"

"Something about serious eyes and eighteen owls?" He feigned nonchalance. "I wasn't paying much attention."

"Yeah. Right. I'll be right back." She went into the storeroom and gave Cassie a few last-minute instructions before saying good-night.

As they crossed the parking lot to his car, Thad asked, "Do you leave her alone in the store a lot?"

"Not too often. It isn't that I don't trust her. She's bright and dependable and does an excellent job. But she's only sixteen, and I worry sometimes about her leaving alone at night. But tonight her mother's picking her up, so that's not a problem."

"You're a good boss."

She appreciated the compliment but wondered what he was basing it on. "Why do you say that?"

"Because you're concerned about her. And she's obviously very fond of you. She was delighted to find out that you had a man in your life."

Lindsey laughed as she got into his car, but by the time he was seated beside her, the mirth had faded. "To be honest...so am I. I'm glad you're here, Thad. I'm glad you're in my life."

As he started the car and backed out, he muttered a good-natured curse. "Why do you say things like that when you know I can't do a damn thing in response? If we're not at the door waiting when the locksmith comes, it'll take another week to get him out here."

"We'll be there," she said, deliberately misunderstanding. "He's not due for another twenty minutes."

"The things I have in mind, sweetheart, can't be done in twenty minutes, not adequately, anyway." Then he smiled, and his glance, for the few seconds he could spare from the street, focused on her breasts underneath the soft blue silk. "On the other hand, twenty minutes could make a fine start."

Lindsey lay her head back against the headrest and laughed. "You know, looking at you, in your fancy suit with your serious eyes and solemn expression, no one would ever guess how sinfully wicked you are inside."

"Only with you, sweetheart." He parked in front of her house and shut off the engine, then stilled her hands when she reached to unfasten her seat belt. "I want you to wait out here while I go inside."

She gave him a chastening look. "Thad—"

"We have no way of knowing if Donny is in there or not. Just sit here and let me have a look around."

"Donny would never hurt either one of us."

"Are you willing to bet your life on that?" He paused. "Are you willing to bet mine?"

She sighed softly. How did he know just what to say to get his way? He knew perfectly well that while she might risk her own life for her brother, she could never do anything that might bring harm to *him*. "All right. I'll wait. I won't even get out of the car until you say it's okay." She drew her keys out of her purse and laid them in his palm.

"Thank you." He got out and started up the walk, switching the keys to his left hand. He wouldn't pull it out here where Lindsey could see, but once he was inside, he needed his right hand free for his gun. While he seriously doubted that Donny would be hanging around—last night he'd come too close to getting caught—he wasn't taking any chances.

The place was all locked up. He made a thorough search, even went into the backyard to check the locks on the garage, before stepping onto the front porch and gesturing to Lindsey.

As she walked toward him, all grace and elegance, he thought about her earlier remark about his appearance and knew that it applied equally well to her. Who would ever imagine that her cool, aloof exterior was merely the outer shell of the hottest, sexiest, most unabashedly passionate woman he'd ever known?

Automatically he looked at his watch. It was ten minutes until the locksmith was due to arrive. Assuming that he was on time, that was ten minutes to start a task that could take the entire night to finish. Ten minutes to get her inside. Ten minutes to kiss her, stroke her, arouse her, undress her, hold her, caress her, love her.

Or ten minutes to just think about doing all those things. Ten minutes to anticipate doing them slowly, so incredibly slowly that they would both die with the need.

She collected her mail from the box, then followed him inside. For a moment, she simply stood there in the doorway, looking at the shards of glass and pottery on the floor. "That bowl was one of the few things of my mother's that Aunt Louise had kept. She had to sell everything else—the house, the furniture, even the pots and pans and dishes. But she kept that bowl, Dad's pocketknife and Mom's wedding ring. Aside from a few personal things—letters and photographs—those were all Donny and I had."

And now they were all gone, Thad acknowledged—the bowl destroyed, the pocketknife in FBI custody, the ring stolen by Donny.

After a moment, she shook off the melancholy. "Let me change clothes and clean that up. Then I'll fix us some tea and see what I have for dinner."

"You didn't invite me for dinner."

She smiled faintly. "I invited you to spend the night so I could ravish you. Of course I'll find it necessary to feed you, too. You did bring some clothes?"

"I wasn't sure you were serious, but...yeah, I stopped by the house on the way to the shop and picked up some clothes."

Her smile grew stronger. "Good. I'll change—"

He stopped her with only his fingertips on her arm. "Don't." He was hoarse, but he knew clearing his throat wouldn't help. At this very moment, because the locksmith had just pulled up out front, nothing would help. "Wait until we're done here...then let me undress you."

She didn't say anything, just nodded solemnly.

The moment was broken by a cheerful greeting from the man outside. Thad brushed past Lindsey, careful not to touch her, and went out to take care of business.

The locksmith was an older gentleman, friendly and chatty. He assumed that Lindsey and Thad were married and called him Mr. Phillips the whole time they talked. Thad didn't mind the mistake, although he would have greatly preferred hearing her called Mrs. McNally instead. They talked about security and crime and the value of a good lock, and when the man was done a half hour later, Thad—knowing that Lindsey would fuss—paid him for his services. Then he went inside, closed the door, locked the new lock and went in search of her.

She'd made herself scarce once the locksmith had arrived, taking advantage of the time to sweep up the broken glass and sort through the day's mail. She had also put something in the oven, something that was just beginning to send a faint aroma through the house.

Slowly he started up the stairs. The last thing he'd said to her was that he wanted to undress her himself. He knew where she was waiting.

Her bedroom door was open a few inches. He stopped in front of it, seeing only a small portion of the room that included a lot of the bed and not a glimpse of Lindsey. Reaching out, he gave the door a slight push, and it swung inward with one little squeak.

She was there, standing by one of the windows, her hands loosely clasped together. She glanced at him, then gestured with both hands toward the window. "I saw the locksmith leave. I'll pay you later."

He shook his head to indicate that it didn't matter, but she insisted. "This is business, Thad."

Trust her, at a time when he wasn't even capable of arguing, to turn his own argument back on him. He simply shrugged. "The receipt is on the hall table." He moved farther into the room, approaching her but as slowly, as patiently, as unhurriedly as he'd planned. How long he could hold back to this pace, he didn't know, but he was going to try.

She watched him and touched the tip of her tongue to her lips. "I—I had this urge to be naked in bed when you came in," she said with an uneasy laugh.

"You know I would never hurt you."

She nodded. "I know."

"I won't make you do anything you don't want to."

"I know that, too." Her voice was uneven. "I'm not afraid, Thad. I've never been afraid of you."

"Then why—?"

"I've been up here since right after that man came, thinking about what you're going to do—what we're going to do. And I'm already so aroused...." Her voice trailed away, and she swallowed hard.

"What I'm going to do is undress you...and kiss you...and touch you in all the places you like to be touched, in all the ways you like to be touched." Now he was close enough to do that, close enough to reach out and touch any part of her, but he didn't. "And then I'm going to make love to you. I'm going to love you so long and so well that to-night, just for tonight, you'll forget the past and love me, too."

Taking her hands, he drew her away from the window with its sheer lace curtains and closer to the bed. Next he removed his glasses and laid them on the nightstand. For what he was about to do, he didn't need to see. Only feel. He began unbuttoning her blouse. It was an achingly slow process, because each button that slipped free revealed a little more of her skin, skin that he had to caress and kiss and occasionally moisten with his tongue.

Even when her blouse was open, he didn't remove it, but slid his arms around her, underneath the fabric, and pulled her close and bent his head to kiss her while his hands stroked her spine. He kissed away what little bit of lipstick remained, bit gently at her lower lip, licked from one corner of her mouth to the other. Sliding his tongue between her lips, he lazily brought one hand to her jaw, silently urging her to open to him, to let him fill her mouth.

When she obeyed, his hand slipped down her throat to rest on the swell of her breast. He could cover her breast with one hand, and he did—a simple lingering touch. Then he began to leisurely rub it, pressing just hard enough to slide the silk back and forth with his caresses, hard enough to make the sheer fabric of her bra underneath scrape pleasurably against her nipple.

Lindsey whimpered deep in her throat, the sound muffled by his tongue in her mouth. She hadn't exaggerated when she'd told him that merely thinking about his love-making had already aroused her. Now her skin felt as if it were burning with fever, and her clothes were a painful barrier that needed to be removed. If she were naked in the cool room, maybe some of the heat that was consuming her would dissipate. But some part of her dazed brain knew that wasn't true. The only thing that would contain this fire was Thad, deep, deeper than ever, inside her.

Her breasts were swollen, her nipples erect and throbbing. She needed his mouth on her bare skin, needed the strong, suckling kisses that he tormented her with. But she also suspected that such kisses at her breasts would shatter her control, would make her explode, satisfying savage need with savage release. And he wouldn't have found the pleasure he wanted in undressing her.

He ended the kiss, then pushed her blouse off one shoulder, exposing her breast, and for a long moment he just looked. She forced her eyes open, forced her gaze down to see what he saw. Her bra was insubstantial, so sheer that it hid nothing, and it was marked, right across the seam where the lace had been sewn, by the crest of her nipple.

While she watched, Thad stroked his thumbnail across the seam, and she gasped, feeling the shock all the way down between her thighs. Then he slid his fingers underneath, dark shadows against her fairer skin, and he pushed the small mound up, free of the lace, free for the exquisite agony created by his mouth.

Lindsey gave a soft, utterly helpless cry. The sensations rushing through her were more than she could possibly bear—yet she did bear them, and pleaded for more. Between harsh breaths and boneless shudders, she begged for it to end—and that it never end. She struggled for control, and demanded to lose it.

Still suckling her nipple, Thad grasped a handful of her skirt and began pulling it up. The skirt was designed to fit every supple curve, so it wasn't an easy task, but at last he could slide his hand underneath to her hips, and he found the heated, damp place between her thighs. He pressed his fingers against her, rubbing, intensifying her pleasure and doubling her need, his caress made all the more intimate by the fact that he wasn't touching her flesh but the silken hose and silky panties that covered her. When her body arched and her muscles became hard and steely, he held her tighter with his arm at her waist and continued, and when the place where he touched her grew hotter and damper and her body, in a sudden flurry of shudders and sighs and voiceless cries, went limp and quivery, he caught her, lowering her to the bed, following her down.

Mindless. Senseless. That was how Lindsey felt. Thad could do what he wanted with her now, and she couldn't protest, couldn't find voice or words, couldn't even find thoughts to express. She could only feel...and what she felt was indescribable. There were still tiny tremors exploding within her. It would take forever to recover from the pleasure he'd brought her.

Then she felt him kneel between her legs, felt his trousers, soft and warm, against her now-bare thighs, felt his manhood, thick and long and unbearably hot, pressing against her, and she felt recovery, swift and miraculous.

She hadn't even realized he'd removed her hose and panties, hadn't known he'd pushed her skirt higher, hadn't seen him unfasten his trousers as he'd teasingly threatened to do this morning. But she knew that now he would fill her. Now he would bring her more torture, more pleasure, more bliss.

Thad entered her slowly, not brutally the way his passion demanded or swiftly the way his need insisted, but little by agonizing little. Her flesh was swollen and exquisitely sensitive and convulsed at the intrusion of his own swollen flesh. When finally they were joined, she gloved him tighter and hotter than ever before.

It was over in mere seconds...and yet lasted forever. Shock waves of sensation washed over him, starting deep inside and rippling out, causing his taut muscles to tremble, his lungs to constrict, his restraint to shatter. He gasped for breath as he strained against her, into her, and he groaned, a deep, low, animal sound as he filled her with the heated liquid of his release.

Long moments passed before he could speak, long moments when all he could do was lie above her, pressing her into the mattress, still intimately joined, feeling the lethargy of intense satisfaction slowly calm his fatigued muscles and his erratic breathing and his thudding heart. When he could finally move, he drew away from her, kissed her forehead, then left the bed. He returned a moment later from the bathroom, his clothing left lying in careless disorder on the bathroom floor, a warm, damp cloth in his hand.

With the gentlest of touches he finished undressing Lindsey, tenderly stripping her naked. Then he sat beside her and used the warm cloth to cleanse her, his light strokes as unarousing as possible, careful not to stimulate her in places already overstimulated. That done, he lay beside her, pulling her near, and placed a light kiss on each closed eyelid.

"That was perfect," she whispered, brushing her mouth across his chest. "Absolutely perfect."

Chapter 9

Thad chuckled softly. "I don't know. I think we could both work a little on control."

She kissed his nipple, and his skin rippled in response. "Sweetheart, we could work on it every day until we die," she said in a low, husky voice, "and I would never gain more control. I would never stop wanting you so desperately. I would never stop needing you." After another brief kiss, though, she added, "But that doesn't mean we can't try."

"Try to improve our self-control? Or try to make you stop wanting me?"

This time it was Lindsey who chuckled. "Nothing could ever do that, Thad."

"Nothing?" He tilted her head back so he could make out her expression. "Not even Donny?"

She scooted along the bed until she was leaning over him, her face only inches from his. "Even when I thought Donny was dead, even when I hated you for taking him from me, I still wanted you," she whispered with a fierce intensity. "I used to lie in this bed at night and cry, not because my brother was dead, but because you weren't here. I used to lie here for hours, my entire body aching for your touch. I used to have dreams that you were making love to me, and would wake up aroused and trembling and needing you so badly that I hurt with it. I've always wanted you, Thad. *Always.*"

"Then why..." He broke off for a moment, considered the wisdom of what he was about to ask, then plunged ahead. "Why didn't you let me know? Why didn't you call me? Why didn't you give me another chance? Do you think you were the only one who was lonely? The only one who had dreams? The only one who hurt?"

"I couldn't. I couldn't let you back into my life until now."

"Now," he repeated, unable to hide the sharp edge of bitterness to his voice. "Now that you know I didn't kill your brother. Now that you know he's still alive. That makes it all right to satisfy those wants and to fulfill those dreams."

"I'm sorry, Thad," she whispered. "I would give you everything that you ever wanted if I only could. I would love you the way you want, the way you deserve. I would wipe out the past, destroy all the bad memories and only remember the good . . . if I could."

"It doesn't matter," he said quietly, finally removing the pins that held her hair back, watching it fall and shimmer in the lamplight. "I don't care what made it all right for you to want me again. I don't care if you ever love me the way you used to. I'll be satisfied with whatever you can give."

Tears glistened in her eyes when she looked at him. "You deserve so much better."

"I spent a long time looking, sweetheart," he said. "I never found anyone better than you."

"Then you weren't looking hard enough." She got up, took her black satin robe from the closet and belted it around her waist. When she came back to the bed, she sat down facing him. "What about Carole?"

"What about her?"

"You must have cared for her. Maybe if you'd tried, if you had given it enough time, you would have fallen in love with her."

He sat up, leaned against the headboard and put on his glasses, then gave her a curious glance. "You really think so?" he asked, sounding genuinely interested. "I still see her from time to time—" He broke off when Lindsey gave him a none-too-gentle thump on the arm.

"What do you mean, you still see her?"

"She works in the same building. I run into her occasionally on the elevator, coming and going."

She moved up to snuggle beside him, and he opened his arms to her. "Is she pretty?" she asked wistfully.

"Beautiful."

"And smart?"

"She has her Ph.D."

She turned her face against his shoulder and said glumly, "I bet she's rich, too, and has gorgeous hair and gorgeous legs and a gorgeous body."

"You ought to see her in a bikini," Thad said in agreement. Then he relented and hugged her tight. "Ah, Lindsey, she doesn't begin to hold a candle to you. She's a nice woman, and we had some nice times. I liked her, but it never went beyond that, because of you. And if it makes you feel any better..." He set her back so he could see her face. "*She* was jealous of *you*. She knew that I was still in love with you, and she knew that was never going to change. And since she was in the market for a husband, that put an end to our relationship."

"How long were you with her?"

His voice was soft when he answered because he knew the answer would hurt her. "Five months."

That was a long time for a casual affair, she thought sadly. It hadn't taken anywhere near five months for her to fall head over heels in love with him. And though he hadn't come right out and said so, Carole must have been in love with him, too. How could she not have been?

She pulled away and slid to the other side of the bed. "Were there other women, too?" she asked petulantly. "Just how many affairs did you have while we were apart?"

"A few."

"And did they also last five months each?"

"No." He didn't try to control the sharpness in his voice. "The first one lasted only one night, and I never even knew the woman's name. I knew all the important things, though—that she was tall and had long legs, that she had brown eyes and long brown hair that she wore pulled back like this." He demonstrated with her own hair, copying one of the classic styles that she had always preferred.

Then he let her hair drop and let his head fall back against the wood. "And so did Carole," he admitted wearily. "And so did the ones in between."

She was ashamed of her petty jealousy. What right did she have to question him? It had been her decision to end their relationship, and that had ended whatever faithfulness or loyalty he'd owed her, too. He'd been free to seduce a different woman every night if he'd chosen to. He owed her no explanations now. He certainly didn't owe her the comfort of knowing that he'd only formed relationships with women who had reminded him of *her.*

Before she had an opportunity to apologize, he rolled his head to the side to look at her. "As long as we're together, Lindsey, I will never be unfaithful to you. I just couldn't do that. But when I met those women, we weren't together. I was alone and miserable, and I—I used them to ease the pain. I'm not proud of that, but I won't apologize to you for it, either."

She rose onto her knees and clasped both of his hands in hers. "I'm glad you found Carole, and this woman whose name you never knew and the ones in between. I'm grateful to them for helping you through a difficult time that was all my fault." Then she offered him a friendly warning. "That doesn't mean I'm not jealous, because I am. I can't bear the idea of you making love to another woman. But I know you would never do it now, and I'm sorry that I made it necessary then."

Aware that he was staring blankly at her, she got up and went to the closet to get some clothes. "I stuck a pan of lasagna in the oven while the locksmith was here, and it should be about ready. Are you hungry?"

He rose swiftly from the bed and caught her at the bathroom door. "Let me warn you, sweetheart, I won't be nearly as forgiving if some man pops up in your past," he said fiercely.

"There hasn't been another man in my life since the day you told me you were breaking it off with...Andrea. That was her name, wasn't it? The chesty blonde with the IQ of a gourd?"

He drew her closer. "That was...two months before I ever asked you out. That was even before I knew I was going to ask you out."

She smiled confidently. "*I* knew."

"How?"

"The way you looked at me. The way you found excuses to touch me. The way you started going home immediately after we finished running instead of sitting around at the park and talking and cooling off the way we usually did."

"That was because I found it impossible to hide how hard I got just being close to you," he admitted. "The first time really took me by surprise. You were my *buddy,* and I was getting aroused watching you run."

She slid her hands over his chest to his shoulders. "No, Thad," she disagreed softly. "I was *never* your buddy. I waited a long time for you to realize that."

There were different types of hunger and different degrees, and he was just beginning to think that maybe satisfying *this* hunger yet again was more important than food when she slipped out of his arms, gathered his clothes from the floor, pushed them into his arms and prodded him out the door. She closed it behind him and turned the lock before he could protest.

Grumbling to himself, he dressed in his shirt and trousers, then went out to his car to get his duffle bag and the suit hanging in the back seat. He heard Lindsey moving about in the kitchen when he returned, but he went back upstairs. There he changed into running shorts and a T-shirt, then hung both suits in the closet amid her dresses. His foolish romantic streak liked the way they looked there.

She gave him a narrow-eyed look when he finally joined her in the kitchen. "Am I to assume from your clothes that you intend to go running after we eat?"

"Five miles on a full stomach would give me indigestion, and your lasagna is too good for that." He leaned over her shoulder to sniff the aroma from the pasta she was cutting into large squares. "You're to assume that I was in too much of a hurry to pick you up to take the time to pack anything beyond what I absolutely needed. You're also to assume that I expect you to be up and dressed by five-thirty in the morning to go running then."

Amused by her nonresponse to his words, he fixed two glasses of tea, then sat down at the breakfast table. Located in a wide bumped-out area of the kitchen, it was surrounded on three sides by windows. Lindsey joined him with two plates of steaming pasta.

"What interest does the FBI have in stolen cars?" she asked as she set his plate in front of him.

He frowned, then remembered his reference earlier in the shop to stolen cars. "Have you been waiting all evening to ask about that?"

"Heavens, no. I had better things on my mind." Her smile left no doubt as to what those things had been. "But as long as we're out of bed and dressed . . . Stolen cars seem pretty small-time for the FBI."

"Usually they are. Report one stolen car to us, and we'll refer you to the Atlanta Police Department. Auto theft doesn't particularly interest us. But make it fifteen to twenty cars a month that are being stolen by the same people and resold in another state, and simple auto theft becomes interstate transportation of a stolen motor vehicle."

"And that does interest you."

He gave her a wry look. "Let's say it interests the Bureau."

Her look was thoughtful and somewhat surprised. What was she thinking? he wondered and after a moment's speculation, he asked her outright.

"You don't like every case you're assigned, do you?"

"Are you kidding? Some are boring, and some are tedious, and I know some are going to be dead ends before I even start. But that's part of the job. You don't like everything about your job, do you?"

"Well, there's not much chance for time off."

"Yeah," he agreed. "And having strangers coming in and handling your things—your cards and your vases and your pottery and your owls—getting things out of order and never returning anything exactly where they found it isn't much fun, either, is it?"

She acknowledged his accuracy with a nod. "I expect myself to be dissatisfied with certain aspects of my job. But not you. You're different."

"How?"

"I don't know," she hedged with a shrug. "You're so professional."

"You're professional, too."

"You're so...gung ho about being an FBI agent. Like you said that day on the porch, the store is just a job to me. I love it, but it's what I do, not what I am. But you *are* your job twenty-four hours a day. I just assumed you loved everything about it—every case, every assignment, every court appearance."

He shook his head, her naiveté taking him by surprise. "There are a lot of things I don't like about the job, Lindsey. I don't like to work auto theft or drug cases. Kidnappings are disheartening, especially when the victims are kids, but murder cases are challenging. Economic crimes are time-consuming and tedious, but my background is in accounting, so I don't mind them." He paused. "But, overall, I like the job. I think I'm contributing something to society and to the country rather than detracting from them, that I'm performing a vital service. Frankly, I can't imagine doing anything else, being anything else."

They finished eating and were washing the dishes when he returned to the subject. "Lindsey, we were together a long time. How could you think that I'm always one hundred percent satisfied with my work? How could you *not* know that there are things about the job I'm not crazy about?"

She rinsed the plate he'd just washed and set it in the drainer, then dried her hands. "Because you never told me. That was one of our problems, Thad, and you never even realized it. I always wanted to be involved in every part of your life, and you would never let me see that part. Practically every time we met after work, you asked me how my day had been, and I told you everything. You knew what jobs I was doing, you knew how I felt about my bosses, you knew the names of the people I worked with—and even the names of their husbands and their kids."

"I was interested," he said with a defensive shrug.

"I was interested in your job, too, but you wouldn't share it with me. After I told you everything that had happened to me, I always asked you how *your* day had been. And you always said the same thing. *Okay.* That was all you ever told me. I never knew what kind of cases you liked or disliked. I never even knew what kind of cases you worked on."

When he started to respond, she raised her hand to stop him. "I know. I didn't need to know. I was an outsider. That's why I never pushed you for details. And I think . . . I think that's partly why I reacted so strongly to the whole mess with Donny. I was no longer on the outside...but you still shut me out."

He cleaned the sink and rinsed it, then accepted the towel from her and dried his hands. "I'm sorry I ever used the word outsider, and I swear I will never use it again. But can't you understand, Lindsey, that I didn't have a choice in keeping the details of Donny's case from you?"

"Part of me does understand. Every aspect of life has its rules and regulations, and I understand the need for them. I especially understand the need when it comes to the kind of work you do. But—" she sighed distantly "—I guess I wanted to believe that when it came to something important, something *really* important, you would be willing to bend or maybe even break a few rules for me. I wanted to believe that, if it ever came down to a cold, hard choice, you would choose me over the Bureau. But you didn't."

"If I'd done that, Lindsey, I could have lost my job. Depending on the outcome, I could have wound up in jail myself. And no matter what the outcome, instead of losing your respect, I would have lost my own. *That* would have destroyed us quicker than anything else could have."

She frustratedly disagreed. "But don't you see? It never would have come to that. No one would ever have known that you'd told me about Donny. They simply would have assumed that he'd decided to turn himself in. Your case would have been settled, you would have gotten the credit and my brother wouldn't have fallen off that bridge."

Taking her hand, he pulled her down the hall and into the living room with him. Once they were settled at opposite ends of the sofa he picked up where she'd left off. "You're assuming that you could have convinced Donny to turn himself in. I don't think you could have. What if I had confided in you? And you had told him, 'Give yourself up, they know you did it, they're going to catch you, make it easy on yourself.' And what if he had decided to make it *real* easy by taking off with that two hundred and some thousand dollars of ransom? My career would have been destroyed—my reputation, my future, everything."

"But Donny wouldn't have run away like that."

"Sweetheart—" Closing his eyes, he ground out a curse. How could she be so intelligent and logical... and so damn illogical? After everything she'd learned about her brother, how could she still hold on to the belief that he was a good man who never would have done anything so wrong as running away from the police?

"You think I'm being naive, don't you?" she asked quietly.

Sighing, he opened his eyes again and shook his head. "I think you love your brother so much that you don't want to admit even to yourself that he was capable of doing something bad."

"And you think that's naive," she persisted.

"Blood ties are strong. You know Donny better than anyone. You love him better than anyone. Understandably, it's hard for you to accept that the little boy who used to run to you to dry his tears could have grown up to become a bad person." He broke off, and his expression turned bleak. "I just wish you had that kind of faith in me."

Lindsey impulsively moved to his end of the couch, making a space for herself between the cushions and his hip where he had no choice but to put his arm around her. "You're the only person in the world that I ever really trusted to take care of me. You're the only one who ever made me feel really safe. I know that you believe you handled that case in the only way you could. You believe you did the right things, and I respect that. I can't agree with it, but I do respect it, and I respect you and I trust you."

I respect you. Three little words. *I trust you.* They brought him a satisfaction that all the wild, passionate lovemaking in the world couldn't match. They made him feel warm. Happy. Proud. They made him feel almost as good as those other three little words he longed to hear would make him feel.

"Thank you," he whispered, giving her a solemn kiss. "Now...could we talk about something else, something a little less grim?"

She was about to answer when the phone rang. She reached over his shoulder and picked it up with a cheery hello.

Instead of silence or the measured breaths that were somehow intimidating, this time there was music. It sounded distant, the sweet tones of the saxophone thin. It was a beautifully haunting tune, with no lyrics, but just instruments meant to accompany the sax, not outshine it.

Lindsey listened for a few seconds, her fingers clenching, her throat dry, her heart pounding audibly, then she whispered, "Donny? Donny, talk to me, please." Her voice gained strength—the strength of anger and frustration and need so powerful that it brought tears to her eyes. "Donny, why are you doing this to me?" she demanded just before Thad pried the receiver from her hand.

He heard just a bar or two of the music before the line went dead. He hung up, then turned to her. "Lindsey, did he say anything?"

She was staring blankly at him, seeing him but giving no sign of recognition. "He loved that song," she whispered. "It was the only thing besides country music that he ever listened to. The first time he ever heard it, he went and bought the tape, and he used to bring it when he came over here and play it over and over and over until I learned to hate it. We used to argue about it, and finally I'd make him turn it off."

And even then he would hum or whistle it. For a while, she'd told him in annoyance, she'd heard the song even in her sleep.

"Lindsey!" He gave her a shake. "Did he say anything?"

She shook her head. "He never does. He just listens to me saying hello."

"Then you've gotten these calls before?"

"A couple of times. Last week."

"What makes you think it's Donny?"

"I don't know. That song..." She raised both hands to her face. "God, he loved that song."

"But you didn't hear the song the other times."

"No." Letting her hands fall, she looked at Thad. "I had no reason to belive it was him the other times, just a feeling. I don't get nuisance phone calls, Thad. I never have. And they came right at the same time—between ten-thirty and eleven."

"This one's early. It's only a little after eight-thirty." He reached for the phone and began dialing. "I'm going to notify Clint Roberts. They'll probably put a tap on your phone. It will record all the calls made either to or from this house. And you can't tell anyone, okay?"

She nodded, then slid away from him when he began talking to the other agent. She wandered around the room, finally stopping in front of the silver-framed photograph of herself with Donny. Cradling the frame in her arms, she studied it for a long time, the mournful strains of that song weaving through her mind.

He'd been a handsome man, tall and slim with shaggy blond hair and blue eyes that could rival any movie star's.

There had been no resemblance between her and Donny—neither physically nor in their characters—but there had been a great deal of love and reliance and dependence. Donny had counted on her to take care of him, to help him when he quit one of his jobs before the next month's rent was paid, to feed him when he was tired of his own cooking or had run out of grocery money, to give him advice that he always asked for but rarely took, to pick up his car tag for him when the old one had expired and to see that his insurance stayed in force even when he forgot about it, to take care of a thousand and one other details for him.

And she had depended on him, too. He had been the outlet for all the love she'd had to give, all the mothering she'd needed to do. Unstable as he'd been, he had been the stability in her life. He was always there, always needing her, and *she* had needed *that*.

Maybe she had smothered him with all her love. Maybe she had stifled whatever independence he'd had by doing so many things for him. Maybe kidnapping the old lady had been his declaration of independence, his way of telling Lindsey that she couldn't run his life for him anymore, that he was capable of doing things for himself, that he no longer needed her interference.

No. She refused to believe that. She wouldn't accept the burden of any further guilt. If Donny had wanted her to quit running his life, he would have told her so. If he had resented all the help she'd given him, he would have told her that, too, instead of constantly asking for more. Kidnapping the old lady had been no different than a thousand other actions he'd taken: quitting his jobs without a moment's notice; buying a car without even finding out first what the payments would be or if he could afford them; taking off for a Florida vacation with fifty dollars in his pocket, no place to stay when he got there and no way to get back home.

All his life he had acted first, then considered the consequences later, if at all. And that, she was positive, was what he'd done with the kidnapping. He had seen a relatively easy way to get a large sum of money, and he'd done it. He had never considered that it was a serious crime. He had never given any thought to the fact that the FBI, and very likely Thad, would be brought in. He had never concerned himself with what getting caught would mean, had never reflected for even a moment on what twenty-five years in prison would mean.

And he was still doing that even now. Any reasonably intelligent crook would have taken the money and gotten as far away from Atlanta as he could. He wouldn't have come back to the city where he'd committed the crime, wouldn't have started spending the money with an arrogance that made the FBI more determined than ever to find him, wouldn't break into his own sister's house twice, wouldn't be making phone calls to her.

But Donny had to come back and play games. He had to flaunt the money in front of the FBI. He had to make this damned call tonight after almost getting caught by Thad on Monday. He had to taunt them, had to say, "Look, I outsmarted you all. You gave me up for dead, wrote the money off as lost, and here I am, alive and well and rich and back home in Atlanta."

She focused again on the photograph. Thad had taken it only a few weeks before the kidnapping. They'd driven out north of Atlanta on a cool October day to have a picnic and admire the changing leaves. She and Donny were both in jeans, and she wore a green turtleneck sweater. Donny wore a T-shirt and a shabby leather jacket, and there were leaves in their hair and on their clothes from their play. Only a few weeks later, he'd traded that worn, old jacket for a brand-new five-hundred-dollar one, the one that had been stolen from the closet upstairs.

"No matter what he did," Thad said softly from behind her, "there's one thing you can always count on. He did love you."

Her smile was sad. "At least that's something."

"They'll take care of the phones tomorrow. If it rings again tonight, let the answering machine pick it up."

She nodded.

He pulled the frame from her hands and returned it to its spot, then drew her back to the sofa. "Roberts and his men finally got lucky. They've been questioning all the clerks at the shops that sell your cards. They had a possible ID at the one in Covington."

On the advice of her distributor, Lindsey had visited as many of the stores as possible, introducing herself to the owners, getting their opinions on which cards worked best and which needed to be changed. The one in Covington was small and charming and family-run. The owner was a white-haired grandmother, and she was helped out by her divorced daughter and her seventeen-year-old granddaughter. It was the granddaughter, she suspected, who would be most likely to remember Donny, and Thad's next words confirmed that.

"The clerk who works afternoons is a high school kid named Lara. They showed her the cards and a half-dozen photographs, including one of Donny, and she picked him out. She said she remembers him because he asked her to help him choose the cards and he was good-looking and funny and charming," Thad said dryly. "Also, he insisted that the cards had to be Lindsey's Blooms, even though they're more expensive."

"So it definitely is Donny. There's no doubt now."

"Well . . . she picked out his photograph, but she wasn't a hundred percent sure. She said it looked like him, and it didn't look like him. Granted, the photo they used is a year and a half old, and it wasn't the best—it was taken that day on the bridge. She did say that he'd cut his hair and put on some weight. If he suffered any injuries to his face when he fell, that could also explain differences in his appearance."

"Just tell me it *is* Donny," she said softly. "In your opinion, Thad . . . do you believe it is?"

He took off his glasses, rubbed them with his shirttail, then replaced them and sighed. "Yes. I do. He knew where the money was hidden. Of course he knew that he sent you Mother's Day cards. He had a key to the house. The only things he took from here were things of significance to him.

He had your father's pocketknife. The song on the phone, and now this.... Yes, I believe he's alive."

Between customers Wednesday afternoon, Lindsey and Cassie sat down in twin rockers and propped their feet on a shared stool. "How's your boyfriend?" Cassie asked.

Lindsey sent a preoccupied smile in her direction. "He's okay. His name is Thad."

"Thad? Is that short for something?"

"Thaddeus."

"That's a weir—unusual name."

Lindsey frowned mildly at her assistant. "Are you younger than I've believed all this time? Thaddeus is a good, strong, old name."

"With the emphasis on *old*. I don't think I've ever heard it before. Are you going to marry this guy?"

"If he asks." It felt nice to be so honest about it, she thought, to not have to worry about love and forgiveness and guilt, to give a simple heartfelt answer to a simple question. Yes, if Thad asked her to marry him, she would do it.

"Do you think he'll ask?"

She watched a mote of dust caught in the bright light of an afternoon sunbeam for a moment before answering, "He almost did once before. I think he will."

"What happened before?"

"A lot of problems."

Cassie got up to wait on a customer, then returned to her seat. "Did they involve the guy in the picture on your desk?"

She'd almost forgotten that photograph was there. "That's my brother Donny. Yes, he was a part of our problems."

"He's cute, but Thad's cuter. And he looks reliable, like you could count on him. And he's got money, besides. What does he do for a living?"

Lindsey turned so she could see Cassie clearly. "He's an FBI agent."

"How neat! I've never met an FBI agent before. Does he carry a gun and arrest bad guys and shoot the really bad guys?"

"Well, I don't know if he's ever shot anyone," she said, with a smile at Cassie's enthusiasm. "But he carries a gun and he arrests people."

"That's really neat. You know, most men of your generation are usually only interested in one thing: themselves. You don't find too many who are willing to risk their lives for what the government pays."

"Men of *my* generation?" Lindsey challenged as the bell over the door chimed. "And what about the males of *your* generation—Tess!"

She stood up to greet her friend and gave Andrew a pat on the back. "What brings you out?"

"I've wanted to come in here ever since you've opened the place, but I never thought..." She ended with a shrug.

She had never thought she would be welcome after the way Lindsey had ended their friendship. Feeling ashamed of herself and sad for all the time they'd lost, she gave her an awkward hug. "You always would have been welcomed."

"I'm glad you're not too busy right now," Tess said with a glance around. "Taking Andrew shopping is murder, especially when there's a crowd. He's not comfortable with strangers."

"You should have seen his eyes light up when you walked in here," Cassie said, leaving her chair and joining them. "There are all sorts of things you can get into here, aren't there, sweetheart?" she asked the baby in a soft, sweet voice.

He raised his head from Tess's shoulder, studied Cassie a moment, then reached for her.

"Wonderful," Lindsey said dryly after introducing her two friends. "I spent several hours with this child on Saturday, and every time I got within his line of sight, he gave me this long, suspicious distrustful look. Two seconds with you, and you're his new best friend."

"What can I say? I have three younger brothers." Cassie took him and started away. "You do your visiting, and I'll just show him around."

"Thanks." Tess let the diaper bag slide to the floor, then arched her back, rubbing down low with both hands. "The only people he's taken to that quickly are his grandmothers and Thad. He still gives Deke's brothers that kind of wary look, and he just started letting my dad hold him within the last few months. So how are you and Thad?"

"Fine."

"I know that smile. It's safe to assume that you're spending more than just your evenings together now, I think." She didn't need the confirmation of Lindsey's blush. "I'm so glad you two are back together. He was miserable when you were apart. If it hadn't been for Andrew, I don't think we ever would have seen much of him the past year."

At Tess's request, Lindsey showed her around the shop, finishing in front of the card section. "Time to take care of business, I guess," Tess said there. "I have to get Father's Day cards for Deke and my dad, and Andrew's birthday is next month, and Deke's got two nephews graduating from high school this week, so…can you help me pick something out?"

They spent the next twenty minutes browsing through the cards, laughing over the funny ones but sharing a preference for the sentimental ones. Finally, her choices made and paid for, Tess called Andrew's name.

He was sitting in the tin washtub, surrounded by soft dolls and clutching a fuzzy white lamb, its ear firmly caught between his teeth. "Oh, Drew," she sighed.

"Some babies have to chew," Cassie said matter-of-factly as she freed the black cloth from his mouth. "My littlest brother ate books."

"You mean he chewed on them," Lindsey clarified.

"Well, he chewed on the cardboard until it was soft enough to tear, and then he ate it."

"How old is he now?" Tess asked as she tried to pry the stuffed animal from the child's arms. It was destined to be a losing battle, Lindsey thought privately as Andrew held on as tight as he could and screwed up his face for an outraged scream.

"Six."

"And he *has* grown out of it...hasn't he?" Tess asked warily.

"Oh, sure. He's about as normal as a six-year-old gets now."

"Let him have the lamb," Lindsey suggested. "I missed his birth and didn't give him a gift then, so let this be it."

Tess prepared to argue, then sighed and smiled exasperatedly. "Thank you. You know, I used to be in control of my life. Really, I was. I went to work, I did my job, I went home. I ate when and what I wanted. I shopped when I wanted and visited my friends when I wanted and went out whenever I wanted. Then I met Deke, and then we had Drew and it's like I have no say in my life anymore. Andrew's in charge, and he's not even a year old yet."

"And you wouldn't change things back to the way they were for all the money in the world," Lindsey said knowingly.

"I don't know," Tess sighed. "I think I would like one quiet dinner without strained peas all over the floor, strained carrots in Drew's eyelashes and applesauce dripping off his hair." Then she suddenly brightened. "Speaking of dinner, can you and Thad come over Saturday? I realize I just painted a really appetizing picture of meals at the Ramsey house, but I'll feed Drew and get him to bed early."

"Let me check with Thad and make sure he doesn't have any plans, and I'll give you a call," Lindsey promised. "It was nice seeing you again, Andrew."

Nestled against his mother's shoulder and chewing on the lamb's ear again, he grinned. It was the sweetest, loveliest, most heart-tugging smile she'd ever seen, Lindsey thought, and once again she envied her friend. Someday *she* would have a baby, too. Someday she would hold Thad's child in her arms and would know the same exasperation, the same frustration Tess did.

Better yet, she would know the same pleasure Tess did. The same joy. The same love.

* * *

That night after work, Lindsey changed into shorts before going into the kitchen to start dinner. Thad had had to work late but had promised that he would be over no later than eight o'clock. It was after seven now, she thought, and wished she had asked him to call before leaving his office, since they were having steak, salad and baked potatoes, and she had forgotten to buy sour cream.

When the phone rang, she smiled smugly. How was that for convenience? Just wish that he would call, and poof, he did. Too bad everything in life wasn't that easy.

But the voice on the phone wasn't Thad's. It was younger, less mature, a little rusty but familiar all the same. God, how familiar! "Hey, Lin," said her brother. "Did I catch you alone, or is the G-man there?"

She almost dropped the phone in her surprise. For a moment she felt as if her nerves were scraped raw with pain and longing and love. How many times had she prayed that the Bureau's presumption that he was dead was wrong, that it was all just a horrible mistake? How many times had she wished for the chance to talk to him again?

And now that she had that chance, she couldn't say a thing. Everything was coming so fast that the thoughts tumbled over each other, confusing her, blocking her ability to speak.

"Lin? You there?"

Finally she managed to whisper his name. "Donny? Is that you?"

He laughed. "Does it sound like me?"

"Donny, where are you?"

"Around."

"You have to tell me, you have to—"

"Uh-uh, big sister. If I tell you, you'll tell the G-man, and I'll end up rotting in prison."

She stretched the phone cord so she could sit down at the breakfast table. "Donny, you have to turn yourself in. They're going to catch you—you know they are—so please just go ahead and turn yourself in."

"You're wrong, Lin. Monday night was the closest any-one's ever going to come to catching me."

"I'd like to see you," she whispered.

"I'd like to see you, too, but not with Thad around. It's too dangerous. Listen, I've got to go."

"Donny—"

"I'll keep in touch."

"Donny!" she shouted, but there was just a hum, then a dial tone at the other end. He had hung up.

"Thad," one of the agents called down the hall. "Before you leave, we've got something here you might want to listen to."

The elevator had just arrived, but Thad turned away from it and returned to the office, where he joined the small group of agents gathered around Clint Roberts and a tape recorder.

"Hey, Lin, did I catch you alone, or is the G-man there?"

Thad's briefcase slipped from his fingers and landed on the floor with a thud, then toppled onto its side. He moved a step closer, shutting out everyone around him, focusing narrowly on the voice on the tape.

"Lin? You there?"

Then came Lindsey's whisper. She sounded...shattered. Then an easy chuckle. "Does it sound like me?"

Roberts stopped the tape and looked at Thad. "*Does* it sound like him?"

"Without a doubt. When did this call come in?"

"At seven-sixteen. On the note inside the Mother's Day card, he called her Lin, too, didn't he?"

Thad nodded. "He always did, except when he was angry with her."

"And G-man? Is that what he called you?"

He nodded again. The way Donny had used it, in a disdainful, derogatory manner, had been his way of insulting Thad without being too overt about it. Even though Thad had disliked it, he'd always ignored it, because any sort of reaction would have shown Donny that he had achieved his goal.

Roberts started the tape again, and it played through to the end of the call, to Donny's hasty goodbye, followed by Lindsey's shout. After a moment's silence, Roberts asked, "Do you think that was him?"

"It sounded just like him—not just the voice, but the inflections, the arrogance, the boasting that no one's ever going to catch him. And the G-man stuff. Everyone knew he called Lindsey Lin, but he only got obnoxious enough to call me that when it was just the two—or three—of us. I can't remember him ever saying it in front of anyone else."

"We have the tape made on the bridge that day and also the one of his calls to the Heinreid house when he finalized the ransom drop. I've already gotten authority to send all three to the lab in D.C. on the next flight out. Gina's taking them."

Thad glanced at the female agent across from him, then gestured toward the recorder. "Do you mind?"

When Roberts shook his head, Thad rewound and replayed the tape. After it ended, he asked, "Where did this call come from?"

"A pay phone. Phone company records show that the calls made before we put the tap on her phone came from the same phone. We're checking out the area." Roberts hesitated, then added, "I'd like to talk to Lindsey tonight."

"I'm on my way over there now."

They drove over in separate cars, arriving one behind the other, and found Lindsey pacing the porch from end to end. She came rushing down the steps to meet them when they entered the gate in the picket fence, and threw her arms around Thad.

"It *was* him all along. I knew it was!" she said excitedly. "I just had a feeling!"

Thad couldn't help but smile at her. At times he saw this case purely from the Bureau's viewpoint: a kidnapper who had eluded arrest once before and gotten away with over two hundred thousand dollars of ransom money was about to be caught. But there was Lindsey's view, too: the brother whom she loved dearly, who had tragically disappeared

from her life a year and a half ago, was about to be found.
She would finally be able to see him, touch him, hug him,
tell him how much she loved him. She would finally be able
to accept that he truly was alive and well, would finally be
able to put behind her the terrible months when she'd believed he was dead.

She gave Thad a kiss right on the chin, then turned to face
Clint Roberts. "Mr. Roberts."

"Ms. Phillips. You've already answered my first question. You have no doubt that was your brother on the
phone."

Still smiling broadly, she shook her head and gave him the
same reasons Thad had offered earlier: the things Donny
had said and the voice and the manner in which he'd said
them were all classic Donny. It couldn't have been anyone
else.

"What are you going to do now?" she asked.

"Exactly what you want us to do. We're going to find
him."

Chapter 10

After Clint Roberts had left the house, Thad explained to Lindsey in more detail just what they would do. The pay phone where the call had been made would be placed under surveillance while the neighborhood where it was located would be thoroughly combed. The tape was already on its way to Washington with the female agent who had assisted in investigating the second break-in. The lab at FBI head-quarters there would run it through a spectrum analyzer, along with the two earlier tapes, for a voice print analysis. That would tell them with scientific certainty what Lindsey already knew in her heart: it *had* been Donny.

She was so excited that she couldn't sit still, and later she had trouble falling asleep. She kept remembering special memories about Donny, kept speculating about where he was staying, when he would call her again, when she would see him, until finally exhaustion claimed her and she drifted off.

She had been so happy.

Now, late Thursday afternoon, Thad sat at the table in one of their interview rooms, Clint Roberts across from him. He knew he'd heard the findings Roberts had just announced correctly; he simply couldn't make his mind acknowledge them.

The voice on the tape, the voice that had called Lindsey Lin and big sister, the voice that had brought her such happiness... wasn't Donny's. Even though it sounded exactly like him, even though no one who had known Donny could distinguish one from the other, it wasn't his voice.

It wasn't Donny who had called Lindsey. It wasn't Donny who had sent her those cards. It wasn't Donny who was spending the ransom.

But someone wanted them to think it was.

Someone wanted them to believe Donny was alive.

And that meant, most likely, that he wasn't.

He looked up and met Roberts's sympathetic gaze. "How am I supposed to tell her this?" he asked hoarsely. "You saw her yesterday. She was thrilled. She believes she's finally got indisputable proof that her brother is alive. She believes that any day now she's going to see him, alive and well and whole. She believes that this whole nightmare is about to end." He uttered a low curse. "And I'm supposed to tell her that it's not, that Donny probably died in that fall after all, that this whole thing has just been a scam to divert suspicion from whoever's really got the money?"

He stood up from the table and paced over to the tinted window. Often, when this room was being used for interviews, there were agents on the other side of this glass, observing and listening to the conversation via hidden microphones. But there was no one there today. There was no one around but him and Clint Roberts.

"I can't do this," he said grimly. "I can't destroy her hopes like that."

"Do you want me to tell her?"

Could he do that? Thad wondered, looking at Roberts's reflection in the window. Could he let a virtual stranger break such news to Lindsey? Could he be that cowardly?

"No." He sighed bleakly. "Thanks, but... no." He returned to his chair and picked up the jacket he'd left hanging there. "Any luck on the surveillance?"

"Not yet. That phone booth is located in front of one business and right across the street from another. We're in the process of getting a list of employees for both. Maybe we'll turn up something there."

Thad simply nodded once, then walked out. He stopped at his desk to clear it off, shrugged into his jacket and picked up his briefcase, then left.

It wasn't even five o'clock yet, he realized as he walked to his car. Lindsey wouldn't get home for more than two hours, and he certainly couldn't break such news to her at the shop. Maybe if he asked, she would leave early and let Cassie close up. Then he could meet her at the house and give her the bad news. Then he would know if he still had a future with her.

What was it she'd told him a few nights ago? *I couldn't let you back into my life until now.* Until she'd become convinced that Donny was alive. Until she could no longer blame Thad for Donny's death. Once she knew the truth, that Donny wasn't alive, that she *could* still blame Thad for his death, would she? Would she force him away the way she had before? Would she hate him the way she'd hated him before?

He stopped at a pay phone and dialed her shop. When she answered, he tried to speak in a perfectly normal tone, tried to display none of the bleakness, none of the fear. She was in such a cheery mood that she didn't notice anything. She agreed to leave early, agreed to be at her house waiting when he got there. Could they run right away? she asked, reminding him that they'd missed it this morning, and he agreed, knowing that once he told her the news, she would forget about running...except maybe to run away from *him*.

Rush-hour traffic was heavy, but even with a stop at his apartment en route, he made it to her house in good time. She was sitting on the porch, already wearing gym shorts, a T-shirt, thick padded socks and running shoes, all in white. She greeted him with a kiss, then ushered him into the house to change so they could get started. She had energy to burn.

He changed into his own running clothes because it was easier to do so than to argue with her. But when he came downstairs again, he insisted that she sit down on the sofa. "I have something to tell you," he said grimly.

She sat down, her feet together and her hands folded primly in her lap. "All right, I'm listening."

He tried to stand away from her, across the room, but he couldn't do it. He wound up sitting on the coffee table in front of her, her hands in his, and quietly, unemotionally, he told her the results of the analysis.

Lindsey frowned at him. "What does that mean—the voice prints don't match?"

"It means—" He stopped, searching for gentle words and gentler tones. After clearing his throat, he began again. "It means, Lindsey, that the voices on the tapes aren't the same."

Now her frown turned into a bewildered stare. "Of course they're the same. They're all three Donny's voice."

He shook his head. "Not the tape from last night."

She snatched her hands away and jumped to her feet, pacing restlessly back and forth. "I *heard* that tape. I *talked* to him. That was my brother, Thad. That was Donny!"

Once again he shook his head. "That was someone who sounded virtually identical to him. Lindsey, the analysis proves that the first two tapes—the old tapes—are the same voice. We know beyond a doubt that it was Donny's voice. *I* wore the wire when the second recording was made on the bridge, and he admitted to the first one, the ransom call. But the third tape, last night's tape, is not the same voice. It isn't Donny."

Her steps slowed until she was standing utterly motionless, staring at him as if she'd never seen him before in her life. For a long, long time she simply stood there. When she finally moved, when she finally spoke, it was with a great deal of control. It was in a voice as empty and blank as if it were coming from the air itself instead of a living, breathing, feeling person. "So what you're saying is that someone is pretending to be Donny. That Donny...that my brother didn't survive that fall. That he really is..."

She couldn't say the word. It wouldn't come. It was too final, too cold, too harsh.

Thad stood up and went to her, but didn't touch her. "I'm sorry, Lindsey," he whispered. "I'm sorry we gave you hope. I'm sorry we let you believe. I'm sorry, God, about everything."

His apology didn't register with her—he could see that in her lifeless eyes. She'd heard too much, was trying to comprehend too much, to understand a simple apology.

He touched her—just his hand on her arm—and she flinched. Her rejection carried with it a dark, fearful blow. He withdrew his hand and even took a few steps away from her. "Lindsey..." he began, but he couldn't think of anything to say except I love you, and he was afraid she wouldn't want to hear that ever again.

If she would just react—tears, anger, hatred, screaming—he could handle any of those things. But this coldness, this emptiness... He didn't know how to respond to this. He didn't know whether to touch her or leave her alone, to comfort her or stay away from her.

Then slowly it disappeared. Life returned to her eyes, she blinked as if waking from a dream and a smile, faint and wobbly and infinitely sad but still a smile, came to her lips. "Are you ready to go now?"

He watched her warily. "Go where?"

"Running."

"Lindsey... you understand what I've told you?"

"Yes. The man who called me on the phone last night wasn't Donny. Which probably means that Donny is dead." She picked up her keys from the new dish on the hall table, found no pockets in her shorts and slid them into Thad's pocket. "You told me from the beginning not to get my hopes up too high. You said I had to be prepared for the possibility that Donny really was dead and that someone was pretending otherwise. And you were right. Now, are you ready to go?"

She didn't wait for his answer, but went outside and began a series of slow stretches to warm up her muscles. Stunned by her acceptance of the news he had thought would devastate her, Thad followed her, locking the door behind him.

They didn't talk as they jogged, setting an easy pace on the mile to the park, then picking it up when they reached the trail. Thad kept watching her, bewildered by her attitude, unable to believe that it had been that easy for her. *He* had shown more shock than she had, and he didn't have near the emotional investment in the matter that she did.

Maybe that was it—shock. People reacted to it in different ways. Maybe she hadn't *really* taken in everything he'd said. Maybe it hadn't registered yet that her brother was dead, that he was never coming back to her. Maybe this was her mind's way of protecting her from a shock she couldn't endure.

They ran two miles, three, then four. When they reached their starting point, Thad automatically turned toward the street for the mile home that would give them a total of five, but Lindsey didn't. He swung around and caught up with her again.

"You want to do more than five tonight?"

She didn't reply, didn't even look at him.

Grimly he stayed beside her through another mile, then another. As they started the seventh, he became aware of the discomfort in his side and knew that Lindsey must be feeling the same thing, yet she gave no sign of it. She wasn't used to pushing herself like this, and her muscles had to be protesting; her entire body had to be. Her hair, usually bouncy in its ponytail, was wet and heavy with perspiration, and her shirt clung to her, her face and arms and legs glistening with sweat. Her breathing was ragged and too shallow and her stride had lost its fluid grace.

Finally he decided to force her to stop, but before he could take action, her steps faltered and she slowly collapsed on the track. Thad caught her, lowering her to her knees on the ground, and she clung to him, muscles trembling, chest heaving, her breaths coming in heartrendingly dry sobs. He knelt beside her, holding her, stroking her hair, pressing his face against its damp softness.

"I only wanted two things in my entire life," she whispered thickly. "You and Donny. For weeks after he died, I cried every night, and I promised God I would do anything if He would just bring you and Donny back to me, if He would just make things right again. And then you showed up, and you told me that Donny was alive after all, and I thought—I thought my prayers had been answered!''

Something gave inside her then, and her tears broke free, streaming down her cheeks, soaking into his shirt. Her fingers curled tighter around his arms until he knew they would leave bruises, but he didn't mind the pain. "I don't want him to be dead!" she cried. "Oh, God, Thad, he's my baby brother! How can he be dead?"

For a moment, Thad simply held her, ignoring the curious looks they received from other runners who had to circle around them. It wasn't until one man, a regular that he vaguely recognized, stopped to ask if they needed help that he got her to her feet and guided her to the bank of the small lake, giving her some measure of privacy for her grief.

She cried the sort of tears that made him ache for her, and made him feel her sorrow as if it were his own. In its way, this had to be even worse than losing Donny the first time, for she had already endured and accepted the pain of his death once. Now she had been offered false hope, only to lose that hope.

He held her in his lap, stroked her hair and whispered words that he knew offered little comfort. He wished he could somehow make it easier for her, but all he could do was hold her. Love her.

Slowly her sobs faded and her tears dried, but Lindsey made no move away from Thad. Without his arms around her, she would surely come apart. He was the only thing keeping her together. And so she sat where she was, her face against his damp shirt, the fingers of one hand clenched tightly around his, and she tried desperately not to think, not to question, not to remember. She just wanted to sit and absorb his warmth. His strength. His love.

But she desperately failed in her attempts. Donny was dead. He hadn't miraculously survived that fall, hadn't spent the past eighteen months recuperating somewhere safe, hadn't come back to Atlanta to reclaim his money or to taunt the FBI or to see her again. Just as the FBI had said months ago, even though his body was never found, Donny had died in the fall from that bridge. The water had been cold, the air colder. The river had been shallow and rocky and flowing fast, and the bridge had been high. He had probably been trapped beneath the surface, wedged between rocks or beneath the brush that had lined the banks.

He would probably never be found.

She had wanted this to end, but not like this. She had wanted the phone calls and the break-ins to stop, had wanted Donny to show himself, to turn himself in. She had wanted to see her brother, to hug him, to tell him that she loved him, to know that he was alive and all right. But she hadn't wanted to find out that the calls and the break-ins were all a game. She hadn't wanted to know that someone who knew Donny—someone who knew *her*—could be so cruel, so vicious, so greedy.

"Who is it?" When she asked the question, she felt Thad stiffen slightly, as if startled by the sound of her voice after such a long silence.

He shifted restlessly, sighed, then answered, "I don't know. We had been operating under the assumption that it was definitely Donny. Everything seemed to point in that direction. There's no other suspect. We were never able to find any evidence of a partner, of anyone else who could have been involved on even the most minor level."

"So they'll continue the surveillance on the pay phone and hope that he calls again so they can find out who it is."

Thad shrugged. "That seems to be our best chance."

"Whoever it is, I hope he rots in hell," she said matter-of-factly.

"So do I, sweetheart."

She pulled away from him, sitting up straight, flexing the muscles in her shoulders. Then she cautiously moved off his lap and onto her knees, rising to her feet. She was testing how far away she could get from him before feeling the loss too acutely. It was no more than a few feet. She extended her hands to him, and he stood up and took them. "Let's go home."

By the time they reached her house, the muscles in her legs were aching. She had overdone it on the running, but something had driven her. She remembered thinking that if she ran far enough and long enough, she wouldn't have to face the news that Thad had given her. She wouldn't have to accept Donny's death yet again. But that had been wishful thinking, because she *had* run until she could go no farther, and the grief had shadowed her every step of the way until she'd given in to it.

After a shower, she fixed dinner while Thad took his turn in the bathroom. Then they carried platters of sandwiches and chips out onto the front porch and ate in the early night darkness. They didn't talk—what was there left to say?—but she drew comfort from his presence anyway. It would be hard to let him go in the morning.

What was he feeling? she wondered, capable at last of considering someone other than herself. Anger, she was certain. Even if she weren't the victim of this hoax, even if it had been a total stranger so cruelly deceived, he would be angry that someone could do this.

Guilt, as well. *I'm sorry we gave you hope,* he'd said earlier. *I'm sorry we let you believe.* Of course he was blaming himself for that, as if he somehow should have known the truth, as if he should have been able to look at all the evidence that said Donny *was* alive and see that he wasn't. But she didn't blame him. He had warned her, had cautioned her against being too hopeful, but she'd been eager to believe. She had wanted to believe so badly that nothing Thad told her could have made a difference.

And maybe he felt a little sadness, too? She couldn't say that Thad had loved Donny, but they had shared a certain friendship, stronger at times than others. When she had begged off, they had often gone to baseball or football games together, and when Donny needed advice that Lindsey couldn't provide, he'd gone to Thad for it. Surely Thad must regret Donny's death, for the sake of their own friendship as well as for her loss.

For a moment, she simply watched him. He was seated at the opposite end of the swing, facing her, so his face was in shadow. She could barely make out any details—the straight line of his nose, the even straighter, grim line of his mouth. He was so handsome when he was solemn... and when he was laughing... and when he was angry. He was perfect. And she loved him.

It seemed silly now, sitting here in the dark and thinking about death and loss, to have denied her love even to herself for so long. Did it really matter that he'd unwillingly been involved in Donny's arrest? God knows, he hadn't wanted her brother to die. It had been a tragedy, a terrible end to the nightmare Donny had brought on himself. But blaming Thad was senseless. It meant prolonging the pain and sorrow. It meant that whether Donny was alive or dead, this whole affair would never end. The ugliness would never stop.

A lifetime had passed since that day on the bridge. A lifetime of sorrow and grief, of anger and guilt. It was time to let it go now. Time to let Donny go. Time to quit living in the past and look toward the future. Time to quit hating and hurting. Time to start loving.

"Thad?"

His response was just a soft sound in the quiet night.

"Are you ever going to ask me to marry you?"

She saw how still he became and knew that she'd surprised him. Had he thought that the news about Donny was a blow too strong for their relationship to survive? Had he believed that once again she would push him away, once again hate him because her brother was dead, once again find some way to hold him responsible? She was sorry that she'd given him so little reason to believe. She was sorry she'd given him so little hope for their future.

After a long moment, he exhaled. "I thought I would."

This time the silence was longer, heavier. She was thinking about how much she liked the idea of being his wife, about how wonderful it would be to lie beside him every night, to have that old-fashioned sort of commitment bind them together, to fill this old house with children and happiness and love. She was thinking that her parents, if they had lived, would be happy with her choice of husband. They would be proud to have such a good man for a son-in-law. And Donny, if he had lived, would be as happy as he could be when it came to Thad. In spite of their differences, Donny had never doubted how much she loved Thad.

"Would we live in this house?"

"If you want."

"And have babies?"

"As many as you want."

"When?"

For the first time since he'd sat down across from Clint Roberts that afternoon, Thad smiled. "Assuming that you quit taking birth control pills when we broke up—" he saw from her blush that he was right "—and considering how often we've made love this week without other precautions, I suppose it's possible we could have the first one in nine months or so. Would that be soon enough for you?"

She smiled. "February," she murmured. "That would be nice." Then she became silent again.

The brief exchange left him hurting somewhere down deep inside. She was talking about marriage and babies—marriage to *him*, babies with *him*—but not about love. It was only natural, he supposed, when you'd lost the last member of your family to want to fill the empty places. Of course Lindsey had aunts, uncles and cousins, but that wasn't the same. They were her relatives, not her family.

It was natural when dealing with death to think about life, and what could represent life better than a baby—a new life, a new hope?

And it was also perfectly natural, he defended himself, to want the woman he married to love him the same way he loved her. It was natural to want the mother of his children to have more than just a fondness for their father.

He had told her he would be satisfied with whatever she could give him. Maybe he had lied just a little. He would be *grateful* for whatever she gave him, but as long as it was less than her complete and total love, he would always want more. He would always want it all.

In his own way he was as greedy as Donny had been. He didn't care about money—easy enough to say since he'd always had more than enough of it—but when it came to Lindsey, his greed knew no bounds. He wanted her love, her respect, her admiration, her friendship, her affection and her desire. He wanted everything. Always. Forever.

But she didn't have to know that. She *couldn't* know it. If she ever felt pressured, if she ever felt that she was cheating him, he would lose her. As much as it hurt not to have her love, not having her at all would be far worse. So he would be grateful and he would, as much as he was able, be satisfied. But he would keep hoping. He would keep praying that someday she would give him more.

Lindsey sighed, but it was more of a shiver. "Would I get to meet your family someday?"

"Would you like to?" Beyond her dismay that they'd sent their children to boarding schools, she had never shown much interest in his parents. Maybe it was because she'd had her own family—Donny, with the possibility for a sister-in-law, as well as nieces and nephews in the future. Now things had changed. The only grandparents her children would have would be McNallys. The only uncles, aunts and cousins they would have were McNallys.

She nodded. "Do you think they would like me?"

He smiled gently at the uncertainty in her voice. "I think my father would love you, and my brothers and my sister would like you very much."

"And your mother?"

"My mother would want to be sure that you were properly sorry for breaking my heart." Reaching out, he found her hand and pulled her across the swing, lifting her so that she straddled his thighs. "Of course, she would only have to look to see that you put it back together again, so naturally she would love you, too."

She rested her head against his shoulder. "I am sorry," she whispered, her voice becoming thick with unexpected tears. "I'm so sorry, Thad."

He set the swing in motion and held her close, patting her back, occasionally whispering softly to her. Finally he took her inside and upstairs to the bedroom. Like a weary child, she let him undress her and tuck her into bed. He sat with her until she was all cried out, until there couldn't possibly be another mournful sob inside her, and still he sat there.

With exhaustion from the tears came sleep. As her breathing slowed and evened out, he bent over, smoothed her hair from her face and kissed her forehead, whispering in the quiet, "I love you, Lindsey."

Eyes closed, she smiled a sweet, innocent smile. "I love you, too," she said with a sigh.

He knew better than to be hopeful. She was exhausted. She was overwrought. She had suffered a great shock, had been forced to endure for the second time the pain of losing her brother. She was too weary to know what she was saying. She wouldn't even remember it in the morning.

He *knew* those things. But the pleasure was too strong to be ignored—the *joy* was too strong. He had thought he would never hear those words from her again. And even though she was exhausted, overwrought and more than half-asleep, they were still the sweetest words he'd ever heard.

Wakefulness came slowly to Lindsey. For a long time she lay motionless as layer after layer of sleep peeled away, until finally she knew it was the middle of the night. The house was quiet, the only sounds that of her own breathing and Thad's mingling with the soft calls of the whippoorwills outside.

Thad lay on his side, and she was snuggled against his back. He put out such heat that extra covers were rarely necessary, even in winter. He'd been so good to her last night, she remembered, so gentle and tender that just thinking about it made her ache with love. Someday she would repay him, she vowed, by being the best wife, lover, friend and mother any man could ever ask for. She would spend the rest of her life repaying him.

Slowly she shifted positions. The movement made her calf muscles ache, and it brushed her breasts against his back and made them ache, too. She was aroused, she realized. Her skin was sensitized, her breasts swollen, her nipples hard and the need that pooled between her thighs was hot and slick and demanding release. Was that what had awakened her? she wondered with a sleepy smile. Or was it that heat that filled her hand, as she covered him, cupped him, and—judging by the length and hardness—aroused him?

She stroked him gently, and he grew harder, then moaned softly. Maybe she should stop and let him sleep. She started to withdraw her hand, but he turned onto his back and trapped it with his own, pressing her palm flat against his arousal. "I was having an erotic dream," he murmured in a sleep-softened, passion-roughened voice. "But it wasn't a dream at all." Raising his arms over his head, he stretched out kinked muscles, straightened his spine, then arched his back. Then he pulled Lindsey into his arms and gave her a long, lazy kiss. "How do you feel?"

She refused to let his soft, concerned question make her think of last night. Instead she nipped at his chin and bluntly replied, "Hot."

He grinned drowsily. "Slide on over here and take me inside you, and we'll see what we can do about that."

She promptly obeyed him, lifting herself over him, reaching down to gently grasp his hardness and guide him inside. He filled her so completely, so tightly, that she couldn't stop the satisfied little groan that escaped her, and it made him chuckle. "Ah, Lindsey, you're a beautiful woman."

Bending low, she gave him a kiss as long and lazy as his had been. Then she tugged at his lower lip with her teeth before impudently pointing out, "Beautiful, huh? It's dark, you're half-asleep, and you don't have your glasses on. You can't even see me."

She was right. All he saw in the dark night was shadows and shapes. But he didn't need his eyes to know that she was beautiful right now. His hands told him. His heart. His soul.

"I could stay like this forever," she sighed, resting her cheek against his shoulder.

"Could you, now?" He reached between them, slipped one finger past her soft curls and stroked her.

Lindsey shuddered and gasped and forced his hand away. Taking his other hand, she lifted them both about his head, forcing them to the mattress with her hands on his wrists, holding him prisoner to the caresses of her body. Even though he could have freed himself at any moment, he didn't. He liked the idea of being her prisoner. He liked letting her have control. He liked being at her oh-so-tender mercy.

She moved against him in exquisitely slow torture, sheathing him, drawing away, sinking again. He watched the sinuous movements of the shadow that was her and knew by the way her breathing quickened, by the way her body tightened around him and by the way her hips arched faster, harder, that she was close to the end. And it was then that he wished for his glasses and lamplight so he could see the pleasure overtake her, so that he could see the flush spread through her body and her eyes close and her lips part, so he could see her face when she reached that shattering completion.

With a measure of control he didn't know she possessed, she became utterly motionless, poised over him, head tilted back, breathing strained. He moved inside her, and she shook her head. "Not yet," she whispered. "I don't want to..." She broke off in a low groan as shivers rippled over her.

"We can always make love again, sweetheart," he whispered to her, and she shook her head again.

"I want this to last...." Slowly she stroked him, up then back down, millimeter by millimeter. Then, denying her own words, she repeated the movement, faster, harder, wilder, until, only moments later, she was shuddering, crying, gasping, and an instant after that the same delicately savage tremors rocketed through his own body as he emptied himself into her.

She sagged against him, her body drained, and as she struggled for breath, she softly cried his name in between her tears. But these weren't tears of sorrow, he realized as he stroked her, quieted her, reassured her. They were tears caused by an overload of sensation, an overload of emotion. They were tears of love.

* * *

Lindsey didn't get up when her alarm went off Friday morning. She reached out from beneath the covers and shut it off, then rolled onto her back, brushed her hair from her face and stared up at the ceiling.

She felt like hell. Her head was aching, her eyes were puffy and sore and the muscles in her calves protested every movement she made, yet there was a sweet ache between her thighs that made her smile with pure, feminine satisfaction. *We can always make love again, sweetheart,* Thad had told her during the night, and they had, more times than she'd thought possible. Slow and tender, fast and near-violent, hungry and hard and hot and wicked. She felt thoroughly satisfied, thoroughly happy, thoroughly loved.

Then the memories of last night came rushing back.

Donny was dead.

How could she have forgotten that? How could it not have been the first thought in her mind the very instant she woke up?

She heard the sound of running water and realized that the other side of her bed was empty. Thad had been so good to her last night—both before they'd gone to bed and after. She didn't deserve it, didn't deserve *him,* but since she had been blessed with this second chance, she was certainly going to take him. She was going to spend the rest of her life with him, loving him and praying that she could make up to him for everything bad in their past.

He came out of the bathroom, wearing only trousers. He was already getting dressed for work, she thought with regret. She wished he would come back to bed and make love to her again, even though she doubted he could find the strength. She wished he would stay with her, wished he would call in sick and spend the rest of the day right here with her. But he had obligations . . . and so did she.

When he realized that she was awake, he came to the bed and sat down beside her. "Good morning."

She gave him a taut little smile.

"How do you feel?"

He had asked her that question last night, and she had answered bluntly, honestly, not how she felt in general but how she had felt at that very moment. Now she gave it a brief consideration. "I've never been hung over, but I imagine this must be what it's like," she said hoarsely.

"I'll get you some aspirin."

She stopped him before he could get up. "Thank you for staying with me last night."

His only response was a tender kiss, then he went into the bathroom, returning a moment later with two aspirin and a small cup of water. Lindsey sat up and swallowed them, then rolled her neck to one side. When she pushed back the covers and reached for her robe, Thad blocked her way. "What are you doing?"

"I have to get ready for work, just like you."

"Lindsey, you can't go to work today. You need—"

"To be alone in this house with nothing to do but think, and nothing to think about but Donny? To spend the rest of the day the same way I spent last evening—crying—only without the benefit of your arms around me?" She shook her head. "I need to work, Thad. I need to get away from here and to stay busy."

"I'll take the day off and stay with you. We can go for a drive. We can get out of the city for the weekend. We can to to Asheville or Charleston or Savan—"

She stopped him with her fingers on his lips. "I need to work. If I'm not there, the shop doesn't open. I can let my personal life go to hell, but I can't let it affect my business. Besides, we're having dinner with Tess and Deke tomorrow night, remember?"

"They'll understand. And your customers will understand. Close the shop for today and let Cassie run it tomorrow."

She shook her head. "Please, Thad, this is what I need to do. I can't let this person upset my life any more than what he already has. I have to stick with my routine. I have to keep my life as normal as possible. I have to go to work. But please, will you come over tonight?"

He raised one hand to stroke her cheek. "Of course, I will. I'll even meet you for lunch, if you'll let me. Sandwiches at your desk?"

"That would be nice." Like a cat greedy for attention, she leaned into his light caress, her eyes starting to drift shut as his fingers performed a magic that aspirin couldn't come close to. But just before her lashes met, when everything she saw was through that delicate screen, she saw the bruises on his arm—five small oval shapes in a pattern that was repeated on his other arm. Immediately she remembered holding onto him at the park, and she knew that she had caused them. Her face flooded with shame. "Why didn't you tell me I was hurting you?" she asked quietly, rubbing one finger lightly over the largest of the ten marks.

"Because I didn't care about the pain."

And even if he had, he still wouldn't have said anything, because he'd known she needed him. He'd known that she had needed someone to hold on to, someone to anchor herself to so her grief wouldn't sweep her away.

She pressed her face against his chest for a long moment, then looked up at him, her voice husky once again. "I don't think I could survive this again without you."

"You will survive because you're strong. Because people are depending on you—your family and friends, Cassie, your customers, everyone you do business with and all those babies we haven't had yet. You will survive because I won't go through losing you a second time."

Just when she thought she would start crying all over again, he gave her a gentle push. "You'd better get ready for work, sweetheart."

They were on their way out the door nearly an hour later when Lindsey noticed the blinking light on the answering machine. She was certain there hadn't been a message when she'd gotten home from work last night; she would have noticed when she'd laid the mail on the desk. She was almost as sure that no one had called while they were running. Maybe while they'd been sitting on the porch... She hadn't been in any condition when Thad had brought her inside to care about messages.

He was waiting at the open door, wondering what was taking her so long, when he, too, noticed the light. He walked over to stand beside her. After a look from her, he pressed the playback button.

There was nothing on the tape—maybe fifteen seconds' worth of silence before the caller hung up. "It could have been a wrong number," he said with a shrug.

She nodded, fully understanding the other possibility, too: it could have been the man pretending to be her brother. She understood, as well, that Thad shared her hope that it *was* the man. For every time he called, he increased the FBI's chances of catching him. And she would willingly take a hundred calls a day from him, would pretend that he was her brother, would act like she was happy he'd called, if it would help catch him.

She pressed the erase button just as Thad touched her arm. "Are you all right?"

She considered it, sighed, then nodded. Yes, she was all right. And with Thad at her side, she always would be.

Chapter 11

Work wasn't the lifesaver Lindsey had depicted to Thad. Even at her busiest times, she still found a few seconds to think about everything that had happened. She spent most of the morning torn between sorrow for Donny, fury at whoever was behind this game and overwhelming love for Thad.

When he left after lunch with a promise to pick her up at seven, she wandered over to the rack that displayed the year-round line of Lindsey's Blooms. There was a series of cards, eight in all, grouped between Birthdays and Friendship under the category of Love. They were I'm-glad-we-met-and-fell-in-love type cards, and she had written every one of them with Thad in mind. There had been a time when loneliness had nearly overcome bitter anger, and she had almost sent him one of the cards. With her luck, that would have been the time when he was most heavily involved with Carole or one of the others, she thought with a smile.

She remembered which one she had almost sent, and she picked it up now. Like all her other cards, it was undeniably sentimental, the kind of card a woman was likely to send a man, but rarely the other way around. The cover showed a redbud tree in full bloom, a faithful rendering of the one in her backyard, and the verse inside spoke of love, of caring and sharing and commitment and forever. Taking a matching envelope, she went into the workroom and sat down at the desk. There, after composing and discarding a half-dozen messages in her head, she finally found the right words—or as close as she could ever get—and added them to the card. Then she sealed it in its envelope and slipped it inside her purse.

After a moment, she picked up the photograph of Donny that had sat on her desk since the day she'd moved in. For a while she looked at him impartially, seeing a tall, thin young man with a boyish grin and a careless attitude so strong that it transcended the camera and time.

Then she sighed softly, a bit sadly. He had been her brother, and she had loved him dearly. For the nineteen years of his life following their parents' deaths, she had made him the center of her attention, the center of her own life. She had placed her needs, goals and desires a distant second to his own. She had devoted herself to him, not only while he lived, but after he had died, too.

But not anymore.

She put the frame back, but not in the center, not in the place of honor. Then she opened the bottom drawer of her desk, reached into the very back, beneath stacks of sketches for new ideas and verses for rejected ones. She drew out the oak frame she had placed there months ago, unable to keep it in her house any longer but unable to throw it away, either. For a moment she just looked at it, at the image of herself and Thad, arm in arm, remembering the day it had been taken, remembering how wonderfully happy her life had been then, how utterly in love she had been. When she'd taken this picture from its place on the living room table and brought it here, she had believed that she would never be happy again. She had been convinced that she would never love again.

Thank God she had been wrong.

She wiped the frame and the glass free of dust with a soft cloth, then set it where the other picture had stood. She would always love Donny, but he was in her past. This—Thad and herself together, happy and in love—this was her future.

This was her life.

Although there were other things she should do—like contact her Aunt Louise and her cousins and pass along the news about Donny—Lindsey readily agreed that evening when Thad suggested they skip going home and go out to dinner instead. And just as an added bonus, he told her with a charming smile as she shut off the lights at the shop, he was even willing to take her to the Comedy Spot afterward to catch Shawn's act.

"I'm impressed by your generosity," she said, really meaning it. Stand-up comedy had never been high on his list of pleasurable pastimes—probably ranking somewhere between having a root canal and being involved in a shoot-out—leading to Donny's insistence that he had no sense of humor. Lindsey knew that wasn't true; he simply found there was little to enjoy about sitting in a smoky club listening to routines that were sometimes painful in their lack of humor when he could be doing any of a hundred other things instead. Adding that to the jealousy he'd recently developed for Shawn, she was doubly touched by his offer.

"Don't be," he said, taking the keys and locking the door behind them before they turned toward the bank to make her daily deposit. "It's a bribe. I expect you to be equally generous when we get home tonight."

"Oh, you do, huh? Just exactly what is it that you expect me to give you?"

He moved to the edge of the sidewalk and gave her a long, leisurely look. She expected a shamelessly sexy response, but when he spoke in a suddenly husky voice, his answer was sweet and touching. "Whatever you want, Lindsey. I'll take anything."

She thought of the card inside her purse and the offer it made: love. The kind of love that he'd given her—free, without demands, without limits. Unconditional. Would that be enough, she wondered, to make him forgive the things she'd said to him, the way she'd turned away from him, the blame she had heaped on him?

She knew it was. He would never punish her for the things she'd said and done when grief had overwhelmed her. He would forgive her because that was the kind of man he was. He would forgive her because he loved her.

And God help her, how she loved him.

She made the deposit at the bank, then they returned to Thad's car. He had already made reservations at the same elegant restaurant he'd taken her to on their first date two weeks ago and had called ahead to the club to verify that Shawn was indeed appearing tonight and find out what time his shows would begin. She suspected that he was coddling her, keeping her busy, away from the house and the phone, but she didn't mind.

Dinner was relaxing—excellent food in a quiet atmosphere with the perfect companion. When it was over, for a moment Lindsey considered telling Thad that he'd done such an outstanding job of arranging it that they could forget Shawn and the club and go on home. But she hadn't seen Shawn in a while, and she needed to tell him about Donny. She decided it wouldn't hurt to delay going home by another hour or two.

The club was crowded when they got there, and the only table they could find was a tiny one against the side wall. Lindsey claimed it while Thad went to the bar to get a beer for himself and a soda for her. By the time he returned, Shawn was five minutes into his routine.

Only half listening to Shawn's patter, Thad scanned the large room, his disinterested gaze pausing at this table or that, watching the different reactions to the act. Some of the customers—the majority, he admitted—seemed to find it hilarious. Some limited their responses to occasional smiles, and only a few, like him, seemed unimpressed.

Suddenly his gaze locked on a couple seated at a center table. The man was one he worked with, one of the agents assigned to the Phillips case. The woman with him had her back to Thad, but he could see enough to know it wasn't the guy's wife. Then she turned and made a slow, lazy survey of the room, and he recognized her, too. It was Gina, the lone female agent assigned to this team. She didn't show even a hint of recognition when her gaze passed over him and Lindsey.

Suspicious now, Thad looked around again, careful not to bring attention to himself. Not even Lindsey noticed his interest in the customers. She didn't notice, either, when he spotted the other two agents standing at the end of the long bar.

He picked up his beer and took a long drink as he looked at the man who held the other agents' attention. Standing center stage, microphone in one hand, and loving every minute in the spotlight, Shawn Howard looked innocent and harmless. But a man didn't draw the FBI's attention by being innocent, and he didn't get himself set up for surveillance by being harmless.

Shawn Howard. Thad didn't want to believe it, didn't even want to let the suspicion completely form. Shawn adored Lindsey. For eighteen months he had been her best friend, her surrogate brother. He had loved her and let her love him in return, at a time when she'd desperately needed to love someone. He had gotten her through that miserable time.

But it made sense. Shawn had been Donny's roommate for two years. He'd been his friend since junior high. He'd had an opportunity to find out about the Mother's Day cards; he'd certainly heard Donny call his sister Lin; he'd probably even heard Donny refer to Thad as the G-man. It would also explain why the intruder had had a key to her house. Everyone had simply assumed that Donny had had his keys with him on the bridge that day, but Shawn could have had them, or sometime during the two years he could have had a copy made.

It explained why the handwriting experts couldn't say for certain that the writing on the card was or wasn't Donny's. Living in the same apartment, Shawn must have seen samples of Donny's writing—notes, a grocery list or something. It had probably taken him only a few hours to turn out a near-perfect copy.

It would also explain why Donny's fingerprints weren't found at the house or on the cards or on the outside of the pocketknife. And why the clerk at the shop in Covington had insisted that the man who'd bought those cards had looked like Donny but different. Tall, slim, blond-haired, blue-eyed and handsome—the description fit them both.

But it didn't explain the phone call. Shawn's voice was higher-pitched than Donny's had been. He had less of a drawl and usually spoke in the rapid-fire manner common to comedians.

Yet weren't impressions a tool of the trade for all successful comedians? How many times on television had he seen and heard impressions of various actors or politicians done so well that the next time he heard that person actually speak, he sounded less like himself than the comic had? Maybe Shawn included such bits in his repertoire.

As if in answer to his silent questions, Shawn moved into the next part of his act. He started with cartoon characters and animals—good imitations that didn't require much talent. Then he moved on to people—former presidents, well-known actors, musicians, even other comedians—with an accuracy that was uncanny.

Feeling sick deep down inside, Thad glanced at Lindsey. She was smiling, a really sincere, happy smile. After the sadness of the past twenty-four hours, it was a treasured gift—and it would disappear when she found out that the man who had made her believe that her brother was alive, the man who had played games with her mind and her heart all for the sake of money, the man who she hoped would rot in hell, was her dear friend Shawn. How could she cope with one more loss when she hadn't yet recovered from the last one?

He leaned across the table, his mouth close to her ear. "I'll be back in a few minutes," he said.

She nodded and smiled again, then turned her attention back to Shawn.

Thad went outside, passing the two agents at the bar on his way. Almost immediately, one of them, a man named Curtis, followed. They walked around the side of the building into the parking lot, where Curtis pulled out a pack of cigarettes and lit one. "What are you doing here?" he asked as he exhaled a stream of smoke. "We weren't expecting you."

Thad pushed his hands into his pockets and took a step back to avoid the smoke. "Haven't you gotten enough of that in there?" he asked, overly annoyed by the minor irritation.

"In there all I have to do is breathe. I don't need a cigarette. Out here I do."

"Is that the pay phone?" Thad gestured with a nod, and the other agent responded with one. He muttered a curse. "I never thought to ask Roberts for the address, or I would have known immediately. It's Shawn Howard, isn't it? He's the one who's been calling Lindsey. He's the one with the money."

"We think so. I guess this means you're not here on business."

"No. I had to tell her last night that her brother is dead after all. Naturally she didn't take it too well. I thought..." He shrugged. "Hell, Shawn always makes her laugh."

"She doesn't suspect anything?"

Thad shook his head. "Where is Roberts? Is he working tonight?"

"He's at the office. He's working on the warrant."

"I'd like to talk to him," Thad said thoughtfully. "You guys are going to stay with Shawn until you pick him up, right? I can take Lindsey home and leave her there without worrying whether or not she's safe, can't I?"

"He won't get out of our sight. Besides, he's scheduled to do another show at midnight. He'll hang around here until he's done."

With a muttered thanks, Thad went back inside. The stage was empty, but he had no trouble finding Shawn. He was sprawled in Thad's seat at their table, talking to Lindsey. For a moment Thad held back, studying her face. There was such affection, such love, there. How badly was she going to be hurt this time? he wondered grimly.

* * *

Lindsey rested her arms on the tabletop and leaned toward Shawn. "I was going to call you today, but...I just couldn't."

His smile immediately faded and was replaced by a look of concern. "News about Donny?"

She nodded.

"Lindsey, what is it?"

She swallowed hard. She kept believing that she was taking this rather well, then suddenly tears would form in her eyes or her throat would tighten or the pain would grow sharp. She knew, from past experience, that it would take time to get over this. Time and love and Thad. "It's not Donny," she said gently. "It isn't Donny who's doing these things. He—he apparently did die in the fall."

"But—you were so sure. The FBI was sure. When—what happened? What made you change your mind?"

"I got a phone call two nights ago. The FBI recorded it, and they compared it to two tapes that were definitely Donny's voice, and...this one didn't match. It wasn't him. It's just someone pretending."

Shawn hit the table with his fist, rattling the glasses there. "My God, Lindsey, I can't believe anyone would do this to you. Are they doing anything to catch this bastard?"

"They've had the pay phone where the call came from under surveillance, so maybe they'll get something there." She looked past him and saw Thad and smiled at him. He made his way through the crowd to stand beside her, and she reached for his hand. "I do believe I saw him smile tonight," she told Shawn in a lighter tone.

"Well, that's progress. You keep bringing him back, and I guarantee we'll get a laugh out of him yet." Shawn stood up and offered his hand to Thad. He had to release Lindsey's to accept it. "Lindsey told me about Donny. God, I was hoping..."

"We were all hoping," Thad said quietly, taking Lindsey's hand again when his was free.

"You're not working on this, are you?"

"No." Thad smiled faintly. "Conflict of interest."

That made Shawn smile, and he looked to Lindsey. "He has potential. He just might have a sense of humor buried in there somewhere after all." Then he grew somber again. "Tell your associates to hurry up and find this guy. And until they do, you take care of her."

"Believe me, I will." He finished his beer, then smiled down at Lindsey. "Are you ready to go?"

She nodded. She stood up and hugged Shawn. "I enjoyed the act tonight," she said, then sighed. "I needed the smiles. Come by sometime this weekend, will you? I've missed you."

With his hand flat against her spine, Thad guided her through the club and outside. At the car, after he unlocked and opened the door, she leaned forward to kiss his cheek. "Thanks."

"For what?"

"For trying to cheer me up. For being nice to Shawn."

That had been one of the hardest things he'd ever done. Knowing what he knew, feeling the way he did, he'd wanted nothing more than to beat that loving, concerned friend act right out of him. But just as he had pretended inside, he pretended now, offering her an easy, careless smile. "Listen, sweetheart, I have to go by the office, so I'm going to take you home, all right?"

"Work? This late on a Friday night?"

"It shouldn't take too long. I just need to check some things."

"Will you come over when you're done?"

"Of course."

"Okay."

It was that easy, he thought with some small amount of surprise, as he got into the car and backed out. There was no annoyance that he was leaving in the middle of their date to work. No resentment that his job had interfered with their plans. No bitterness that instead of making love to her, he was going to leave her alone in the house that only this morning she'd been so eager to get out of.

"I'll make it as quick as I can," he told her as he walked her to the door. "I'll be back before you have time to miss me."

She unlocked the door, then turned and wrapped her arms around his neck. She gave him a long, sweet, lazy, hungry kiss that sent desire spiraling through his body and caused his immediate arousal. When he pulled her hips against his and she felt it, she ended the kiss and gave him a seductive smile. "I already miss you."

She pulled away, leaving his arms empty, and for one cold instant leaving his heart empty, as well. Then she smiled again as she slowly closed the door. He waited to hear the click of the lock, then for a moment just stood there, rubbing the back of his neck with one hand. He didn't *really* have to go to the office. If he had to know more about Howard, he could call Roberts and get everything over the phone. Then he could leisurely undress Lindsey and satisfy—at least, temporarily—this need that she had stirred in him.

But he didn't want to discuss this on the phone in her house. He didn't want her to have the slightest suspicion that something was wrong until Shawn Howard was locked up safely away from her.

He was more than halfway to his office when he glanced at the passenger seat and saw the envelope there. The color was difficult to describe—soft crimson, he would say. It was definitely one of Lindsey's. Had it fallen from her purse when she'd gotten out of the car? He didn't think so. It was arranged too neatly in the center of the seat, as if it had deliberately been placed there. As if she'd wanted him to find it.

The moment he'd parked, he picked up the envelope and turned it over. The flap was sealed on the point, and he easily pulled it open, sliding the card out. He hardly glanced at the front, only skimmed the printed message inside, but focused immediately on the handwritten note. Her writing was beautiful, the style more like calligraphy than script. The card was definitely intended for him—the note was headed with his name—and it was about love and forgiveness: how she had thought she could never forgive him for his part in Donny's death, how her bitterness over that had almost destroyed them, how she knew now that *she* was the one who needed forgiveness.

He hadn't caused her brother's death, she had written, nor had his job. Only Donny could be held responsible for what had happened to him. And only *she* could be held responsible for what had happened to *them*. She had resented his job, had resented the secrecy it had required, had resented that his loyalty to the Bureau had been greater than his loyalty to her. She had known in her mind that she was being unfair and irrational, but had refused to see it with her heart because it was too painful. Now it was too painful to remain blind to the truth, too painful to continue to deny her love.

I do love you, Thad. In spite of how desperately I tried not to, I always have. And I always will. Please forgive me.

It was signed, simply, *Lindsey.*

Smiling tenderly, he read the note again, then read the printed message, then finally looked at the front. Bless her, how had she known how badly he'd needed to hear those things? And how had she known that written words such as these, words that had been carefully planned and thought out, were so much more convincing than anything she might have said in person?

Regretting his decision to leave her, he replaced the card in its envelope and slipped it in the breast pocket of his coat. Then he got out and went inside, finding Clint Roberts and three other agents at work in the office.

"Curtis said you'd shown up at the club," Roberts remarked. "We've been waiting for you."

"What have you got on Shawn?"

"A phone call was made to Lindsey's house last night at nine-fifteen. The caller hung up when he got the answering machine and went into the Comedy Spot. Here's his picture." He slid a grainy photograph across the desk. "It took us a while to find out who he was. According to his credit history, he's living way above his means, but he isn't in debt. So where's his money coming from?"

Thad looked at the photo. Where, indeed? Had he been Donny's partner, or had he simply discovered the money after Donny's death and found it an opportunity he couldn't pass up? "When are you going to pick him up?"

"As soon as we can get a warrant." Roberts gave him an exasperated look. "It's late Friday night, not exactly the best time to be doing our kind of business in Atlanta. We had to track Frank Harris down at a party out in Marietta, and he's trying to find a judge."

Thad nodded absently, still studying the photo. Frank Harris had taken over the job of U.S. Attorney more than two years ago. He was a good man, a good prosecutor and he always worked well with the Bureau. He would get them what they wanted as quickly as possible.

There was nothing more to learn here, and Lindsey was at home waiting for him. Thad returned the photograph to Roberts and started to say good-night when one of the other agents interrupted him.

"Curtis just called in. Howard left the club."

"I thought he had another show at midnight," Roberts protested.

"He does. Apparently, he's skipping it. They thought he was heading for his apartment, but about halfway there he changed his mind." The agent paused, then glanced at Thad. "It seems he's going to Lindsey Phillips's house instead."

And Lindsey was home. Alone. Where *he'd* left her. Swearing under his breath, Thad started for the door. He heard Roberts yell his name, but he was already stepping into the elevator, punching the button for the ground floor. If Howard hurt her, if he even so much as scared her, Thad would kill him. It was that simple.

When the doorbell rang, Lindsey glanced at her watch. Less than thirty minutes. Thad had made good time. She didn't bother to look out the window, but unlocked the door and swung it wide open. "That didn't take you—" When she saw Shawn, her smile faltered, but only for a moment. "I wasn't expecting you."

"You changed the damned locks, didn't you?"

She stared blankly at him. "Yes, I—I did. How did you know that?" Then she saw the keys he was holding in his hand, keys that were secured on a painfully familiar chain, and her fingers tightened on the door.

"You told me everything else. How did you manage to forget about the locks?"

She moved to close the door, but he was quicker. He shoved her back, stepped inside and slammed the door behind him. While she stared dazedly at him, he reached back to secure the lock, then started toward her. She backed away until the edge of the hall table was biting into her legs. "You, Shawn?" she whispered brokenly. "You were the one who sent me those cards? Who put that money in my account? Who broke in here? You were the one who called me, pretending to be Donny? Why? *Why?*"

He ran his fingers through his hair. "What else could I do? I was sitting on over two hundred grand, Lindsey. Two hundred thousand dollars! And I had no way to spend it without bringing attention to myself...unless everyone believed that Donny was still alive."

"You bastard!" she spat out. "You were my *friend!* You knew how badly his death hurt me! You knew it almost killed me, too! How could you make me think he was alive? How could you make me go through losing him again?"

"I didn't have a choice, Lindsey. Can't you see that?" Shawn sighed heavily and let Donny's keys fall to the floor. They were useless now. He didn't need them.

She stared at them, at the brass oval painted with a gleaming black 1965 Mustang. That was Donny's car—an old beat-up black Mustang that had been made before he was born. He had loved that car. And he had loved this friend. And Lindsey had loved him, too. That made his betrayal even harder to accept.

"Get out of my house." She heard the demand, then realized that it came from her. She started toward the door, intending to open it and somehow force him to leave, but he stepped in front of her.

"I don't want to hurt you, Lindsey."

She started to mock that, but then he pulled his hand from his pocket, and in it was clutched a small, nasty-looking gun. She stepped back so suddenly that she almost tripped. Where was Thad? she wondered desperately. How long would it take him to finish his business and come home? She wanted him here *now,* wanted him here to put a stop to this, to arrest Shawn and send him away.

But almost immediately she amended that. How would Shawn react to Thad's arrival? If he found it necessary to pull a gun on her—she, who couldn't hurt a fly—how big a threat would he consider Thad, an FBI agent, who carried his own gun?

Her voice trembling, she said, "Shawn, put the gun away, please. You don't need that here. Come into the living room, and we'll talk. I—I'll try to understand what you've done. Maybe—maybe I can even help you."

Uneasily she forced herself to turn her back on him, to start into the living room. A moment later she heard the creak of wood that indicated he was following her. She sat down on the sofa, her hands clenched tightly together, but he had too much nervous energy to sit. Instead he paced back and forth, sometimes pausing to peek out the front curtains. "Is someone out there, Shawn?" she asked, sounding calmer than she felt.

"Yeah, four cops or FBI agents or whatever. They followed me from the club. It's their fault I'm here." He turned suddenly to look at her and waved the gun to make his point. "After what you told me at the club, I was just going to go home, get the money and leave. I was going to disappear. I didn't intend to threaten anyone. I didn't intend to have to use *this*." He looked for a moment at the gun as if he hadn't seen it before, then remembered his explanation. "But they were at the club—they were there when you were, watching me. Did you know that? Did McNally tell you?"

She shook her head.

"Of course not. Good old Thad. You can always count on him to keep his mouth shut when it counts. But they followed me when I left. I decided I couldn't risk it, not by myself. I needed an advantage. I needed a way to guarantee that they'd let me get my money and leave—some kind of insurance. And of course I thought of you. McNally would never let them endanger your life. If he knew I had you, he would make sure I got away safely. He would make sure no harm came to you.''

"You mean to use me as a hostage?'' Her voice went up sharply on the last word. There couldn't be any more surprises, she thought bitterly. She'd had enough. To think that Shawn—good, sweet, gentle Shawn whom she'd known and loved since he was fifteen years old!—could do such a horrible thing! That he could be so cruel, so cold, so evil! It was more than she could take in, more shocking information than her mind was capable of processing.

"I won't hurt you, Lindsey,'' Shawn said earnestly, crouching in front of her. "I swear, if you just do what I say, I won't hurt you. I just want to get out of here. I want to be left alone with my money.''

"*Your* money?'' She gave a shudder. "Shawn, that money isn't *yours!* It belongs to that poor old lady's family! It's ransom, stolen money, dirty money!''

He gave her a chilling smile. "Donny didn't share your disgust. He spent nearly thirty thousand of it before he died. He wanted me to give the rest of it to you. He honestly thought you would take it. He was a fool.''

Lindsey shrank away from him, frightened and angry and repulsed. "You were Donny's partner in the kidnapping.'' She said it flatly, expecting a confirmation. Instead he denied it.

"I wouldn't kidnap an old lady. I didn't know anything about it until the day he died. I came home from work and found a note on my bed. It said McNally thought he was going to arrest him, but he was wrong. Donny had no intentions of going to prison. He was weak, you know? He always wanted everything taken care of for him, and he knew that there was no way in hell anyone could take care of the mess he'd gotten himself into this time. If he let McNally arrest him, he'd wind up in prison for sure, and it would have killed him. So he killed himself.''

Lindsey shoved him away and jumped to her feet, hugging her arms across her stomach. "I don't believe you," she whispered, but there was no sound to her voice. Then it came, strong and thick with tears. "Donny didn't kill himself! He *fell* from that bridge! He was struggling with Thad, and he fell! He didn't *want* to die! It was an accident, a terrible accident!"

Shawn gathered her into his arms, persisting even when she struggled against him. "I knew McNally would never tell you the truth. He'd rather let you blame him than tell you what a weak, spineless coward your brother was. But it's true, Lindsey. It was in the note Donny left me. That's why he chose that particular place. He went out there the weekend before to make sure the bridge was high enough, to make sure he would die. He couldn't face prison, Lindsey. It scared him like nothing else ever had."

She didn't believe him, couldn't believe him! Not her brother! Donny loved being alive. He would never kill himself! Yet what he said made sense. It was like Thad to hide the truth if he thought it would hurt her and let her blame him instead. And it was like Donny to look for an easier way out of whatever predicament he found himself in. Besides, why would Shawn lie? At this point, what did he have to gain by lying or to lose by being honest?

She felt the tears stinging her eyes again, but this time she didn't know if they were for Donny, for Shawn, for Thad or for herself. They blocked her throat when she tried to speak, and she had to give herself a moment to regain control. Then she freed herself from Shawn's embrace and walked away. "So Donny deliberately jumped from the bridge. How did *you* get the money?"

"He'd hidden it in my car—he'd had the keys because I had borrowed his that morning. That was why I had the key to your house. Anyway, his note said that he wanted me to give the money to you. You deserved it, he said, after everything he'd put you through." Shawn laughed.

"He was stupid enough to think you'd keep it. But I knew you wouldn't. I knew the first thing you would do would be to call McNally. You'd turn it over to the FBI, and they would give it back to the old woman's family. And they were rich, Lindsey. They already had more money than they knew what to do with, you know? And I'd never had any, never in my entire life. I had always struggled for everything, and suddenly here was two hundred and twenty thousand dollars. Do you even know how much money that is, Lindsey? Have you ever imagined it? Two hundred and twenty thousand dollars in tens and twenties?''

This time his laughter was more frightening, more reckless. It scared Lindsey all the way down to her toes.

"I drove out of town to a secluded spot and counted it that night. It would take me years to earn that much money, and there it was in my car, and it was mine. All I had to do was wait—wait for all the fuss to die down, for everyone to forget about Donny and the money." He shook his head grimly. "Then I realized that they were never going to forget. The bills had been marked—I'd read that in the paper. The first time one of them showed up at the bank, bingo! So I had to have a plan. I had to make them believe it was Donny. I had to make them believe he had survived. And that meant you, as well, Lindsey. I didn't want to hurt you, but you had to believe, too.''

She broke in then. "You'll never get away, Shawn. You just said that there are four FBI agents outside, and Thad's due back any minute now. You think they're going to let you take me out of this house? Do you honestly think they'll let you escape?''

He drew her attention to the gun again. "If they value your life, they will. It's sort of the same thing Donny did, you know? That old woman's kids valued her life, and so they gave away two hundred and fifty thousand dollars to save it. McNally values your life, and so he'll let two hundred and twenty thousand dollars walk away to save you.''

"But Thad's not in charge out there. Thad isn't involved in this case. He has no say in what happens,'' she quickly pointed out.

"He won't let anyone endanger your life,'' he insisted. "God, the man is so much in love with you that he'd kill for you.''

She fixed a cold stare on him. "Then he might kill *you*. Have you considered that, Shawn? Have you thought about whether or not this money is worth dying for?"

"He won't," he said confidently. "Because when we leave here, you're going to protect me."

"Like hell I am. You're not my friend—"

The ringing phone interrupted her, and she automatically reached for it. By the time Shawn yelled at her not to answer, she already had the receiver to her ear.

"Lindsey, are you all right?" Thad demanded.

She was so grateful to hear his voice, and so grateful that she'd left the card for him in the car, so that, no matter what happened here, he would always know how she felt. "Yes, Thad, I'm okay. Shawn and I are talking."

"Is he armed?"

"Yes."

"What does he—"

Shawn jerked the phone away from her. "McNally, are you out front?"

Losing that slight contact with Lindsey stung, and left Thad feeling raw, and angry. "Yes, I'm out front, you bastard." Then he took a deep breath, struggling to turn off his emotions and to think, to act, strictly professional. "I can't talk to you, Howard. I'm putting Special Agent Roberts on the—"

"No! You, McNally. I want to talk to you."

Thad looked at Roberts, who was listening in on the call. Roberts shrugged, signaling for Thad to continue. "What do you want, Shawn?"

"I'm bringing Lindsey out in a minute. We're going to get into my car and go to my apartment. After I get my money, we're leaving the state. She has to go with me, you understand, but once I'm safe, once I'm someplace where you can't find me, I'll let her go and give her money to get back home, okay?"

"I can't agree to that."

"Look, don't make me hurt her, Thad. I don't want to do that. I just want to get away with my money."

Thad felt an icy feeling crawl down his spine. When he replied, his voice was deadly low. "If you hurt her, Shawn, I'm going to kill you. That's the only promise I can make."

An instant later the line went dead, and so did everything inside Thad. He looked at Roberts, who almost immediately looked away. His avoidance confirmed what Thad already knew: they weren't going to let Shawn walk away. They couldn't. They would kill him if necessary.

And Lindsey? Dear God, what would happen to her?

Shawn disconnected the call, then dropped the phone to the floor. With the gun he gestured toward the door. "Come on, Lindsey, let's go."

She was leaning against her desk, her arms folded over her chest. "No."

"Damn it, Lindsey—"

"I'm not going anywhere with you, Shawn." She laughed, and it bordered on hysterical. "You call my brother a weak, spineless coward—and look at you. You're afraid to leave this house unless you can hide behind me. *You're* weak, Shawn. *You're* the coward."

"Shut up," he ordered, starting toward her.

But Lindsey couldn't stop the words, couldn't dam the hatred and derision and fury that flowed out. "On top of all that, you're stupid. You're stupid if you think they'll let you waltz out. You're stupid, Shawn, if you think anyone out there cares enough about me to let you go free."

"Shut up!"

His shout made her flinch, but she kept on, goading him, pushing him, prodding him. "All your threats and your little gun—is that what it takes for you to feel like a man, Shawn?" she taunted. "You're big and strong, but you can't even stand up to a woman like me without that gun. You're not a man, Shawn, you're—"

"*Shut up!*" He screamed the order in her face and this time raised his hand, intending to hit her, to make her obey. She saw the intent in his eyes, blue and enraged and belonging to a stranger, felt it in the menace that emanated from him, and she cringed, preparing for the blow, preparing for the pain, but it never came. He took a step back, then another, and his hand fell harmlessly to his side. He seemed stunned, Lindsey thought—by the fact that he'd almost hit her? Or by the fact that he couldn't?

He *couldn't* do it. He couldn't even hit her. How did he ever expect to be able to use that gun on her?

Maybe he didn't. He'd been driven here by desperation, convinced that she could help him, convinced that he could make her help him. But he'd been wrong. The only way she would help him was if he used physical force, and he couldn't bring himself to do that. He hadn't sunk that low.

"I'm going out, Shawn," she said in an even, flat voice. "I'm going out to Thad."

He didn't seem to hear her.

She stepped around him and walked to the door. The key was still in the lock, and she turned it. The jingle of the keys sounded loud in the sudden, harsh silence of the room, and must have penetrated the fog that surrounded Shawn, because he whirled around. "Get back here!"

She paused, but didn't turn around. She opened the door, pushed it all the way back and stepped onto the porch.

"I'll kill you, Lindsey!" he screamed, starting toward her, his arm extended, the pistol wavering in his unsteady grip. "I swear to God, I'll kill you!"

She reached the top of the steps. Her breath was coming in harsh rasps, and tears were silently sliding down her cheeks. She was waiting for him to prove her wrong, thinking with each step that now he would do it, now he would shoot her, now she would die. But she reached the bottom of the steps, and she was still alive.

Thad met her at the end of the sidewalk, yanking her through the gate, drawing her to safety behind a van parked in the street. Dimly he heard someone—Clint Roberts, he thought—ordering Howard to put down his weapon, but Thad's attention remained focused on Lindsey. She was shaking, and her eyes were closed, and she was crying the most heartrending silent tears.

"Lindsey, sweetheart, it's all right," he murmured, holding her close, rocking her back and forth in his arms.

"It's all right, honey. He can't hurt you, sweetheart. He can't hurt you now."

She laughed, a terrible, desolate sound that made his blood run cold, then she opened her eyes and looked at him. "Don't you understand?" she asked sorrowfully. "He never could."

They offered to let her make her statement the next morning, but she insisted on doing it that night. She sat on the sofa, looking calm and in control, waiting to begin, and Thad stood near the window, watching her, seeing the fatigue etched into her face. He wished he could sit beside her while she talked, holding her or touching her.

She'd hardly even looked at him since she'd come out of the house. She had let him hold her while she cried, but she had remained stiff, unyielding, the way she might with a total stranger. She had listened to his whispers of love as if she didn't even understand the words.

She had scared him senseless.

Did she blame him for this, too? Was that why she held herself so distant? Had she already figured out that he'd known when he left her here alone that Shawn was the man who had been tormenting her? His refusal to confide the details of his cases with her had already destroyed them once. Was it going to happen again tonight?

When everyone was settled, she began talking. Her voice was level, but occasionally he heard the quiver she tried to hide. She told them how Shawn had gotten Donny's keys, about the note her brother had left for him that day, and how Donny had hidden the money in Shawn's car.

"What did the note say?" Roberts asked.

Lindsey hesitated, then her gaze met Thad's across the room. Her eyes were empty, but there was something dark and cold there that made him shudder. "He told Shawn what he had done, told him that Thad was going to arrest him that day. He told him where the money was hidden and to give it to me. And..." She broke off and swallowed, but her gaze never wavered from his. "And he told him that he was going to kill himself rather than go to jail."

Feeling sick all the way into his soul, Thad turned away from her. He had shielded her from that truth for a year and a half. She wouldn't forgive him for hiding it from her. He had no doubts at all about that. Added to all the other things he'd kept from her, she would *never* forgive him.

She talked on, but he didn't listen, didn't hear. All he could think of was how badly he'd screwed up with her. It wasn't fair, he thought morosely, that he could love a woman so much and never be able to do the right thing in her eyes. If he'd ever mishandled a case as badly as he had mishandled this relationship, he'd have been shown the door immediately.

That was probably what Lindsey intended to do as soon as everyone else was gone.

"Why did Howard come here tonight? Why did he decide to take you hostage and leave tonight?" Roberts asked.

Lindsey sighed, then glanced at Thad, but he wouldn't look at her. She noticed he'd been edgy every since they'd come inside, reluctant to touch her, going to stand clear across the room instead of here beside her where she needed him. But what did she expect? Because she had demanded it, and because he had trusted her, he had confided in her, had told her things about this investigation that she hadn't needed to know. And she had betrayed his trust by passing every bit of that information on to the suspect in the case. She had almost made it possible for Shawn to escape; she might even have gotten Thad into trouble. He had every right to avoid her. Every right to hate her.

"I told him—" She glanced again at Thad, at his back, since that was all she could see, then swallowed hard and looked away. "Tonight at the club I told Shawn about Donny. I told him that the call had been recorded, that the voices didn't match, that the phone where the call had been made was under surveillance. He knew he was about to get caught, and he thought... he thought taking me hostage would ensure his escape."

"Why did you walk away from him? He was threatening to kill you, and you walked out the door."

She smiled uneasily. "He couldn't hurt me."

"How did you know that?"

"I didn't mean to, but I provoked him, and he was going to hit me." From the corner of her eye, she saw Thad finally turn around again. She felt his gaze on her. "He couldn't do it. And I figured if he couldn't hit me, he certainly couldn't shoot me. So I told him that I was going outside to Thad, and I walked out."

Roberts asked her a couple more questions, clarified a few points, then he and all his agents left. She hardly noticed. It was Thad who showed them to the door. When they were gone, he returned to the living room, and restlessly wandered around, waiting for her anger, her blame, her order that he leave.

Finally she stood up and confronted him, but there was no anger in her eyes. Only sadness. Only sorrow. "I'm sorry."

The apology caught him unprepared. He blinked and looked at her. "For what?"

"Blaming you for Donny's death when you risked your own life for him. I know now that there was nothing you could have done—nothing I could have done—to save him. Even if you'd told me everything, he still would have died because that was what he wanted."

"You would have known that eighteen months ago if I'd told you the truth."

She shrugged as if it didn't matter. "I'm sorry about tonight, too."

He was careful when he replied to keep his voice completely neutral. "If I'd known that you had told him everything, Lindsey, I never would have left you alone here. I never would have given him the chance to threaten you."

"I know." She blinked away the moisture that stung her eyes. "God, for months I blamed you for what I saw as your poor judgment in handling Donny's case. Now look at my own. I almost ruined everything."

Thad hesitantly touched her face. "Don't blame yourself, Lindsey. You were fooled by someone you trusted. It's not your fault."

"Can you forgive me?" she whispered.

He stood motionless for a moment, then relief rushed over him. *That* was why she'd been so distant—not because she'd blamed him for all his past silences but because she'd blamed herself, because she thought she had betrayed him. For the first time in two hours, he managed to smile. He pulled her into his arms, and she came willingly this time, her body molding to his. He slid his fingers beneath her hair to her neck and urged her even closer for a kiss. "I guess I have to, sweetheart," he said with a low, sexy chuckle, "because I damn sure love you."

Then she kissed him, her tongue slowly dipping into his mouth. When she withdrew, she tenderly touched his face and in a husky, sweet voice that sent shivers down his spine, she said the words he'd waited a lifetime to hear.

"I love you, too, Thad. I truly do."

Epilogue

"What are you doing?"

Lindsey was on the third rung of the step stool when Cassie's question, sharp and demanding, echoed around her. Bracing herself with one hand on the wall, she looked down at her assistant and indulgently smiled. "I'm going to dust the cottages here on the top shelf."

"No, you most certainly are not." Taking her arm in a firm grip, Cassie guided her right back down to the floor. "You're going to go over there and sit down and put your feet up. *I'll* dust the cottages."

"Cassie, the baby's not due for another two months."

"Maybe not, but your husband's due here in about ten minutes, and if he found you on top of that step stool, there would be hel—" she broke off at Lindsey's admonishing look, then substituted "—heck to pay. Go on now and sit down."

She hated to let a teenager boss her around, but Lindsey knew it was easier to give in than to argue. So she went to the rocker, sat down and propped her feet on the hassock while she watched Cassie nimbly climb the ladder.

Although she wouldn't say so to Cassie, it felt good to sit down, she admitted as she tilted her head back and closed her eyes. Her back hurt down low and showed no sign of letting up until the baby was born. It seemed that most of her evenings lately were quiet ones spent at home where Thad could rub her back or her aching legs or her puffy feet. He was good about that, and about cooking most of their meals and doing most of the housework and the shopping and all of the lifting and stretching and bending.

He was especially good about loving her.

The baby moved, and she shifted, too, searching for a more comfortable position. It almost wasn't fair, she thought as she clasped her hands over her stomach, for one person to be as happy as she was these days. Even Shawn's trial, conviction and subsequent transfer to a federal penitentiary hadn't done more than dim the edges of her happiness. By the time he'd been sentenced to prison, she and Thad had already gotten married. She had already met and fallen in love with every member of the McNally family. She had already found out that she was pregnant, that come February she and Thad would finally have the baby they wanted so much.

Once the bitterness and anger had faded, she'd felt sorry for Shawn and still did, but sometime in the last seven months she had also stopped hating him for what he'd done. With Thad's help, she had dealt with Shawn's betrayal. She had accepted it, forgiven it and moved on.

Now her life revolved around happier things. Her husband. Her new family. Her renewed friendship with Tess and Deke Ramsey and Andrew and their tiny newborn daughter Rebecca. And her own baby. Thad's baby.

The bell above the door sounded as someone came in, but Lindsey made no effort to get up to greet the newcomer. Her woman's intuition told her it was Thad, come to pick her up as he did most evenings. She had fussed that she was perfectly capable of closing up the shop and driving home alone, but privately she was grateful that he'd ignored her and kept coming anyway. It was a pleasant way to end the workday and shift into their evenings together.

Thad waved in response to Cassie's silent greeting, then approached his wife in the rocker. Her eyes were closed, her mouth was curved into a sweet smile, and her hands rested on her belly. She looked so peaceful, so lovely, he thought, his throat tightening at the sight of her.

He stopped a few feet away and took a moment to simply look at her. There was no sign on her face of all the emotional turmoil she'd gone through last summer. It was smooth, unlined, beautiful. Her hair was fixed as primly as ever, and her dress, though much roomier than she liked, was as elegant and flattering as ever.

He had always doubted the claim that pregnant women were more attractive, more radiant, but Lindsey definitely was. The only thing he missed about her slimmer days was the antique diamond wedding band he had placed on her finger six months ago, the band that proclaimed to the world what he knew so well in his heart: that this woman was *his*. But these days her fingers were too swollen for jewelry, and so the ring had been relegated to a spot in the laquered box on her dresser.

And that wasn't a change that had sat well with Lindsey, he remembered with a grin. Unlike Tess, whose entire weight gain with Rebecca had been limited to her stomach, *she* was getting fat all over, Lindsey had wailed self-pityingly the first day her ring had refused to slide onto her finger.

But she was beautiful. Still beautiful. Always beautiful.

And she was happy.

And she *was* his.

Slowly she smiled and, without stopping her rocking or opening her eyes, she asked, "Do I look like a beached whale?"

"You look like the woman I love." He lifted her feet and sat down on the hassock, then slipped her shoes off and began rubbing her left foot. "I don't need to ask how your day was. You look tired."

She moaned softly as he switched to her right foot. "I *am* tired. I think you were right. We *are* going to have to hire someone to help out until the baby's born. Cassie and I can't do it alone." Then she opened her eyes and looked at him. "And how was your day?"

"I got a new case."

"An interesting one?"

He shrugged. "One offered as a reward for a job well done."

"Then why don't you look like a man who's been rewarded?"

"Guess what kind of case it is."

She studied his expression, filled with dismay, for a moment, then smiled delightedly. "Stolen cars?"

He nodded. "I did such a good job on the investigation last summer that when a new auto theft ring began operating in Atlanta, they gave it to me."

"Ah, the burden of being bright, talented and very efficient."

"Talking about me?" Cassie asked teasingly as she joined them. "It's seven o'clock, folks. I'm going home."

"Be careful, Cassie," Lindsey said softly.

She got her things from the office, then passed them again on her way out. The bell dinged once, then the shop grew quiet. For a long time, they simply sat there, looking at each other. Then Thad stood up, rested his hands on the arms of the rocker and gave his wife a kiss, slow and gentle and achingly tender. "Lindsey, my love?" he murmured.

"Yes, Thad?"

"Let's go home, too."

* * * * *

This is the season of giving, and Silhouette proudly offers you its sixth annual Christmas collection.

SILHOUETTE

Christmas Stories

1991

Experience the joys of a holiday romance and treasure these heart-warming stories by four award-winning Silhouette authors:

Phyllis Halldorson—"A Memorable Noel"
Peggy Webb—"I Heard the Rabbits Singing"
Naomi Horton—"Dreaming of Angels"
Heather Graham Pozzessere—"The Christmas Bride"

Discover this yuletide celebration—sit back and enjoy Silhouette's Christmas gift of love.

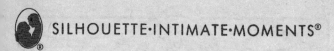

COMING NEXT MONTH

#409 TWILIGHT SHADOWS—Emilie Richards

When a friend's wedding party ended with bullets being exchanged instead of just ordinary vows, Griff Bryant discovered someone was out to get him, and he needed help—*fast*. However, capable *and* gorgeous private investigator Kelley O'Flynn Samuels gave "bodyguarding" a whole new meaning....

#410 NOWHERE TO RUN—Mary Anne Wilson

Psychiatrist R. J. Tyler had chosen to focus exclusively on the teaching side of his field. Yet, drawn by the vulnerability and fear in Lyndsey Cole's eyes, he made an exception. He had to help her remember who her attacker was, before it was too late. But was his heartfelt determination professional...or personal?

#411 LONG WHITE CLOUD— Marilyn Cunningham

When Kiri MacKay inherited an island from the father who'd abandoned her as a child, she wanted nothing more than to sell the entire estate and be done with it. Then she met wildlife biologist Noel Trevorson, and her determination wavered. His arguments against the sale were persuasive, his kisses seductive. But was he after her—or her island?

#412 BAD MOON RISING—Kathleen Eagle

Schoolteacher Frankie Tracker thought she'd gotten over her adolescent crush on Trey Latimer. But the moment he returned to town, she knew trouble lay ahead. For Trey the man was twice as exciting as Trey the boy. And this time, *she* was a fully grown woman.

AVAILABLE NOW:

#405 PROBABLE CAUSE
Marilyn Pappano

#406 THE MAN NEXT DOOR
Alexandra Sellers

#407 TAKING SIDES
Lucy Hamilton

#408 ANGEL ON MY SHOULDER
Ann Williams

Angels Everywhere!

Everything's turning up angels at Silhouette. In November, Ann Williams's ANGEL ON MY SHOULDER (IM #408, $3.29) features a heroine who's absolutely heavenly—and we mean that literally! Her name is Cassandra, and once she comes down to earth, her whole picture of life—and love—undergoes a pretty radical change.

Then, in December, it's time for ANGEL FOR HIRE (D #680, $2.79) from Justine Davis. This time it's hero Michael Justice who brings a touch of out-of-this-world magic to the story. Talk about a match made in heaven . . . !

Look for both these spectacular stories wherever you buy books. But look soon—because they're going to be flying off the shelves as if they had wings!